The SACRED CIRCLE

Rachel James
author of *The Kindred*

CRIMSON ROMANCE

F+W Media, Inc.

This edition published by
Crimson Romance
an imprint of F+W Media, Inc.
10151 Carver Road, Suite 200
Blue Ash, Ohio 45242
www.crimsonromance.com

ISBN 10: 1-4405-7481-2
ISBN 13: 978-1-4405-7481-8
eISBN 10: 1-4405-7482-0
eISBN 13: 978-1-4405-7482-5

Cover art © 123rf.com

*For Mom and Dad, who kept the magic alive
throughout their sixty-four years of marriage.*

Acknowledgments

My heartfelt thanks go to Julie Sturgeon, Imprint Manager for Crimson Publishing. Her ability to magically transform from editor to creative muse in the blink of an eye can only be labeled as "mind-blowing."

To Lauren Spielberg, editor and magician extraordinaire. Together we conjured up the right words, at the right time, in the right place. Thanks, thanks, and thanks!

A special thank you to the Crimsonistas. Your daily pics of man candy cast a spell over me no charm or amulet can ever break.

Hugs and kisses to all the readers who read and loved my first novel, *The Kindred*. Your praises, both in person and by e-mail, have evoked a life-long magic that can't be altered, reworked, or undone.

THE DARK TIME

Green Sapphire Coven—Fifteen Years Ago

The dark time descended without warning. The furry, brown moon hogs were the first to react, abandoning the Sacred Clearing and burrowing themselves deep underground. The cicadas and crickets were next, silencing their voices and burying themselves beneath nearby twigs and dirt. The cool night breeze vanished simultaneously, along with the disappearance of the full white moon. A towering Saguro cactus suddenly split in two, toppling to the ground with a thunderous crack. The shock wave reverberated beneath the ground, traveling along a dirt pocket and towards the group of teens standing in the middle of a Sacred Circle. Five seconds later, the rush of energy hit the edge of the painted circle and jumped it, jarring the occupants with a seismic jolt of electricity.

Thrown off balance by the chaotic spray of energy debris, the group lost control of the birthday ritual they were building. The cone of power collapsed in on itself, showering Sally Carver with its cave-in rubble first. She crumpled to her knees, knocking into her sister, Brenda, who took the second hit. Startled by the tumbles, Eileen O'Connor reached out to cradle her best friend's fall, only to find her own frame jolted by a sizeable eruption of energy. Ten seconds later, she was on her knees, alongside Sally and Brenda. Marla Curtis watched in horror as the trio clutched their heads and doubled over. Seconds later, a thrust of energy jarred her ankles, shins, and thighs and she joined the others on the ground.

Flustered, Brianna Sage and Devlin Janus linked hands, using each other as an energy source to regain control of the cone of power. Any other day, the joining would've worked, but the dark entity bent on escaping its home world to a new one, unleashed a raw series of energy smudges as a warning to back off. Ignoring the energy dust assaulting their palms, Devlin and Brianna held on, invoking aid from the Ancient Ones.

"Lord and Lady protect us, keep us from harm; protect your sons and daughters, and empower our charms. We stir the Ancients to be here this night; to travel upon their spiritual light. We call on the Ancients, the old ones, the wise; to comfort our fears, and heed all our cries. Give us protection from the darkness and cold; shower our spirits with your knowledge of old."

The air above their heads stirred, and then turned icy. A second later, a pinwheel of colors announced the arrival of the Ancients, who immediately misted through a seam of the energy vortex, and showered the circle with a pale lavender hue. The energy surge halted the dark entity's escape and sucked it back into the vortex, like water through a straw.

Devoid of power, the busted ritual righted itself and settled down. The Ancients vanished behind the entity, leaving the cool night breeze to find its natural state of flux again. A second later, the bright white moon reappeared from behind a cloud, and the clearing took on a shimmery glow. Off to the left, a lone cricket trumpeted the all-clear signal, and the night took on its rhythm and flow again.

Released from the spell, Devlin and Brianna crumpled to their knees, dazed by the upset. Across the way, Marla roused. She staggered to her feet, clutching Devlin's shoulders for balance.

"What happened?" she asked.

"The ritual tanked," Devlin replied. "We've taken a huge hit of electricity, but we're coming around now." He clambered to his feet, helping a stumbling Eileen recover her footing. "We'll be fine."

"What went wrong?" Eileen asked, rubbing her goose-caked arms, and looking around the clearing.

"Don't know." Devlin replied, helping Sally to her feet.

"You went wrong." Brianna accused, tottering to her feet and knocking his hands away as he tried to help her up. "You didn't stop the shanking."

"Me? I wasn't emceeing the circle. You were."

"You should've caught on sooner that the spell was tanking. You're older, more experienced."

"A circle can't have two masters, and you know it; but if it pleases you to blame me for this, go ahead." He whirled around, giving each girl the once-over. "Any headaches? Dizziness?" They shook their heads and then Sally gave a shriek.

"Brenda!" The group turned en masse, as Sally fell to her knees alongside her sister. "Brenda!" She shook her shoulders, blubbering her name hysterically. "She's not responding." She shook her sister harder, until Marla halted her fingers.

"Quit it, Sally. You're shaking her brains out."

Sally's gaze lifted to Marla's, and Devlin recognized the angry glint surfacing. He had to ward off the coming confrontation between the pair, or there would be another body lying alongside Brenda's. Once again, he took charge.

"Go find Doctor Ellis, Marla. Tell him what's happened."

She was off in a flash, tearing up the incline and over the ridge.

Devlin hid a relieved sigh. One crisis averted.

"It's cold, Devlin," Eileen stated, "and the animals have all gone quiet."

Devlin chose to ignore her words; they had to focus on Brenda.

"Something bad's coming," Brianna remarked, sitting back and hugging her chest. "I can feel it."

Devlin glanced at her shadowed face. Something bad had already come, he thought, *we just don't know what its name is yet.* He peeped at Brenda's grey pallor and winced. Should he send Eileen for the healing stones?

"Go wake Charles and Sienna, Eileen," he said, suddenly. "They need to be told about Brenda."

"Wake them? It's after midnight." She wrung her hands. "I can't wake them. They'll know what we've done."

"You go wake them, Eileen. Now!"

His autocratic command had her scrambling up the incline like Marla before her. A moment later, sounds of sliding shale split the air. Whipping around, the trio searched the ridge for a falling figure.

"Nothing," Brianna stated, "Just a last minute moon hog burrowing underground."

"Something bad *is* coming," Sally remarked, with a shiver. "You can feel it in the air." She bent again, shaking Brenda. "Wake up, Brenda! Please!" Her tone was panic-stricken and, hearing it, Brianna stilled her fingers. Sally's head lifted and she contemplated Brianna's stare, with a busted sob. "Don't let her die, Brianna. You can bring her back; you know secret ways."

Brianna's fingers pulled back.

"Secret ways? What on earth are you talking about?"

"You have powers. Use them—on Brenda."

A stunned look crossed Brianna's features.

"I don't have the power of life and death, Sally. No High Priestess does. We must wait for the Elders to tell us what to do."

"Brenda could die before they get here. You must use your powers to save her now."

"Brianna doesn't have any special powers yet," Devlin interjected, annoyed. "None of us do. We're kids; barely out of training."

Another sob echoed.

"The ritual was supposed to be fool-proof. Brianna said it was. We wouldn't have tried it, if she hadn't insisted it was safe." She glanced at Brianna. "This is all your fault. You lied to us."

Brianna flushed under the jibe.

"The spell was safe, Sally, I swear it!"

"For you, maybe, but for the rest of us?"

"Stop arguing!" Devlin muttered. "Help me turn Brenda over. I've got to inspect her back."

The girls complied at once, and Devlin lifted Brenda's blouse and inspected the area along her spine closely. No rash, no burn scar. He raised Brenda's skirt and examined her legs and thighs.

"Anything?" Brianna whispered.

"No puncture wounds. No rash or burn marks."

"We've got to do something." Brianna emphasized. "She's been out too long. Take a guess. Could it be a parasite, or a smudge?"

"Parasite?" Devlin's head whipped up. He scanned the circle around them. "We cut a door out before Marla and Eileen left, didn't we?"

The girls' gasps were audible, and though he couldn't see their faces clearly, he knew the answer was "no, they hadn't." The girls had left without protection, and possibly taking a ride-along entity with them.

As if reading his thoughts, Brianna hopped to her feet and began walking around the inside of the circle line.

"I walk the circle once around, to cleanse and bless this hallow ground. I walk the circle three times more, to open the portal that unlocks the door. As like meets like, and dark meets night, I bend the river to catch the light. One will stay and three will go, time unbends and healing flows."

A ripple of energy doused the circle and, feeling the gentle breeze, Devlin scooped Brenda into his arms and strode from the circle. Sally followed closely on his heels, calling softly to Brenda as they disappeared over the incline and into the darkness.

Left alone, Brianna's mind spiraled to a dark place. If Brenda died, it would be her fault, and no matter how many "I'm sorrys" she said, her world would never be right again. She shivered at the thought; hugging herself again. If Marla and Eileen succumbed to an energy sickness, it would be her fault, too. The thought so sickened her that she collapsed to the ground and burst into tears.

. . .

The waiting room was eerily quiet—except for the occasional gurgle of a water fountain. Slouched in a chair on the far wall, Brianna sat brooding. What was taking Doctor Ellis so long? It had to be bad news. She bit her quivering lip. She would never forgive herself for the havoc she had caused. How could she have been so selfish? Thinking only of gratifying her wants, her needs. She had been arrogant, and it was likely her best friend would pay for her sin.

Brianna heard movement by her chair and glanced quickly to her right. Great. Now she would have to endure a character-shredding lecture from Devlin. She watched as he slumped back in the chair, with a guarded look.

"I want to tell you something, Brianna … " he finally muttered.

"Leave me alone," she exclaimed, jumping from her chair and moving to a vacant chair on the other side of the room. She sprawled out and went back to her brooding. If she had to hear one more sermon about witches who betrayed their heritage, she'd scream. Didn't anyone realize she knew how bad she had acted? How reckless she had been? No one could berate her harder than her own conscience.

She heard movement again, and when she glanced up, she found Devlin towering over her, his shoulders hunched and his hands tucked into his front jean pockets.

"You need to listen … "

The waiting room door slammed open, cutting off his sentence and startling the pair. Devlin whirled first, while Brianna bolted to her feet, an eager expression coating her face. The look died immediately as she recognized the lanky figure of Francis Lord poised in the doorway. She plopped back down in her seat, trying to ignore the rising energy level in the room. Francis' anger was palpable. She could feel it saturating the walls and furniture, and even the air around her.

Spotting her wilting posture, Francis charged across the space. He stopped in front of her chair, his lips curling to a sneer.

"You just had to show off, didn't you? Prove to Brenda and Sally how superior your skills are to theirs."

Brianna fidgeted in the chair, tears trembling on her eyelids.

"Leave me alone, Francis. I can't bear another lecture right now."

His eyes blazed amber fire.

"You don't get it, do you? You constructed a ritual in secret; and worse, you constructed it on unconsecrated ground."

Devlin pulled alongside Francis, gripping his shoulder.

"Take it easy, Francis. Can't you see Brianna feels bad enough already?"

Francis knocked Devlin's hand from his shoulder.

"Don't tell me to take it easy. It isn't your girlfriend who's fighting for her life in there."

"No, and it isn't yours either!"

Francis flinched at the slur, and then losing his temper, he shoved Devlin hard. Devlin stumbled back, careening into a chair and sliding it sideways. He was on his feet quickly, lunging forward and grappling with Francis.

Brianna watched in horror as the pair locked arms and wrestled angrily. Hearing the sound of a fist clobbering jaw, she jumped to her feet.

"Stop it, both of you! Your insults are maddening."

The pair tore apart, chests heaving, glaring at each other with unbridled fury.

"What's going on here?"

The sharp question had the trio spinning around rapidly. Spotting her father and mother positioned in the doorway, Brianna took a step forward, a wobble in her voice.

"How's Brenda? Is she okay?"

Her father moved into the room with a determined stride, and Brianna knew the news was not good. *Something bad is coming*, her inner voice repeated. She bit her lip as her father stopped just short of the trio.

"Brenda died about fifteen minutes ago," he said, quietly.

Brianna fumbled for a chair and sank down. Brenda dead! Shocked, Francis emitted a sob and tore from the room. He bumped into the group hovering in the doorway and pushed by their shoulders with careless defiance. Devlin sank to a chair, silent and defeated.

Charles Sage studied the bowed heads and defeated postures.

"I'm so sorry, Papa," Brianna whispered, raising her head. "I don't know why this happened."

Her father's voice held an odd twinge of disappointment.

"You constructed an unsacred circle on unhallowed ground without permission; that's how it happened. You have shamed your heritage, as no other hereditary witch has ever done."

Brianna's tears choked her.

"I'm so sorry."

Her mother settled alongside her father, taking charge of the conversation.

"The laws are specific here in the coven, Brianna, and it pains me to be the bearer of bad tidings. However, what you've done— the Dark Time you've caused—cannot be overlooked. We live by the creed of harming none, as you well know." She signaled over her shoulder. "The Council has voted unanimously to banish you from the community for your sin."

Brianna's head shot up. Banish!?

"Mother, I … "

Her mother held up her hand.

"The vote has been decided, and it cannot be undone. You must leave the coven."

Devlin hopped to his feet.

"It's my fault, Mrs. Sage. I knew what Brianna was set on doing and I didn't stop her. In fact, I helped her construct the circle. If anyone needs to be banished from the coven, it's me."

Her words were clipped.

"You *are* being banished." Shocked, Devlin fell back in his chair, listening to her further recriminations. "Your behavior in all this has been disappointing … reprehensible, really. The Council is in agreement that you can no longer be trusted. You will pack your suitcases and leave the coven immediately." Her gaze darted back to Brianna, and for the first time, her voice broke miserably. "Your father and I l-l-love you very much, and we shall always wonder where you are and what you're doing. Though we will be forever apart, we will send our loving thoughts to you, and pray for you each and every d-d-day." She broke off speaking, seeking a hankie from her skirt pocket, and blowing her nose with it. Composing herself, she gave Brianna one final glance. "Blessed be, dear." She whirled around, and then unable to stop herself, she re-whirled and met Brianna as she hopped from her chair and flung herself into her mother's arms.

"I love you, Mother," she bawled. "I love you!" Her sobs shattered the room and, hearing them, her father encased her and her mother in a tight bear hug. Brianna's face tucked into his chest. "I love you, Papa."

"And I you, daughter. Blessed be!"

The pair released Brianna and then joined the somber group waiting at the door. En masse, they exited the room, leaving an anguished silence behind them. Bereft, Brianna backed up and dropped into a chair, losing herself to a dark despair.

Beside her, Devlin stirred.

"We'll go together. I'll get a job; I'll protect you … "

Appalled by his words, Brianna sprang to her feet and rounded on him.

"Leave together?! I'd rather eat a bag of dirt than go anywhere with you!"

He ignored her insult.

"Your parents will marry us. I'm eighteen, you're seventeen … "

Revolted by such a horrid thought, she responded sharply.

"Marry you?! I wouldn't marry you if you were the only man left on Earth! I'd rather rot in hell! No," she railed, "I'd rather you rot in hell!"

She whirled on her toes, determined to put as much distance between her and Devlin. Marry him? Not if her life depended on it! Skirting the open doorway, she marched down the hallway. Get married and spend the rest of her life with Devlin. He was a slime ball for even suggesting such a thing.

CHAPTER ONE

PRESENT DAY—WASHINGTON D.C.

Hacking coughs split the air, followed by a series of raspy moans. A second later, a loud sneeze bounced off the green walls of the room. Fumbling in her jacket pocket, Brianna pulled a tissue out, and swiped her runny nose. This cold was getting the best of her, and she wished with every fiber of her being that her spirit guides would whisk her away to some tropical island where they never heard of burning lungs and clogged nasal passages.

She dropped her forehead to the desk, and gave into a second set of coughs. If she ever learned who had given her this nasty virus, she would place a curse on their head that couldn't be reversed. Her office door creaked and Brianna realized her assistant, Janet, was responding to her lacerated coughs. She took a deep breath, willing herself to shore up her energy. A strange rattling in her lungs made her clutch her chest again, and all thoughts of making conversation fled into a graveyard of dead sentences. She hated being sick. It was a tremendous drain on her system. And to make matters worse, she was becoming light-headed. If she didn't know better, she'd think something bad was in the wind.

"That cough could use a little Wiccan magic, blue eyes."

The voice was raspy and deep, and Brianna's head snapped up at the statement. She studied the chubby figure crossing the door frame, and voiced her surprise.

"Good heavens, Tommy, who told you I was sick?"

"I have my sources." He approached her desk, studying her cracked lips and ruby-red nose. "I warned you not to travel at this time of year. Perhaps now, you'll listen to me." Her laugh turned into spastic coughs, as Tommy dropped into a chair across the desk from her. He plopped his briefcase on the edge of her desk, and slid back in his chair. "Well, let's get to the point while you still have breath to speak with. Do we have a deal or not?"

Brianna dabbed at her dripping nose.

"Not—and he wouldn't say why, damn him!"

"Probably doesn't like doing business with witches." Tommy teased.

Brianna frowned at his words.

"Don't make me sorry I told you about my background when we became partners, Tommy. And for your information, the coven I grew up in frowns on using magic to manipulate people for one's personal gain."

"Too bad. You could use a magical make-over right now. Your hair is a mess, your mascara is flaking, and your tall frame is hunched over like Quasimodo."

Brianna raised a hand to her hair, brushing a stray tendril behind her ear.

"Don't be shy, Tommy. Tell me what you really think."

"Don't make jokes. When you're unwell, I take it very seriously."

"That's because I'm rarely ill." She stifled a pressing sniffle, and tossed her tissue into the trash can under her desk. A light chuckle sounded as Tommy crossed his legs, and fidgeted with the seam of his trousers.

"I warned you to take your time with this buyout. There is no hurry to liquidate all of your assets at once just because you've decided to make major changes in your lifestyle. Hurried choices can be disastrous, you know."

Hearing his words, Brianna shivered. A moment later, the air around her head stirred, and she glanced up. There it was again—the feeling that something was brewing in the wind. Was spirit attempting to warn her she should be on her guard? Or was she being warned it was much too late to worry? She heard the loud mewl of a cat's cry in her ears, and drew in her breath. There. That disturbance was definitely a ripple of something sinister. Where had the cry come from? Janet's office?

Strong hands gripped her fingers, startling her.

"Here now, what's wrong? You've gone completely white."

"Did you hear it?" Brianna queried.

"Hear what?"

"A cat crying. It sounds hungry—or in pain."

"I didn't hear anything. Are you sure you heard a cat?"

"I heard a cat, dammit!"

A hand waved in front of her face.

"Hey, don't bite my head off. I'm no warlock with super-sonic hearing, you know."

Brianna grimaced, clutching his hand.

"Don't humor me, Tommy. I have a feeling something's wrong."

His expression turned serious.

"I'll have Janet call maintenance to check the nearby offices."

He sprang from his chair and exited the room, leaving Brianna to bite her lip in frustration. Why had she snapped at Tommy? He was her best friend, and his friendship meant everything to her. Besides, cat cries just didn't dance on the wind, no matter how real they sounded. She was ill, and the cries were just figments of her sick body.

Tossing back her shoulders, she made a face at the painting on her wall. She may have heard a cat crying, but without knowing the source, there wasn't a thing she could do about it. She felt a light touch on the side of her cheek, and jumped.

"You're spicy hot," Tommy stated. "That's not a good sign. Fevers often cause hallucinations."

"I am not hallucinating, Tommy, I heard a cat … no, don't say anymore. I know it sounds crazy."

"Damned crazy," he muttered.

"Well, it wouldn't be the first time I've been called crazy, so sit down, and stop worrying about me."

"I can't help it. You're the most rational person I know—next to me—and if you're hearing cats that aren't there, there is great cause for worry."

"It's more than being sick, Tommy."

"What the hell does that mean?"

"It means that I have this feeling of dread that I can't shake—as if someone has just died."

Tommy angled around the desk, and retook his former seat.

"You're on overload—too much work, and too little sleep, and for what? Why are you pushing things at such a breakneck speed?"

Brianna didn't answer right away. She could tell Tommy the truth—that she had been feeling a disturbance somewhere in the fabric of time for months, and was worried by it. He would understand her fears. After all, they had no secrets from one another. He might be a man of art and science, but he had added the power of magic to his vocabulary since meeting her.

Still, she didn't want to involve him in her childish fears unless she had to. If only she didn't sense that the disturbance concerned him in some way. She could feel it pulling both of them towards the past, instead of the future. And worse, she felt herself being dragged back—towards old relationships that she had vowed to keep buried forever. Besides, she shouldn't be able to gauge energy levels anymore. Yet, she could feel the energy in the room around her as if she had conjured up a cone of power, complete with the Guardians of the Watch Tower. No, she stopped her thoughts. She had no intention of revisiting that kind of pain ever again. Not for anyone. She gave a tired sigh.

"Have you ever made a decision you wish you could take back, Tommy?"

"Only every time I sit across the bargaining table with you."

"I'm serious."

"So am I." He heard her sigh again, and threw out his hand. "Okay. Are we talking a complete do-over here? Or just a small, magical tweaking?"

"I'm talking a total re-do, a chance to relive a moment over again, and make a different decision."

"My God, woman, you own two foundations and a wildlife habitat. What else do you want?"

"Mind-blowing sex would be nice."

She heard a busted chuckle.

"Surely you can conjure up a willing partner with some simple romance spell you know." He saw her frown and held up a finger. "None of that matters now. What matters is your damn decision to alter your life."

"Don't get me wrong." Brianna stated. "I am genuinely proud of what I've accomplished with the foundations. But somewhere along the way, the dream became so twisted that it no longer resembles the dream I started out with. Now, I just want to find my roots again and start over—preferably with a quiet, respectful man who loves children."

Tommy scooted his chair forward, and then settled back.

"You need a strong-willed husband, blue eyes. Any other kind, and you'd run rough-shod over him." He switched thoughts rapidly. "Now that you're revamping your life with mind-blowing sex instead of business, I guess a merger of Sage Industries is out of the question, huh?"

"I haven't sunk that low yet." Brianna snatched a tissue from its holder and blew her nose. "Well, you've heard my bad news; how did it go in Texas?"

"Damn charlatans. They let me fly all the way out there, and then just as we hit the bargaining table, they sent word they were passing on the buyout."

"Did they give a reason?"

"They said they're looking to liquidate their holdings, not acquire more."

"It was a good deal, Tommy."

"For you, it was. But let's face facts. Big corporations bypass great deals all the time. It's not personal. It's just business. We'll find another buyer. D.J. Corp isn't the only game in town."

"No, but he's the best. His projects are always environmentally sound. He doesn't drill the hell out of the land or the sea, and his wildlife habitat in Wyoming has an ecosystem to die for."

Another sigh emanated.

"I did my best in Texas, Brianna. I hope you believe that."

Brianna gave a matching sigh.

"I know you did your best." She squared her shoulders. "Let's start making phone queries again. Perhaps D.J. could recommend another corporation that might serve as well. What do you think?"

"I'll call Jake Rogers and find out." He reached in his coat pocket and withdrew his Blackberry. He began making notes on the pad, and Brianna took a moment to study her calendar.

A second later, the phone jangled on the desk, startling them both. Annoyed, Brianna snatched up the receiver, and held it to her ear.

"What is it, Janet?"

"Brianna?"

The voice was low and unfamiliar, and Brianna tucked the receiver closer to her ear.

"Who's this? Can you speak up? The connection's bad."

The voice came online again, steady and loud this time.

"Brianna?

Her pulse skittered.

"Papa?" She clutched the front of her blouse. "Am I dreaming your voice? How in the world did you find me?"

"I've always known where you were, Brianna—right from the day you left my side. I've followed your career closely over the years, too. I'm extremely proud of who you've become."

Brianna's chest tightened. *Déjà vu, Brianna*, her inner voice nudged, *déjà vu.*

"What's wrong, Papa? Why are you calling?"

"There's been an accident."

Brianna squeezed the front of her blouse, his words freezing her brain. Sudden tears welled up, followed by another heaviness centered in her heart.

"Its mother, isn't it? I felt something in the wind—a hint of something bad. How s-serious is it?" she asked.

"Very serious. The entire congregation has fallen ill."

"Good heavens! What from? Have you determined the cause?"

"Our best guess is a busted ritual."

A shadow of alarm touched Brianna's face, and a warning voice whispered in her head again. *Déja vu, Brianna, déja vu.* To her dismay, her voice broke slightly.

"And m-mother?"

"She's gravely ill. I don't think she's going to make it. That's why I'm calling."

Brianna bit her lip to control a sob.

"Can she be moved to a critical care unit in Tucson for treatment?"

"No. She collapsed while performing a ritual, and until we determine what occurred prior to her collapse, we can't let outsiders get involved. We attempted to intercede on her behalf, and well, I don't need to tell you what can happen when an intercession fails."

Brianna's eyes bordered with tears again.

"You must call 9-1-1 immediately. Mother needs to be airlifted as soon as possible. I can meet you in Tucson some time tomorrow afternoon." She glanced at her calendar. "I can catch the red-eye flight out tonight."

A weary sigh emanated in her ear.

"That won't do, Brianna. I'm suffering from the energy sickness, along with the members. I am unable to travel at the moment."

Brianna heard a raspy cough and winced.

"You must let me come home, Papa. I can help."

"I wish you could, but when you left, all ties to the coven were broken."

An unexpected surge of anger had Brianna lashing out.

"That was fifteen years ago. It has no bearing on this incident. I have read the Book of Shadows, and I know what's written in terms of who succeeds whom in a crisis. There's no doubt in my mind, I have to come home and assess the situation."

Her father's cough came through the line again.

"It took a long time to put the Dark Time behind us, Brianna. Please don't make a mockery of our laws by going against them again. I only called you … in case this is goodbye."

Silence descended on the other end of the line, and Brianna suppressed a sob.

"Papa … "

The line went dead, and Brianna's hand shot to her mouth. He had hung up on her. Her hand suddenly fell away. It was clear the Dark Time had descended again without warning, and this time, her mother's essence had taken the hit. She replaced the receiver slowly, wishing she could replay her father's words in slow motion. Her mother had been performing a ritual when it tanked. No, her mother didn't make mistakes like that. Then what? *A clever attempt at murder?* Her inner voice threw up. She shunned the thought, but then thought better of it. Why would the Elders attempt to alter a ritual if they didn't suspect foul play?

She banished that thought, too. She wasn't going to start suspecting that a sinner had entered the clearing and attacked her mother. Her mother's collapse had been an accident caused by spirit, and her father had let the Council try to reverse the outcome—with disastrous results. What had made him do such a foolish thing? She wouldn't know until she asked him in person. Or saw her mother.

Snatching up the phone again, she punched in Janet's extension.

"Ready for the next dose of Nyquil?" Janet teased.

"No, I need you to call the airport and book the earliest flight to Tucson for me. And book a rental car."

"Will do." The line went dead and Brianna replaced the receiver.

"Do you want me to fly home with you?"

Brianna glanced up, suddenly remembering she wasn't alone in the room. She covered her mouth with shaking fingers.

"Thank you, Tommy, but no. You've got to stay here and find a buyer for my company. It's more important than ever now. I'll sign the power of attorney over to you before I leave."

He leaned forward in his chair.

"Are you sure this is what you want to do?"

Her voice drifted to a whisper.

"I'll conjure a protection spell for the pilot and passengers before we take off," she replied.

"That's not what I meant, and you know it. We're talking about you walking back into the lion's den when you've vowed to never go into the den again. Bad blood doesn't dissipate over the years, you know; sometimes it just hibernates."

Brianna began chewing on her lower lip, her eyes darkening with pain.

"I have to go home, Tommy, and that's that."

He didn't offer any other comment aloud, but she saw him frown. She looked away, clamping her lips to imprison a sob. The past was the past, and though she needed it to stay dead, she couldn't sit and wait for word of her mother's death. She felt ice spreading through her stomach at the thought, and she suddenly burst into tears.

Alarmed, Tommy sprang to his feet and circled the desk. He threw his arm over her shoulders, comforting her with his warm embrace and sly wit.

"Here now, blue eyes, forget what I said. If you have to go home, I'll support you. I'll even find one of those magical books of yours and conjure up a spell for you to use." He squeezed her shoulders, and Brianna slipped her arms about his waist and hugged him.

"You're the best, Tommy. I knew you'd understand." She brushed her cheeks against his belt buckle. "If I don't go, and Mother dies, I'll never forgive myself."

"And if they slam the gates in your face?"

"I'll lose my soul."

"What's one little soul among many?" Tommy teased, shaking her shoulder.

Brianna squeezed his waist.

"You are treading on sacred ground with that statement, Tommy. Every soul counts in the scheme of things."

"Even your damaged one?"

"God, I hope so," she said, slipping her hands from Tommy's waist. She leaned back in her chair, swiping her drenched cheeks with a tissue. "All better now," she said, tossing it under her desk. A long sigh emanated as Tommy re-circled the desk and fell into his chair again. His sly wit re-surfaced at once.

"I know we've bantered about witches and warlocks over the years, but just how good of a witch are you, anyway?"

Brianna's head shot up, a mischievous glint entering her eyes.

"Change the subject, Tommy, or you'll find out first-hand just how good I am."

He held up his hands, making a cross with his fingers.

"Stay back, you evil, blue-eyed vixen."

Brianna laughed at his sarcasm.

"Crisis averted," she croaked.

"And without using black magic against me." He gave her a toothy grin, dropped his hands, and hopped from his chair. He hauled up his briefcase, rapping it on the edge of her desk before turning.

"Just say the word, and I'll fly home with you, Brianna."

She studied his serious expression.

"This is something I have to do alone, Tommy. And," she pointed a finger at him. "You need to find a buyer for the company ASAP."

He nodded, then turned from the desk, and exited the door. Watching him go, Brianna gave a relieved sigh. Thank goodness, Tommy knew when to push, and when to back off. If he had pushed things, she would've come unglued, for sure.

Torn by an influx of conflicting emotions, Brianna began drumming her fingers along the desktop. What had really happened to her mother in the circle? She didn't know; she only hoped that when she arrived in Green Sapphire, she'd find that the Elders had misread the signs, and things weren't as bad as her father implied. Her mind replayed Tommy's words: "And if they slam the gates in your face?" She frowned immediately. If, when she arrived, she was barred from the property, she would work her way south along the back roadway, and enter the compound through the outer property bounds. She was going to determine for herself what happened to her mother, and nothing and no one was going to stop her. No one was going to hurt her mother and get away with it.

CHAPTER TWO

PRESENT DAY—DALLAS, TEXAS

The "Do Not Disturb" sign hanging on the doorknob came loose and flew away as the door slammed open, and Jake Rogers, Devlin's partner, strode to his desk. A file sailed into Devlin's line of vision, and he raised his head.

"Good morning to you, too," he quipped with a lop-sided grin.

"Don't 'good morning' me. I've been up all night."

Devlin leaned back in his chair.

"It's nice to see another ecological egghead bogged down in mud. My last two days have been spent training field engineers who don't know shit about the earth, or even give a damn about it. I welcome the chance to talk to someone who actually knows what I'm talking about—even if that someone needs a bath and clean shave."

Jake plopped into a vacant chair.

"What can I say? Digging mines turns me on."

"Now, you see there, that's what I'm talking about." Devlin stated. "These young go-getters I'm saddled with are interested in mining the earth for profit, rather than finding cures for radiation sickness, cosmic rays, food chains, and ozone layers."

"Profit versus extinction. That's always been man's dilemma, and his heartbreak," Jake responded.

"Well, I'm here to prove that man can live in harmony with his environment, instead of drilling it all to hell. Even the plankton in the sea deserves that much courtesy from us."

Devlin saw the busted smirk.

"Yee-haw! Let's dunk the bastards."

Devlin tossed his pencil across the desk at Jake.

"Spare me your good-old-boy personality so early in the morning, huh? Why are you disturbing me when I clearly asked not to be disturbed?"

Jake caught the pencil, and used it to pound the file he threw on the desk.

"You backed out of the Sage proposal. Why?"

"I realized it's not for us."

Jake sported a frown.

"You axed the deal at the last minute, though. That's not like you."

"You know my personal history, Jake," Devlin said, turning his attention to the file. He flipped it open, studying the scrawled signatures.

"Commune living, blah, blah, blah," Jake touted.

"It's a little more interesting than that," Devlin said, glancing up.

"Like I said, blah, blah, blah. No bullshit this time. What's going on?"

"I thought I could mend some fences by buying Brianna's company, but I've realized I can't."

Devlin heard a brief chuckle.

"Touché. Now, let me tell you the real reason you won't broker this deal, old buddy."

Devlin flipped the file shut, leaning back in his chair again.

"I can't wait to hear this."

Jake ignored his sarcasm.

"You have a 'thing' for the beautiful Brianna."

Devlin's chair hit the floor.

"Where the hell did you come up with that reasoning?"

"It's the only plausible explanation. You're a handsome, heterosexual male with needs, yet you constantly shun the ladies who throw their panties in your direction. Only one reason to do that; you've got the love bug bad."

Devlin saw a familiar smirk, but before he could comment on it, a loud jangling erupted from the phone on his desk. He pressed the intercom button on the speaker box, glad for the interruption. Jake's musings were getting close to subjects he had long ago deemed nobody's business but his own.

"Devlin here."

"Devlin, it's Charles."

"Charles?" Devlin paused, running a list of names through his head. Charles in Toledo? Charles in Santa Ana? And then it hit him. "Good lord, Charles, how did you find me?"

"I've kept track of your whereabouts for years," he replied. "However, I had to call the A.A.P.G. to get your number."

"I'm flattered," Devlin remarked. "It's certainly good to hear your voice after all these years. How are things?"

"Things are bad. Sienna's dying."

"What?!" Devlin's chair bumped the desk, and he snatched up the receiver. "Did you say she's dying?"

"Yes. She fell ill during a Sacred Circle ritual, and you know better than most what that means. Several members of the congregation, including myself, are showing signs of respiratory problems. And we have one casualty in the making—a young teen. We've tried to pinpoint the cause, but we've failed."

Devlin swung his chair around, glancing out the bay window with a frown.

"Call the paramedics, Charles. Every second you delay seals her fate."

"I wish it was that easy, but you know involving outsiders right now isn't an option—not until we determine the cause."

"Does Brianna know?"

"Just hung up from telling her; said my goodbyes to her, now to you."

"Goodbye?" Devlin heard a fractured cough, then a clear voice again.

"I should've fought harder for you and Brianna to stay all those years ago. If things go really bad from here on out, promise me you'll take care of Brianna. You have our permission to marry her and have lots of babies, by the way."

The phone line went dead, and Devlin listened to the dial tone in dismay. Marry Brianna and take care of her? He wished that with every breath he took; however, if there was a love spell for accomplishing that, he hadn't found it yet. He swung his chair back around, hanging up the receiver and rapping his knuckles on the desk. Sienna Sage in a coma from conducting a Sacred ritual? Not possible. High Priestesses didn't fall ill during rituals. *Not without help*, his inner voice nudged.

Bolting up from his chair, Devlin strode to the washroom on his left, and doused his face. He was feeling the urge to hop a plane and tell the Sisters of Fate to be damned.

"I can cover the NASA meetings, Dev. We're turning down the proposal anyway."

Devlin shook his head, grabbing a towel.

"You've got to be in Montana Wednesday. If we lose that meeting, we stand to lose two million in change."

An annoyed growl emanated.

"Gee, Dad, I thought we were partners. Since when don't you trust me to conduct simultaneous business meetings?"

Devlin wiped his face, and tossed the towel to the sink.

"Get the hell out of my office and let me read the field training schedules." He skirted around Jake's lounging figure, and strode back to his desk. Sinking into his chair, he prepared to return to his reading. A hard rap on the edge of the desk had him looking up in surprise. He watched as Jake tumbled back into his vacated wingback.

"I know I've scoffed at your coven background for years, but I heard enough of that conversation to know that Brianna Sage's mother is seriously ill. And it doesn't take a rocket scientist to deduce that you should call Brianna Sage right now and try to patch things up with her."

Devlin gave an exhausted sigh.

"And say what? Let's get together and conjure up a healing spell to save your mother? Trust me, if I did that, she'd spit in my face and do everything she could to screw me over."

"Wow! That's a lot of hate, brother. Still, that's no reason to refuse to call her and try to patch things up. She needs a friend right now, I think."

"Mind your own business, Jake."

"You are my business, remember? If you're unhappy, I'm unhappy. That was our agreement when we first formed this company." He leaned forward, and lifted the phone receiver. "Call her—before she conjures up a part-time lover who isn't you." He offered the receiver to Devlin, who scowled as he took it.

"You don't know what you're asking of me by doing this, Jake … " He began punching in numbers on the phone, hoping to God the call would go directly to Cloisters' voice mail.

"Cloisters, here."

"Tommy? Devlin Janus."

"Janus? Thought I heard the last of you yesterday."

"Bad pennies always turn up," Devlin joked, "I'd like Brianna's cell phone number, if you have it handy."

"No can do. She's on her way home to pack and she's not taking any calls."

"She's going somewhere?"

"She's off to Tucson for a couple of days. Family business. Can I have her call your cell when she has a chance?"

"She'll be back in a few days, you say?" Devlin asked, evading his question.

"Or three or four. Her mother's seriously ill. She has no clear timeline for her return at this point."

"I see. Well, give her my cell number when you have a chance. And, Cloisters?"

"What?"

"I've changed my mind. I'd like to buy Sage Industries—if it's still available. Can you fax the papers over?"

"Got Brianna's power of attorney letter in my hot little hands," he chuckled. "I'm just itching to use the power."

The line went dead, and Devlin replaced the receiver. He leaned back, perusing Jake's gleeful grin.

"There, your precious ego has been stroked once again. We are now the proud owners of Sage Industries. I hope that makes you happy."

"As happy as a clam swimming in marinara sauce." he replied.

Devlin waved him away.

"Get the hell out of my office before I terminate our partnership."

"I'm already gone, partner. See you at lunch."

CHAPTER THREE

AIRPORT—TUCSON, ARIZONA

Following the crowd, Brianna stepped onto the tarmac, her gaze scanning the foothills surrounding the airport. It was good to stretch her legs after eight tedious hours of flying. If only she had the time to curl up in the nearest motel and sleep for a solid ten hours. Her mind had reached overload sometime around noon, and her body was paying the price for it. Sore back, stiff muscles; she had it all.

Bending, she lifted the handle of her suitcase and struck out for the terminal entrance. At least her cold was better. Her nose was no longer running like a sieve, and her lungs had started producing fresh air again. Of course, yesterday had been a blur; her scheduled meetings rearranged, her suitcase packed and re-packed. And then a sudden snowstorm had developed and delayed her early morning flight to mid-morning. And now, after the long hours of sitting, the sun was lowering in the west, and she was so hungry she could eat a bear. Did she have time for a quick bite before picking up her rental car? It didn't make a difference, she was going to eat. The egg and cheese sandwich she had eaten for breakfast had dissipated long ago, leaving her lightheaded and woozy.

"Hello, Brianna."

The figure loomed in front of her, and Brianna took a hasty step back. She studied the handsome face, mesmerized by the light green eyes scanning her own face. Her heart tripped in recognition. It couldn't be. Not after all these years.

"Dev … lin?" she sputtered.

"In the flesh."

He took the suitcase handle from her fingers, and guided her forward with a light prod. It took all of Brianna's willpower not to shrink from his touch. However, if she balked, the gesture would be noticed. And being noticed at the moment was the last thing she wanted.

"Are you passing through, Devlin?" she asked, following him under an arrow pointing towards the baggage claim area.

"No. Your father tracked me down yesterday, offered me a cryptic goodbye, and then hung up the phone."

"Me, too." Brianna felt the sting of tears on her eyelashes, and immediately changed the subject. "Was your flight any better than mine?"

"Much better. I arrived this morning with only an hour delay."

"Have you been waiting for me to fly in?" Brianna asked in surprise. He didn't respond, merely side-stepped a senior couple who had stopped suddenly in front of them to read the arrival/departure board. Winding around them, he took stock of their surroundings, and then angled left. Spotting a second exit sign, he guided her towards the front of the terminal. As they walked, Brianna realized he wasn't going to answer her question. It was obvious that he had been waiting for her flight, though she couldn't fathom how he knew which flight she would be on. Her decision to come had been last minute at best.

She stole a peek at his profile. The years had been very good to him. His boyish looks had turned into a mature ruggedness that reeked of working outdoors. She could even smell a hint of balsam in his aftershave. He was as tall as she remembered, and drat it, a lot more handsome. He wore no wedding band, but then lots of married men didn't these days. Her intuition said he wasn't married, though; just having hot, steamy sex whenever possible. His body looked remarkably sculpted beneath his shirt and jeans.

She was sure once aroused, his body would twist with the hard knot of need, and the resulting sex would be mind-blowing.

Brianna pulled her gaze from his body to the walkway ahead. It was none of her business whether Devlin had mind-blowing sex. And it was certainly the height of stupidity to be admiring his body and picturing some lucky woman lying beneath him, writhing in ecstasy.

Her gaze found his profile again. Where had he settled over the years? Out west? Back east? Wherever it was, he had kept true to his upbringing. He belonged to the land and it showed. Passing the last of the ticket counters, she felt a tug on her elbow and turned, content to be guided towards the outside walkway.

"Your father mentioned a respiratory problem," Devlin finally advised, "The scene at Green Sapphire must be pretty depressing, and once you arrive, the rumors will spread your mother is beyond help."

Brianna shoved her purse higher on her shoulder, side-stepping a toddler headed towards the entrance door at a breakneck speed.

"I don't give a damn about what the congregation thinks," she replied, watching as the boy's mother scooped him up before he got trampled underfoot. "I'm here to get to the bottom of what happened, and then do what I can to make the Elders rectify it." Reaching the main terminal, Brianna paused for guidance. "Have you rented a car for the drive home?"

"Yes. It's close by. I've canceled your rental." He switched direction, walked a few yards, and then noticed she wasn't following. He swung back, contemplating her posture. "Look, I get it, we've never been friends, or likely to be, but if we are going to help your mother, we have to work the problem out together."

"Like last time?"

He grinned at her.

"Hopefully, not."

Her lips twitched slightly. The serious boy she had known as a child had grown a sense of humor since leaving the coven. And this new Devlin was upsetting her normal balance in the world with his playful charm and winning smile. Why had her father tracked them both down after all these years? He knew their history together. Oil and water—two chemicals that never mixed.

Reaching the front terminal doors, Brianna swept through, and lifted her gaze to the setting sun. The warm weather was heaven for her chilled bones; however, now that she was at a resting place, she could feel her body starting to wilt. Feeling a trickle of air tease her ankles, she turned to find Devlin exiting the doors. He pointed to their left and started out towards a row of assorted vehicles. Brianna fell into step behind him, refusing to be the first to continue their conversation. It was clear by his quiet tread he was respecting her personal space. She was sure he would continue to do so until they reached Green Sapphire. And then what?

He picked up his pace, disappearing around a black stretch limo and out of sight. Left in the semi-darkness, she realized the old Brianna would've found a rock and clobbered him over the head for blatantly leaving her without a flashlight to see by.

Hearing a whistle, she angled around several more SUV's, finally spotting him waiting for her in front of a black Jeep Liberty with Arizona plates. He had dropped her suitcase by his feet, and appeared annoyed with her lagging gait. She purposely slowed her steps. Let him be the one to stew now. Tit for tat. Oil and water. Seeing the slow down, he fished in his pocket for the car keys.

"Have you been ill? You look tired."

Brianna felt a sting of tears and blinked them back.

"Does hearing cat cries dancing on the wind count? Or a heightened sense of awareness that your life has become an episode of *The Twilight Zone*? Or perhaps, it's the cryptic messages my brain is sending me."

"Like what?"

"What happened in the circle? Why did it happen? Who's responsible for it? When did the ritual go wrong? At the start? Near the end? Where will the answers come from?"

His fingers touched her lips.

"We'll get all those answers, I promise you."

She swallowed convulsively as he dropped his fingers and swung about. They'd find the answers together. He sounded so sure of the words. And so sure that she'd agree. Why had she ignored her instincts and come alone? If only she had taken Tommy up on his offer to accompany her on the trip. Instead, she had given him her power of attorney and demanded he find a new buyer for the foundation as soon as possible. And though she had been disappointed that he agreed to the suggestion, she knew she couldn't expect him to drop everything to babysit her. Still, she wished she wasn't facing the Elders with Devlin by her side. They would misinterpret the pairing and automatically assume they had built a life together after leaving the coven.

Appalled by a sudden vision of being swept into Devlin's arms and kissed soundly, she banished the thought to her "never bring this up again" file. Her coat was suddenly wrested from her fingers, and she realized Devlin had unlocked the passenger door and was holding it open for her. She slipped onto the front seat cushion, ducking when he tossed the coat over the front seat into the back. The door clicked shut beside her, and a moment later, she felt a breeze on her back as Devlin opened the rear hatch and tossed her suitcase in alongside his. Skirting the tail light, he then joined her in the front seat. As he fired the engine, Brianna clasped her seatbelt.

"I never meant to grow into this bitter person, Devlin. I had great hopes for being happy."

"So did I." He gave her a brief glance as he strapped himself in, and then slipping the car into reverse, he angled out of the parking space. Two left turns later, he was concentrating on the exit signs overhead, and ignoring Brianna completely.

Totally depressed, Brianna fell into a mind-fugue filled with self-doubt. Had she been wrong in taking her bitterness out on Devlin? In all her guilt-filled days, she had never once given thought to the pain he must've endured for admitting blame for Brenda's death. She had only thought of herself and her banishment from the community. Looking back now, she realized he must've gone through his own personal hell—alienated from the people he had longed to serve.

"I took the liberty of buying dinner for you in the airport," he said, letting the Jeep settle into a leisurely pace on the Interstate. "It's only fast food, but I imagine after the day you've had, even a Cuban sandwich will taste like a steak." He reached behind his seat, grabbed a bag from the floorboard, and flung it into Brianna's lap. "I had to rearrange a NASA meeting from today until next week, and it took a lot longer than I expected. I managed a brief dinner of a Burrito Supreme and soda myself."

Brianna popped the bag open.

"Food! You're an angel," she declared.

"Really? I'm an angel?" He gave a wry grin. "What have you done with the bossy, sassy Brianna that I once knew?"

"She'll be back as soon as she finishes eating." Turning her attention to the inside of the bag, she studied the wrapped hoagie. "This looks heavenly." Reaching in, she pulled the sandwich out and undid the wrapping. She took a bite, and then brought her gaze back to Devlin, who was flashing a can of Coke in front of her face. She dropped her sandwich and took the can, popping the tab and taking a quick sip. Another can waved in front of her face.

"Open the can for me, will you?"

Brianna placed her can and bag between her jean-clad legs and took the offered can. He was ordering her about, as if he owned her. Perhaps she should open the can and hurl the liquid in his face. No, the surprise shower could send the Jeep hurtling off the road and into a ditch. She wasn't quite ready to die to stroke his alpha male ego. She wiped the top of the can, popped the tab, and then handed it back to him. He took a quick sip.

"I want you to know that when I left Green Sapphire, it was your father's wish that I not look back," he stated. "I've kept that promise. I'm sure you did the same, so the less we talk about whom did what to whom, and how much it hurt, the easier it will be to get through these next couple of days."

Brianna was stunned by the quiet force of his words.

"You spoke with Papa before you left? I didn't know."

He didn't take the hint to embellish on the story and she didn't have the courage to push him. She didn't remember him visiting, and neither of her parents had said a word to her about him before he left the coven. When had they met, and what had been said?

"Change the subject, Brianna," he cautioned, seeing her mouth open. She snapped it shut, and then taking his advice, she changed the subject and began munching on her sandwich again.

"Did Papa give you any hint of what type of ritual Mother was doing when she fell ill?" she asked between bites. "He was purposely vague on the phone."

"Sorry, he only said she had lost consciousness during a ceremony. We didn't talk long. He muttered 'goodbye' and hung up on me."

Brianna couldn't contain a shiver.

"Have you ever heard of a High Priestess collapsing inside a Sacred Circle during a ritual? I haven't." He didn't answer, his attention diverted by a sudden gray shadow streaking across the road in front of the Jeep. The car lurched and then hugged the road again. Glancing down, she studied the last section of her sandwich. "What type of ritual could Mother have been doing?" she asked, "Could it have been a binding spell? They aren't foolproof. They can backfire."

"She'd do a protection spell before ever trying a binding."

"Perhaps I'm the cause."

She heard a brief chuckle.

"There's the Brianna I know. It's all about you ... no, don't hiss. I can't imagine anyone digging into your past and coming up with your coven background, can you?"

Brianna pretended to think on it, glad he didn't know that she had revealed her past to Tommy. Swallowing the last morsel of meat and cheese, she peeked in the bag again and found a bag of unopened potato chips. Withdrawing it, she popped open the bag, enjoying the delicious tang of salt on her tongue.

"Stranger things have happened though," she remarked. She dabbed a speck of saliva from the side of her mouth. "Thanks to the Internet, it's hard to keep anything a secret permanently."

"True," he agreed, taking a swig of soda. "Following your train of thought, her illness appears to be personal, which would lend itself to someone in the coven interfering with the ritual."

Brianna didn't even attempt to hide her anger.

"If I find out that evil was spawned in a coven member's heart and mother was the recipient of that evil, I'll ... " She swallowed her salty chip, surprised when it slid down so easily. "Well, let's just say, I'll not take the news gracefully."

"That fact will work in our favor once we arrive," Devlin stated. "We no longer have a vested interest in the commune, which will allow one of us to pick up on any negative energy that may be lingering and confront the Elders about it."

Brianna took a quick swallow of Coke.

"I may not have been part of the Wicca world in years, but I promise you I still know a thing or two about casting spells."

"Can that kind of talk. It's bad karma."

"It would be justice all around."

Brianna heard a light sigh.

"It's clear you haven't changed much since leaving home." He reached over and helped himself to a chip from the bag. He popped it into his mouth.

"Why did you come, Devlin? You don't owe the coven anything; not anymore."

He looked startled by the question, but took another swig of soda before answering.

"You can't imagine how convincing your father's goodbye was. He said he had made the same phone call to you. Knowing you, I knew how you'd react. You'd come home for your mother's sake, and when you did, I knew you'd need an ally."

Brianna was floored by his reasoning. They weren't friends; he had no reason to be interested in her welfare, especially since she had shredded his character to pieces the last time they had met. *I hope you rot in hell.* Hadn't that been what she had hurled at him? She studied his profile and knew without question, he wouldn't judge her for her actions—past or present. And she knew too, his reasoning said a lot more about her character than his. She tossed her head at him.

"Do you realize that this is first time we have managed to go longer than a minute without sniping at each other?"

"God sends a miracle every so often," he responded, grabbing her napkin and wiping his mouth.

"Don't be rude. You know that we both excel in the art of bad behavior. You have only to look back and see that when Papa paid more attention to you than he did to me, my behavior became atrocious. And then so did yours."

"Is it as simple as that, do you think?"

"It's not about simple when you're nine," Brianna answered. "It's about being paid attention to. Besides, everyone expected you to marry me, and I hated that, especially since you weren't a born coven member."

"Ah, yes, the proverbial outsider," Devlin said, with a grimace. "Always on the outside, looking in."

Brianna saw the scowl that followed and knew she had touched a nerve.

"Perhaps we should change the subject," she said.

"I'm actually enjoying this one."

"Well, I'm not, and if we continue on this track, I might be tempted to remind you how lucky you were to be in the running as the next High Priest of the coven. That's why I was so jealous of you."

"Funny, I thought it was because my appointment would mean that you would have to marry me when you came of age."

Brianna crumpled the bag in her lap between her fingers.

"Now you're just being spiteful. You know my parents would have never sanctioned a marriage between us. We would've killed each other before the wedding ceremony was over, and how would that look listed in the historical pages of the Coven Book of Shadows?"

"Sorry to burst your bubble, Cinderella, but the marriage was already arranged, except for the 'I do's' and the Joining."

Brianna blanched.

"You're joking. I'd never have married you."

"Too bad. You would've made a gorgeous High Priestess." He stole a peek at her face, and Brianna blushed at the lop-sided grin he gave her.

"You're teasing me."

"Maybe."

Brianna snorted.

"Everyone knows you had the hots for Brenda back then. Why do you think Francis disliked you so much? She was everything he wanted in a girlfriend and a wife. And she had a crush on you."

"She had a crush on me? I wish I had known."

"You did know," Brianna scoffed, "Don't you dare deny it."

He grinned again, and then shrugged nonchalantly. Brianna turned her attention to the roadway, digesting his earlier words. When had her parents arranged a marriage between them? They hadn't, she knew; it was inconceivable that they would favor Devlin over Jordy Skyler. Jordy Skyler was her soul mate; the love of her life. She watched the flashing shadows out the window.

"You're pouting."

Brianna turned in her seat.

"Actually I was thinking of Jordy Skyler."

"Him? Don't tell me you still have the red hots for him after all these years."

"You never forget the boy who gave you your first real kiss," she sighed.

"Nor the man who gives you a kiss that melts your soul," he responded.

Stunned by such a romantic insight coming from him, Brianna returned her gaze to the flashing landscape. She wasn't going to start fantasizing about soul melting kisses, not with the clean smell of Devlin's aftershave teasing her nose. *What about all those rippling muscles and his sculpted body?* her inner voice prompted. She ignored the question, opening her purse instead, and pulling out her compact mirror. The reflection that slid into view seconds later revealed a woman tired, worn-down, and not at all sexy. Her mascara streaks were flaky; her eye liner fading. She pulled the dropped napkin from the seat and wiped away the black marks streaking the underside of her eye socket. Then reaching into her makeup bag, she pulled out a lipstick tube and began smearing it on. A few moments later, a chuckle sounded and Brianna halted her movements.

"What?"

"Nothing, just amused by your attempt to improve on perfection."

Brianna gave a haughty sniff.

"As my friend Tommy Cloisters would say, 'There is no such thing as perfection, blue eyes. There's only a hopeful illusion of it.'"

"I like this Tommy Cloisters. Perhaps one day, you'll tell me how you met such a sage philosopher?"

Brianna snapped her mirror shut, and re-pocketed it in her purse. Settling back, she turned her gaze to Devlin's profile.

"Perhaps one day you'll tell me where you went after leaving Green Sapphire, and what you've managed to accomplish since leaving."

"It's a deal," he nodded. He leaned over and turned the radio dial. "Care for some music?"

"Yes, something soothing." Brianna laid her head back against the headrest. "Something that makes these last horrible days a distant memory."

"Done. Cat nap if you can," he advised, seeing her shoulders sag.

The dulcet tones of Josh Groban filled the Jeep a few seconds later and Brianna tuned into the soft, soothing melody. In a matter of minutes, the rocking of the Jeep had her dropping into a deep sleep.

CHAPTER FOUR

A FEW MINUTES LATER

Devlin lifted his foot from the accelerator, noticing the needle approaching eighty. He hadn't meant to reveal his feelings quite so openly, but he had no intention of letting Brianna plunge herself into a pity party. He preferred her anger. And even though she appeared to have forgiven him for that day in the circle, he hadn't forgiven himself for it. He should've felt the spell going wrong as it shifted. But he had been so intent on pleasing Brianna that he missed the signs. Thanks to a foolish, boyhood crush, he had managed to kill Brenda, his confidence, and any chance of pursuing Brianna romantically in the future.

But that was then and this was now, he grimaced. He was fifteen years older and wiser—and certainly more realistic about pursuing Brianna as a permanent bed partner. *Right*, his inner voice supplied. *You just keep pretending you aren't attracted to the clean smell of her hair, or the disturbing way the air around her seems electrified. And her lips?*

Devlin checked the rear view mirror, studying the green eyes glittering back at him. Forget her lips. Focus on the stupidity that robbed her of her heritage. And for God's sake, stop replacing the Dark Time with visions of her body flexing rhythmically beneath yours in all-out ecstasy. They were driving home together, nothing more. Home! The word was laughable. Green Sapphire hadn't been a home to either of them for a very long time.

Turning his head, he gave Brianna's body a raking glance. He had broken every promise he made to forget the past. And he had done it on a whim, hoping that things might be different between

44

him and Brianna now that their lives had intersected again. How masochistic was that?

Feeling the Jeep drift off the roadway, Devlin guided it back with a soft turn of the steering wheel. Hopefully, Brianna would remain asleep for the rest of the trip. Without her pointed questions, he could study her unobserved. His gaze raked her body again. She was still a ravishing blonde, with an hourglass figure. Her lips were sensually rounded and just begged to be thoroughly kissed. And the musky-rose flush that stained her cheekbones? It made him want to see what other flush might be produced if his naked body claimed hers.

He put a brake on that erotic thought—and the insane desire to stop the Jeep and make love to her on the spot. Would the Sisters of Fate look kindly on such an act? Hardly. Then why had they thrown them together again, and filled him with hope that this time he could win her love?

His gaze centered on the illuminated blacktop in front of the Jeep. There was a way to trap her in a loveless marriage, but his pride couldn't stomach it. If he couldn't have her love unconditionally, he didn't want her, period. However, somehow in the next couple of days, he intended to tell her he owned D.J. Corp and that he had bought her company, lock, stock, and barrel. His pride couldn't stomach holding on to that lie any longer either.

Switching his thoughts, he leaned over and replaced the current music with a James Blunt CD. The soothing tones softly reverberated and he returned his attention to the road ahead. The Jeep was eating up their hundred-mile drive at an astonishing rate. He could see the outlying mountain range in the distance already. The Sapphire Lake cutoff was ahead, no further than thirty-five miles.

He let his mind replay Brianna's earlier question. What had gone wrong in the Sacred Circle? Anything, he knew. A pissed off elemental, an intruder stepping into the circle at the wrong time, the door between worlds left open. He squelched that thought. No, he'd not go there. He'd rather think a pissed off elemental had latched onto Sienna's essence and she was unable to fight off the powerful energy. If that were the case, he was sure they could find a way to make amends to the elemental and send it safely back to its home realm. Groveling would probably be part of the process, but it would be a groveling worth doing.

Thirty minutes later, he switched CD's again, and exited the expressway onto the parkway cutoff. As the car settled back into a steady rhythm, he tuned into Brianna's energy level. She had gone dead to the world when the music started, and she hadn't flexed a muscle in at least thirty miles. What was she dreaming about? None of your business, he cautioned. Enjoy the peace and quiet.

Ten miles later, he realized he was nodding off under the steady hum of the tires, and if he didn't find some way to keep his mind occupied, he'd literally fall asleep at the wheel. He stole a peek at Brianna, surprised to find her eyes wide open and studying him.

"Penny for your thoughts," he stated.

"I was thinking about the power of three—how one little thing you do comes back to you in triple force."

"Three times bad, three times good," Devlin quoted.

"Umm, but how does it relate to Mother's collapse? She's never had a hateful thought for anyone. And all I can do is wonder what she could've done to have the power of three boomerang back on her in such a terrible way."

"Perhaps, the boomerang wasn't meant for her," Devlin said. "The karmic lesson may be for the person—or entity—that interrupted the flow of energy in the circle."

"Or me."

Devlin's foot jerked from the gas pedal.

"That's absurd."

"Why? I hurt my parents beyond belief when I willfully disobeyed the Wicca creed. And I broke every principle of faith that I once cherished by wishing harm on you. As if that wasn't enough, I went out into the world and exploited the very people I admire to get them to do what I wanted. So much for the principle of 'blessed be' and 'harm none,' don't you think?"

Devlin digested her words. It was certainly possible that karma owed her a few lessons for her selfish behavior, but he didn't think she was owed the death of her mother as part of that karmic recompense. Should he confess his sins of betrayal to make her feel better? No, she'd not understand; she'd think he was humoring her. He heard a weary sigh, laced with annoyance.

"Alright, let's hear it. What else do I owe you an apology for?"

So much for turnabout, Devlin thought. He followed her second sigh with one of his own.

"We've said it all, I think."

"Well, if we've said it all, then you're just holding a grudge against me for no good reason, and that's just plain stupid."

"I'm stupid?"

"Yes, stupid. I've apologized for wishing harm on you, and if I can humble myself to make an apology, I don't see why you can't. After all, it's not as if I did anything wrong that day."

"No, of course not. You were a saint. It was my fault."

"Exactly. You were the careless one."

"If I remember right, you were emceeing the circle."

"Under your eagle eye. It never dawned on me that you thought I was capable of conducting the ritual on my own. After all, I was only seventeen."

"You've been conversant in Sacred Circles since you were twelve. Why wouldn't I trust you to know what you're doing? Your parents certainly did."

"Of course. Blame Brenda's death on them now."

The slur was cutting, and Devlin wondered why he was letting her get away with such a cheap shot. Had she not once in the past fifteen years thought that Brenda's death might sit squarely on her head? He glanced out the side window. He should've followed his first instinct and let Brianna drive herself home. And more importantly, he should've gone to Florida as planned. Why had he changed his mind? *You still have a "thing" for her,* his inner voice chided. Right. Stupid is as stupid does.

He focused on the roadway ahead again, praying their conversation was truly at an end this time. A loud sigh escaped Brianna's lips.

"Don't you think I know that I mishandled the spell that day?"

"I think that accidents sometimes happen," Devlin interrupted. "It's no one's fault; energy just collides. Let's drop the subject, huh?" He stepped on the gas pedal and brought the car up to a steady seventy miles per hour. It settled under the rush of fuel, giving him time to wish he could turn the clock back a few minutes. Right now, falling asleep at the wheel was preferable to regurgitating an incident that he thought he had buried long ago.

"I never thought I'd want to discuss that day with you."

"Don't then," Devlin cut in. "We were both there; we know what happened. We paid the price. Enough said."

"How long were you ill?"

"Drop the subject," Devlin stated, turning his attention to the CD player. She fell silent, but not for long.

"Don't tell me you weren't ill; I was. We both know that a bout with a powerful negative force can cause an illness to linger for months. How long were you down?"

Devlin ignored the question, hoping his silence would persuade her he had no intention of discussing the past anymore. He pressed the "start" button and listened to the soft, soothing tones of Il Divo. Liking their sound, he turned the music track up. The music disappeared a moment later.

"You may as well answer me. You know what a brat I can be when I set my mind on something."

Devlin turned the music back up again, ignoring her statement. Once more, the music disappeared from his hearing.

"I mean it, Devlin. I need to know the answer to the question—now more than ever."

Devlin gave a huge sigh.

"Look, the punishment fit the crime. You miscalculated the level of your energy, and by the time I realized the error, the ritual tanked."

"And because Brenda was standing behind me, she took the hit."

"Right, so we deserved exactly what we got. Now, drop the subject before I'm forced to toss you out of the car."

"You, and what army of witches?"

Devlin frowned at her sarcasm; however, before he could utter a sarcastic retort, a thumping erupted from beneath the floorboards, and the rear of the vehicle began to fishtail along the blacktop. Lifting his foot from the gas pedal, he tapped on the brakes, hoping to short-circuit the inevitable spin the Jeep seemed headed for.

Twisting the wheel hard-left, he fought to keep the tires from skidding across the swale into a nearby ditch. To his relief, the car righted itself under his jerk and came to a complete stop. Tuning into the silence, he held onto the wheel, listening for the sound of spinning tires. Nothing. At least they weren't dangling over some unseen drop-off. He had hit an animal, nothing more.

"What the hell did you hit?"

"Some damn animal crossing the road."

"Well, that was careless of you."

Her words had him dropping his head, and lightly banging his forehead on the steering wheel.

"Ever mind the Rule of Three," he quoted. "Three times what thou givest returns to thee. This lesson well thou must learn. Thee only gets what thou dost earn."

"I hope you're not suggesting that I caused the animal to cross the road and get killed?"

Devlin rolled his head to the side, his gaze sweeping Brianna's face.

"You *are* a brat, you know—a beautiful one, but still a brat." Lifting his head, he shoved the Jeep into park and exited the vehicle. Angling around the rear panel, he fished in the hatchback for a flashlight. Finding one, he checked the undercarriage on both sides of the car. No structure damage; no smell of gas or burning metal. And definitely no animal carcass caught in the wheel well. He swung the beam behind him, and over the roadway. A lump lay sprawled in pieces not far from the beam. A car door slammed a moment later.

"What have you found?"

Devlin turned the beam onto the mauled lump in the roadway.

"A splattered roadrunner."

She spun about, fixing her stare anywhere but on the diced carcass.

"Are you sure we hit it? Maybe we just ran over the carcass."

"We hit it, Cinderella. So much for my becoming your Prince Charming."

"Don't be an ass!" she sniffed, swinging back around. "Now, are we stranded or not? If we are, it's clear the power of three belongs to you. I'm simply along for the ride."

"Rubbish," Devlin grumbled, tossing the flashlight back through the open hatch and slamming the trunk down hard. "I'm quite sure you've never just been simply along for the ride on anything."

"Are we stranded or not?" she hissed.

"Not."

"Good. I'd hate to leave your murdered body alongside the road for some damn animal to feast on."

He laughed at her words and then spun her about with a hefty shove towards the passenger door.

"Stop being so bloodthirsty and get back in the car. We're almost at the coven turnoff."

She entered the Jeep again and Devlin followed her lead. In less than a minute, they were on the road again, eating up the miles and settling into a companionable silence. Before he knew it, they were passing mile marker 34 and turning onto the perimeter road leading into the compound.

Approaching the front gate, a screech blistered Devlin's ears.

"Stop!"

He slammed on the brakes, sending the Jeep skidding along the dirt roadway with a vicious twist. He heard a door opening before the Jeep had even come to a full stop. The door slammed hard behind Brianna as she dashed out, ignoring his shout to wait. He shoved the car into "Park" and launched himself out of the car after her.

"Have you lost your mind?" he asked, intercepting her at the front bumper.

She grabbed his hand, startling him into silence. Linking her fingers with his, she reached into her blouse and hauled out a jeweled Pentagram. She settled herself in a reverent posture and then lifted the Pentagram upward.

"My golden shield protects me from all that may wish to harm me. I ask that this be done for the greater good of all. Blessed be—I am safe." She turned, and slipped the pentacle from around her neck. She flashed it at Devlin. "Your turn."

He grinned at her, and then holding the pentacle aloft, he repeated the prayer. When they were back in the car, and the Jeep was sailing through the gates, he ventured a comment.

"You're one smart witch, Miss Sage."

She grunted.

"I'm not taking any chances. Sometimes, a negative environment throws off splintered, harmful energies that just beg to be smudged."

The Jeep sailed through the interior compound gate, and Devlin lifted his foot from the accelerator, wondering if Brianna sensed the energy shift in the air.

"I've noticed," Brianna replied, as if reading his mind. "My suggestion would be to put the 'pedal to the metal' and see if we can outrun the feeling."

Devlin increased the vehicle's speed to forty-five, his mouth twisting into a grimace.

"Given our time away from here, we shouldn't be feeling anything at all."

"Well, remember, we used to be about 'blessed be' and 'harm none.' I don't imagine spirit differentiates between the old days and now."

"Right, so let's just carry on, and chalk the feeling up to good old-fashioned nerves."

"I like that suggestion. So mote it be."

Devlin brought the vehicle to a cool fifty-miles per hour and the Jeep sailed through the last of the interior gates without any further jerks, bumps, or unease. That is, until they reached the middle of the compound and found the Main Street plaza totally empty—except for a black streak flashing in front of the car at breakneck speed. Devlin hit the brakes, watching the cat disappear into the shrubs alongside the front bumper.

"Damned crazy cat!" he muttered.

"Cat? Where?" Brianna came alive, bending across his lap and glancing out the window. She searched the bushes for a pair of glittering, yellow eyes, unaware of the effect her sprawled body was having on his lower body. In seconds, she was back in the passenger seat, grousing. "If there's a cat about, we need to find it. It may belong to mother, which means it will know something we don't know."

"You are not going to bond with a cat, Brianna, no matter how bad things get," Devlin said. She looked startled by the suggestion, but wisely held her tongue as he took his foot off the brake. "I mean it," he emphasized, stepping on the gas. "You are not going to throw away your life in D.C. on the off chance a damn cat knows something about something."

"How do you know I live in Washington?" Brianna asked. "I didn't tell you."

"You flew in on a plane from D.C."

"I could've changed planes."

"Drop the subject," Devlin stated, "Concentrate on the matter at hand."

She snapped her mouth shut, doing as he suggested, and glancing at the storefronts they were passing.

"Where is everyone?" she finally asked, "Surely the entire congregation can't have fallen ill in such a short time."

"Perhaps the Elders initiated a house quarantine—to insure there'd be no further outbreak."

"I didn't see any warning signs signaling that, did you?"

Devlin's gaze scanned the center street gazebo.

"No, but they might not have had a chance to post the signs."

"They're probably conducting prayer vigils in the Healing Center."

"Leave it to you to make excuses for their poor judgment," Devlin stated. He stepped on the gas pedal, towards the row of buildings at the end of the main drive.

"I'm not taking sides, Devlin. I'm becoming alarmed."

"Well, stow your fear before it gets the better of you. It's up to us to keep our heads on straight while we're assessing how bad things really are."

"It feels contagious."

"Stow that kind of thinking as well. I don't relish ending up in a bed alongside your parents."

"No. And I don't relish having to call the local police and say 'excuse me, my parents are witches in your jurisdiction, and someone seems to have placed a terrible curse on them. Can you send a team out to investigate?'"

Devlin ignored her sarcasm, concentrating on getting to the clinic as fast as possible. Three turns later, the Jeep braked to a stop in front of a three-story stone building. He studied the row of wreaths covering the sidewalk and clinic doorway. His glance drifted to Brianna, who was chewing on her lower lip.

"Let's not think the worst yet," he advised. "Let's assume that this incident is a freak accident of nature. If we go from that premise, we should be able to zero in on the problem and rectify it."

He saw a look of alarm stain her face and knew her thoughts had flown back fifteen years.

"Neither of us is going near a Sacred Circle again," she said. "We're here to give moral support and offer suggestions. Outside of that, we're not going to get involved."

"You're not my keeper, Brianna."

"I mean it, Devlin. We're visitors here, nothing more."

"Well, then the sooner we get out of this car and find Doctor Ellis, the sooner I will no longer need you as my babysitter."

"So mote it be," Brianna stated, lifting the door handle and pushing the door open. Her smile was grim as she slipped from the front seat into the shadows of a single streetlight, but he had no chance to offer an answer. Her door slammed shut with a soft clunk.

Frowning, Devlin slid from the Jeep. They should've never come home. The current incident was like something out of an Exorcist film, where none of the characters had the slightest skill or knowledge to thwart an evil possession.

"Earth to Devlin," came a hurried call.

Devlin snapped his mind back to reality, slamming the car door shut and joining Brianna at the front of the Jeep. He gave a long sigh.

"Ready. Set. Go."

CHAPTER FIVE

THE CLINIC

"No use stalling," Brianna said, studying the bouquets of flowers lining the sidewalk in front of them.

"It's not about stalling," Devlin replied. "It's about staying grounded and being prepared for anything."

He was right, Brianna knew. There was coven protocol to follow. Without the council's blessing, their stay in the coven would be drive-in, drive-out. They had to find Doctor Ellis and elicit his backing before they met any of the other Elders, and then when they had secured his blessing, they would push for information on what had occurred in the circle to cause her mother's unconsciousness.

Had she opened a portal between worlds and forgot to close it? No, she had thought long and hard about that question during the plane ride, and she had come to the conclusion that her mother didn't make those kinds of mistakes. She had been conducting Sacred Circles for decades. If anything, her mother had been interrupted during her ceremony, and been unable to close the portal.

"There's Brad," Devlin stated. "I called him from the airport, by the way. Told him to expect us."

Brianna squinted, studying the figure striding out of the shadows.

"He looks old and worn down," she commented.

"Solving an epidemic would turn anyone's hair white."

"Amen."

Stepping into a pool of light, the doctor's expression came to life. He offered his hand to Brianna as he reached her.

"You've grown into the spitting image of your mother, Brianna." His gaze shot to the man beside her. "Thanks for the heads-up call, Devlin." He held his hand out and Devlin shook it, nodding.

"Good to see you again, Doctor."

"Call me Brad. We're way past 'doctor' now." His gaze swung back to Brianna. "I was floored when Devlin called and said you were coming. I can't guarantee your being here will be received gracefully by the members, though."

"What about visitors? We didn't see any warning signs posted that the commune was closed to visitors," Devlin said.

A surprised look crossed the doctor's face.

"The commune shuts down for a month every year at this time. Didn't you know?"

His question sent an odd prickling along Brianna's scalp, and she took it as a warning. What was spirit trying to call her attention to? The commune's closing and how it tied to her mother? Or her jitters at being thrust back into her past so rapidly? She brought her gaze back to the doctor.

"Don't you find it odd that this incident occurred right at this time, Brad?"

"No, I didn't think it odd—at least, not until this moment."

"What are you thinking?" Devlin asked.

"It's as if this incident was pre-planned," Brianna replied. "The timing, I mean—so as not to include outsiders. You and I both know from experience that spirit never follows a plan. But this all feels staged to me." Her hands indicated the area around them. "The energy hanging about the grounds is off; not a lot in some places, but certainly bold in others." She studied the men's baffled expressions and changed the subject abruptly. "I'd like to take a look at Mother as soon as possible. If her energy level is off the charts, then we will know that she is the cause of the illnesses occurring and take steps to remedy it."

A quick shake of the doctor's head occurred.

"We tried that; it didn't work."

"Yes, but I haven't offered a solution."

"True; however, we've a more pressing problem—namely, invoking the Dispensation Law with your father."

"And how do we do that?" Brianna asked.

He fished in his pocket.

"With this." He hauled out the Coven Pentagram and flashed it at the pair. "If you evoke the dispensation, it will buy you a twenty-four hour free ride pass with the Elders. Do you remember the words?"

Devlin took the Pentagram from his fingers.

"She remembers." He handed the amulet to Brianna. "You do remember, right?"

She made a face at him and then turned, following the doctor up the clinic steps.

Entering the main foyer behind him, Brianna shivered at the eerie silence. She hoped the rest of the clinic wasn't as depressing as this. She could already feel the tension in Devlin's hand on her arm. Unlike her, though, he was successfully concealing his rattled nerves.

Reaching the elevator, the ends of Brianna's hair suddenly lifted from her neck. Now, what was that for? She glanced over her shoulder at the walls behind her.

"If I didn't know better, I'd think a negative presence was residing in the hallway."

Devlin's gaze followed hers.

"Can that kind of talk. Concentrate on concocting a letting go spell for the community instead. The Universe will reward your efforts."

The light above the elevator door popped on, followed by a light "ding," and Brianna slipped inside the cage before the door was half-way open. The door finally closed and she gave a sigh of relief. A moment later, she spoke up.

"The energy in the compound could be off because a negative entity hitched a ride on Mother's essence sometime during her ritual, and she didn't notice."

"That would explain her collapse," Devlin replied, "but it doesn't explain why so many members of the congregation have been struck down. Of course, it would if the ritual tanked because of carelessness."

Brianna dismissed the thought.

"Mother doesn't make those kinds of mistakes."

The elevator "ding" came again, and the cage door slid open. Brianna scanned the corridor ahead, holding the door open with her hand before stepping out. A typical clinical setting; nothing to indicate stalking entities.

"Turn on a few more lights, Brad," Devlin stated, as if reading her thoughts. "There's nothing comforting about shadows." He stepped from the elevator and headed for a lighted area, about halfway down.

"Hold on," Brad cautioned, plucking at his shirt sleeve. "I need you both to follow me. Francis' son, Danny, is seriously ill. I need you to read his aura for any blemishes."

Brianna frowned. It was just like the doctor to expect they still knew how to recognize a blemished aura after all this time.

"Noted." Devlin said. He sketched a wave at Brianna. "We'll trust our instincts as we go. Hopefully, what I don't see, you will, and vice versa."

Brianna gave a relieved sigh at his words. For a moment, she thought he meant to abandon her. In the elevator, she had experienced an insane, brief desire to lean against Devlin and fit her fingers in his. What would he have done if she had? *Pull away,* her inner voice supplied. *Dropped your fingers like a hot potato.*

The doctor moved to the first door on their left, and following, Brianna peeked in. She studied the long-legged figure leaning over the bed. Eerie. That was the message relayed to her brain. Her gaze swept the series of tubes crisscrossing the bed, and she craned her head to view the occupant under the sheets. Young. Obviously, Danny Lord.

"What are you doing out of bed, Sally?"

The hunched figure standing next to the bed swung about, clearly startled by the doctor's question. Brianna recognized the freckled face of Sally Carver at once. Some things never changed, she mused. Sally was still flashy in dress and sporting a hair-do fresh out of the seventies. The stocky woman straightened her shirt top, and stepped away from the bed.

Even sick, Sally was a marvel in hooped earrings and bangle bracelets. The sound of clinking metal was amplified in the room as Brianna saw her eye the doctor, and then move onto her and Devlin. Her recognition was instant.

"What are *they* doing here?" she demanded. She took a formidable stance in front of the bed, glaring at the pair, and then the doctor. "Surely, you are capable of finding a solution without bringing in outsiders. After all, you have been attending to our ills for decades. Did they even consult the Council before coming here? I don't remember hearing Francis talk about it."

"Fortunately for all of us, you're not in charge of the coven," Brad said, "Charles is."

Sally's expression soured at the doctor's insult, and Brianna was sure the pair had butted heads many times before. She could see why. The vibrant personality that had marked Sally's younger years had vanished completely, leaving a matronly snob in its wake. And she had, what? Ended up marrying Francis after her sister's death? It was hard to believe the pair would find comfort in marriage, but then opposites were often drawn to each other. However, right now that didn't matter. The energy level in the room needed to be brought back to a pleasant decibel.

"We are not here to interfere with coven matters, Sally. We came because of Mother—to get to the bottom of her collapse.

You know as well as I that mistakes can be made at any time when it comes to Sacred Circles."

"Are you insinuating that a member of this coven caused her collapse?"

"Not at all," Devlin interjected, "I'm sure we'll find her collapse was a freak accident." To Brianna's surprise, Sally's hostility quickly evaporated.

"Of course, it's freakish. It's what I've been telling Francis for days."

"In that case, you'll have no objection to Brianna and Devlin taking a look at Danny for a moment with me," Brad said. A myriad of expressions ranging from outrage to compliance crossed Sally's features, and Brianna wondered how she managed to shift from emotion to emotion so quickly. Sally suddenly swayed on her feet and Brad snatched her elbow. "I've warned you not to overdo it, Sally. This illness is draining your system. If you continue to push your body to the point of exhaustion, you will find yourself in worse shape than Danny."

Tears welled at his words.

"He's my angel. I don't know what I'll do without him … he looks so helpless…"

Brad took her arm, guiding her towards the doorway.

"Go and rest, so I can bring Danny back to you healthier than ever."

She gave him a weak smile, and Brianna saw the aura surrounding her frame slip from red to grey. Her shoulders sagged unexpectedly, and she collapsed against the door jam with an agonizing sob. Devlin rushed to her aid, throwing an arm around her shoulders.

"Rituals can be reversed. We found that out when we were ten, remember?" He shook her shoulders. "You mustn't give up now. Brad will find a way to reverse this illness."

Brianna saw Sally's eyes come alive, with shades of the girlfriend they once knew. She clutched Devlin's hand.

"I'm sorry for being so mean-spirited before. I'm tired and cranky, and feeling worse by the minute."

"You must go back to your room and lie down," Brianna advised. "Rest and sleep has always been the best cure for tired lungs."

She nodded then whirled, disappearing out the door.

"You still have a knack when it comes to her, I see," Brad said, heading towards the bed. Reaching it, he pushed the boy's bangs away from his forehead and signaled the pair forward. "Danny doesn't appear to be getting worse; however, he doesn't appear to be getting any better either." He stepped aside. "Tell me what you think."

Brianna crossed to the bed, surprised to find her hands damp with sweat as she touched the handrail. Fear. The word resembled a shock wave jolting her brain. She didn't like that message. It meant that she hadn't really convinced herself until this moment that the coven had come under serious attack from an unknown source. But now, seeing the boy's pale skin and shallow breathing, she was sure his condition wouldn't be so easily diagnosed without some intuitive insight.

"Anything?" Brianna jumped at the question. "Sorry, didn't mean to startle you." Brad wrapped his fingers around Danny's wrist and monitored the beats. "Danny was the first to arrive in the clearing. He found your mother and immediately came searching for your father."

"And he was the first to come down with the bug?" Brianna asked, studying the boy's flushed skin as he roused from his sleep. "May we touch him, Brad?"

"At your own peril, I'm afraid."

"Well, I don't see how you expect us to give you our opinion on things if we can't touch people. Besides, your warning is too late.

I'm already terrified." She reached out and brushed the boy's face and neck with the back of her hand. His vacuous gaze centered on her face as he felt the touch.

She bent down, offering him a smile. "I know you feel like you're on fire," she said, "but I have just the magic to cool you down." She patted his hand. "No more worrying, you hear?" He gave her a reluctant nod and closed his eyes. Brianna turned from the bed to find Devlin studying her curiously. She addressed his unspoken thoughts. "Hope can do more than magic sometimes. If he thinks he will get well, he will." Reaching out, she withdrew a pencil and notepad from the doctor's shirt pocket and scribbled on the first sheet of the pad. "I want you to fix this potion and give it to Danny. If my grandmother was right, it should work its magic in about three hours."

He glanced down at the note, his right eyebrow lifting in surprise as he read the three lines.

"You can't mean it's this simple?" he remarked.

"The earth is an amazing storehouse for miracles, Brad. They're simple and direct. They are never packaged with glitz and glamour."

The doctor folded the note and nodded his thanks.

"I'll have Francis scrape up the ingredients from Sally's shop. The mixture will be dispensed in less than an hour." He studied her curiously again. "You're more High Priestess than you realize." He tossed a wave over his shoulder. "Marla Curtis is recuperating two doors down—Eileen's next door. They appear to be holding their own though; no other symptoms, except for hacking coughs … why the startled look?" he asked breaking off.

"I just spent the last week with a horrendous cold and a hacking cough." His features became alarmed, and Brianna held up her hand. "No, I'm not contagious. I got sick prior to Mother's collapse and was well on the way to recovery when you called."

"An omen of things to come, do you think?"

"It's hard not to see the correlation at the moment," Devlin said. "However, I don't put much stock in coincidences. I'm mentioning it because Brianna believes in the concept of 'what goes 'round, comes 'round.'"

"You're talking about the power of three now."

Brianna didn't confirm or deny his statement; instead, she turned her attention back to the boy in the bed. She lifted the covers atop his body and scanned his arms and legs. No bruises or welts, and his aura was a pale lavender hue at the moment.

She dropped the covers. It was a safe bet that Danny took one look at her mother, panicked, and then fled the clearing.

"Anything jumping out at you now?" Devlin asked.

"Nothing. Perhaps, that's why I'm so scared," she replied. "Energy sickness usually comes with a definite pattern. Welts or bruises on the body, a high fever, alternating hot flashes, and cold sweats." Brianna nodded at the bed. "Danny's skin is warm to the touch, but not hot. And I don't see any signs of a rash or bruising. If he's the worst of the doctor's patients, then we should feel encouraged."

"But you're not," Brad stated.

"No, and I won't be until I learn what occurred prior to Mother's casting of the circle."

"And if you learn she had help in going down in the circle?"

"I'll make the bastard pay."

"I don't like the sound of that." Brad shook his head. "It's not at all Wiccan."

"Or Christian." Devlin replied, stepping from the bed and heading for the door.

Brianna followed more slowly, catching sight of Brad's grin at her.

"I'm glad you're both here," he said. "It's good to have logical, no-nonsense individuals making hard decisions for us."

Brianna's hand flew out as she took a half-turn back.

"I'll remind you you said that when the going gets tough, and you're damning us to hell."

He laughed and Brianna re-whirled, slamming into Devlin's chest. He grasped her shoulders at the same time she clutched his chest. The very air around her suddenly turned electric, and her pulse began dancing with excitement. For a brief moment, she thought Devlin was going to lower his head and kiss her. But when she looked up, she found him grinning boyishly at her. His hands moved slowly; too slowly, skimming her torso lightly and traveling to her waist. Once there, her heart lurched as he balanced her weight and kept her steady. To her horror, she blushed like a giddy girl of seventeen and pulled out of his arms. She emitted a choking laugh.

"Next time, give a girl a warning you're going to crush her toes."

"If there's a next time, I'll crush more than your toes."

Brianna turned a vivid scarlet at his insinuation. Thankfully, he turned on his heel before he could see her reddened cheeks. A moment later, his fingers beckoned her from the hallway. Taking a deep, unsteady breath, Brianna squared her shoulders. Next stop, a surprise reunion with her father.

CHAPTER SIX

A FEW MOMENTS LATER

Brianna stopped just short of the open doorway, taking another deep breath. Was she ready to face her father again after all these years? Ready to mend fences with the Elders? She didn't know, and the curling in the pit of her stomach was proof that she might not be ready. Her dry mouth said it, too.

"No pain, no gain." Devlin quoted, giving her back a forceful shove. She stumbled into the room, giving Devlin a damning look over her shoulder. He ignored the look, content to lounge against the door frame and study the room before them.

Catching her balance, Brianna spotted her father propped up on two pillows. Good Lord, he looked terrible. It was as if the current illness was being directed at him, as well as her mother. Seeing his head turn at her clumsy entrance, she moved to the bed. Once there, she dangled the Pentagram in front of him. She chanted softly.

"I stand here in your guardian light; empower this amulet with all of your might. Dispensation of a day is all that we ask; please accept this request as the Council's new task." She lowered the Pentagram. "Hello, Papa." She bent and wrapped her arms around his shoulders and gave his back a soothing pat. He returned the hug and then pushed her away, brushing his left cheek quickly.

"Dispensation granted, daughter. Bless the Goddesses for bringing you here." A sudden spasm of coughing derailed his greeting, and his hand shot to his mouth for cover. A minute later, his voice was quivering. "As you can hear, I'm in bad shape. It's as if whatever happened to your mother has latched itself on to me."

Brianna shook his arm.

"Devlin and I will pinpoint the problem for you."

His gaze shot to the doorway, and Brianna saw him smile. He held out his hand for Devlin, who moved and shook it firmly. With his free hand, he reached out for Brianna. "My two magic makers finally here. I can rest easy now." His gaze swung to the chair across from the bed. "I know Sienna has a fighting chance now that Devlin and Brianna have come, Francis. They've only to examine the circle and tell us how to make things right."

Brianna looked at the lanky figure rising from a chair. Merciful heavens! Francis was still lurking in shadows and eavesdropping.

"You're full of surprises, Charles. I wish I didn't have to put a damper on this homecoming, but as First Elder, I must. We cannot have outsiders dictating our destiny. It is against coven protocols."

"Throw me out. I dare you!" Brianna declared, recklessly.

Devlin interrupted her impending tirade. He focused on Francis's mulish expression.

"Neither Brianna nor I have any intention of interfering with coven matters. We are here to give advice only. If Charles thinks we can be of help by taking a brief look at the circle, we will do it. So the question now becomes, what will you need from us in order to release the clearing back to the Council?"

Brianna saw a surprised look cross Francis's face, and his gaze shot to her father.

"They don't know?"

"Know what?" Brianna asked, following Francis' scrutiny of her father. A sudden prickling on the ridge of her neck had Brianna catching her breath. Bad news was coming. She could feel it.

"I didn't tell you everything when I called," her father replied. "About your Mother, that is."

Brianna fumbled for a chair and sank down.

"She's not ... "

Her father's hand reached out from the bed.

"No, no. She's alive … "

"Thank goodness!" Her father fell back against the pillows and Brianna felt a brief touch on her shoulder. She nodded at Devlin. "No hysterics yet, I promise you."

"Good girl."

"She was Drawing down the Moon in a special binding ceremony," her father rallied. "There had been a report of an un-Sacred Circle being created."

"My God, Papa! You let her go into the clearing knowing that? What were you thinking?"

"That your mother could take care of herself; she always has."

"Are you sure she wasn't conducting a protection ceremony? You don't need to Draw down the Moon to bind a sinner."

"I can only assume that is what she was doing. She left the cottage without a word to me."

"Performing a ceremony without back-up was a risky thing for her to do under the circumstances," Devlin said.

A set of spasms contorted her father's chest, cutting off any reply he would've liked to make. Alarmed, Brianna jumped from her chair and grabbed his fingers.

"Enough talking. Francis can fill us in on the rest."

Her father shook his head, rallying his strength.

"Don't go baiting Francis. He may be the only person that can aid you in collecting evidence from the clearing."

Brianna made a face.

"The evidence has already gone underground, we all know that. Francis is purposely being a horse's … " She felt Devlin's hand along her upper arm, and brushed his fingers away. "I'm not going to insult Francis. I just want to remind him of the proper protocol when comforting a High Priest under the weather."

"I can't wait to hear what you think that is," Devlin muttered.

Brianna rumpled her nose at him, turning her attention to Francis, whose scowl was almost as fierce as her own. His next words were terse.

"You have no authority here, Brianna, and even though you have been clever enough to evoke the Dispensation Law, it's only bought you one more day in our midst." He held out his hand. "The Pentagram, if you please. It will need to be cleansed and purified before being returned to the Sacristy."

His pointed barb didn't go unnoticed.

"I have no desire to rule anyone, Francis," Brianna remarked, ignoring his outstretched hand. "but you are mad if you think I came all this way to be shunned by the Elders." She waved her hand towards the bed. "I am not going to let anyone sweep the illnesses occurring here under a rug."

"Are you insinuating that the Council had something to do with your mother's collapse?" Francis asked. "And that we now intend to hide what happened to her?"

That was what Brianna thought, but she didn't have the courage to say it out loud, especially when she had no proof of any wrongdoing by the Council. Beside her, her father contained another hacking cough.

"What has Brad recommended for Mother?" Brianna asked. "Has he tried a healing wash?"

"No, I haven't," Brad replied, entering the room. "None of us have the purity to do it at the moment." He crossed to the bed and lifted her father's hand, measuring his pulse. Her father's eyes re-opened and he flashed a weak smile at the doctor.

"Look here, Brad," Devlin stated, stepping forward. "Something is going on that you're not telling us. I can feel it around your auras. What is going on?"

"And you had better have a damn good reason for keeping it a secret." Brianna threw in. "All this secrecy smacks of a cover-up."

"I couldn't tell you everything when you called," her father said. "In case, you didn't come."

"We're here, so spill the bad news," Devlin muttered.

Her father blew threw his cheeks, glancing at Devlin, rather than at her.

"Sienna's body is still in the circle in the clearing. We are unable to get past the energy barrier."

"What!" Brianna fumbled for her chair again, and dropped down. "She's still inside the circle? You've left her inside the circle?" She covered her face with her hands. "How could you keep that vital piece of information from us?" She peeped through her fingers at her father. "How could you be so cruel? Do you realize how much time you've wasted by keeping this a secret? You've wasted days that we could've used to save Mother's life."

"We tried to get her out, Brianna. The attempt failed."

Brianna's temper flared.

"You can't manipulate spirit, Papa. I know that better than anyone." She whirled on the doctor. "How long has she been unconscious, Brad?"

"Four days, maybe five."

"Five!" Brianna covered her face with her hands again. "Five days down!" A weight settled on her shoulders and she glanced up at Devlin's face. A stray tear escaped her right eye. "Have you ever heard such garbage? They left her in the circle. They've m-m-murdered her." Her voice cracked on the words.

"No one's murdered anyone," Devlin advised. "We're going down to the clearing right now, and by God, we're going to repair the problem."

Brianna's tears dried instantly.

"Have you lost your mind? We are not going to repair anything. Not even to appease our guilt over past mistakes."

"Brianna."

Brianna hopped to her feet.

"No, I don't want to hear it, Papa. You attempted to reverse a spell without knowing its source and look what's happened." She whirled around, glaring at both Francis and Devlin. "No one is going to try any type of repair—until I give the word. There have been enough reckless acts already. It's time for some logical assessments for a change." She rounded on Francis. "Is there anyone who hasn't come down with the bug besides you, Francis?"

He ignored her question, turning his back on her, and retaking his former chair. He shot her a mutinous glare, and then shifted his attention to the outside window. Seeing his slouched posture and mulish expression, Brianna's anger edged up a decibel; however, before she could utter a scathing retort, Brad intervened.

"Rufus is still healthy, and so are some of the teens," he said.

"Where can we find Rufus?" Devlin asked, clutching Brianna's elbow and pulling her towards him.

"In his office," Francis finally spoke up. "But if you think you can convince him to let you examine the circle, let me warn you, you cannot step foot in the clearing."

"Why the hell not?" Brianna hissed.

"You aren't married," he gloated. "The Sanctity Law clearly states that no unmarried man or woman can enter the Sacred Clearing once they are of age."

His words floored Brianna, but she didn't let it show. Instead, her mouth formed a perfect rosette.

"Oh, dear, didn't anyone tell you, Francis? Devlin and I married years ago."

Shock siphoned the blood from his face and Brianna would've laughed if she hadn't heard the intake of breath mirrored by Devlin. Francis' gaze dropped to her ring-less hand and then to Devlin's left hand.

"You always did love making a mockery of our laws, Brianna," he stated.

"No, it was you I loved making a mockery of," she replied.

Devlin quelled the rivalry at once.

"Can the insults, you two. We've a pressing problem to solve. We need to get Rufus's permission to examine the clearing and we need to get it now." Francis started to rise from the chair; however, Devlin waved him down. "It's best we face Rufus on our own, Francis."

"Like you did fifteen years ago?"

For the first time since they had arrived, Brianna saw Devlin's demeanor darken.

"Careful, Francis, you're treading on thin ice here. I still know a thing or two about spell making, and I'm not above proving that to you."

Francis blanched at the threat, and then slouched deeper into his chair. Noting his posture, Devlin pushed Brianna out the door, and down the hallway. Nearing the elevator, Brianna balked at his aggressive shoving.

"Stop pushing me, I'm not a vacuum cleaner." Reaching the elevator, she jammed the "down" button rapidly.

"Neither of us can afford to act like brats," Devlin replied. "We have to sound grown up and confident—even if we aren't."

"Do you honestly think either of us is ready to face a Sacred Circle again?"

"Not without the Council's blessing."

"That's not what I meant."

"I know what you meant."

"It is forbidden for an unmarried couple to enter a Sacred Clearing; we forgot that. So unless you can conjure up a wife in the next few minutes, we are screwed."

Devlin stuffed his hands into his back jeans pocket.

"Our problem will be solved if you consent to marry me in the next few minutes," he countered.

"That isn't funny." Brianna shot him a withering glance. "We have to find a way to circumvent the Sanctity law."

"Rufus will never agree."

"He'll have to. Otherwise, I'll make so many allegations of attempted murder, his head will spin."

A black scowl saturated Devlin's features at the threat. He snatched her arm and shook it.

"Don't even think about pushing him. If you do, we will be ousted from the commune before our twenty-four hours is up."

Brianna jerked free of his fingers.

"Stop bossing me around. I outrank you, thanks to my heritage."

He took a step back, his expression one of impatience. And then he grabbed her elbow and shoved her into the now open elevator cage. In less than a minute, they were moving through the downstairs lobby, and out the front door, into the full fledged darkness of night. Reaching the sidewalk, Brianna slowed her steps.

"I didn't mean what I said back there," she apologized. "You bring out the worst in me. You always have."

He sighed at her words.

"I'm not your enemy, Brianna."

She sighed even louder.

"I know that ... no, don't say it. I'm not your babysitter either, but I need to know that we are both on the same page here." She saw his mouth open. "No, I need your assurance right now, or I swear I will invoke my rights as High Priestess and toss you out of the commune."

He took her elbow again, this time more gently; however, his words were anything but gentle.

"You may be used to browbeating clients in your daily life, but don't try that bullshit on me. If by some miracle, we get permission to enter the clearing, neither of us will be attempting any secondary ritual in an effort to resolve this problem—even if you've thought everything out in that level-headed brain of yours.

Disrupting a spell always results in disaster. Mother Nature sees to it."

Satisfaction pursed Brianna's mouth.

"We are on the same page at last. We will examine first, talk it out, and then make a decision together."

"Unless of course, a hasty marriage is the best option," Devlin added.

Brianna's hiss was out before she could stop it.

"Don't make me cast a spell on you instead of Francis." She felt her elbow gripped harder, followed by a strong push towards a grassy swale.

"Don't get your panties in a twist, Rapunzel. Being married to you doesn't have the same fascination it once did. It sounds more like a prison sentence now."

Brianna didn't bother to hide her laughter.

"See, I knew we were on the same page."

"Well, hold that thought, because if I remember right, Rufus Lord never liked either of us very much. One misplaced threat, and he'll have the Council come down on us hard."

"You think he knows we're here?"

"Is the Pope Catholic?"

"Right." Brianna frowned. "Let's get a move on. Patience is not my strong suit."

"Amen to that."

CHAPTER SEVEN

ELDER OFFICES

The Healing Center was empty except for the sound of falling water, a fact that pleased Brianna more than she could say. She needed to hear something soothing for a change, and she only hoped that her current feeling of calm wouldn't desert her during their upcoming meeting with Rufus Lord. She glanced at the far end of the room, to the etched rock formation called Spirit Fountain. At least they had retained the beauty of the building in its purest, physical form.

"Try not to be a rotten brat when we get in there, huh?"

Brianna crinkled her nose, entering the narrow hallway ahead of Devlin's mock bow. She had never learned the art of holding her tongue; however, it was rude of him to remind her of it. After all, they had just agreed to work together. She passed a pastel mural on the wall, and then another, impressed by the serenity of the pieces. Had Rufus chosen the paintings? It was hard to imagine, given his sour disposition and chilling stare.

Reaching the back offices, Brianna heard raised voices and instantly recognized the deeper of the two. She bustled down the corridor and through Rufus's open door.

"Tommy! For heaven sakes! What are you doing here? However did you find me?"

Her colleague's grin was amiable, a total contrast to his rumpled clothes.

"It wasn't easy. This place isn't listed on any GPS tracking map in the known world. I have to say, however, I can see the fascination in living here. The nearest neighbor is what? Fifty miles away? Plenty of room for casting spells and shit."

Offended by the glib obscenity, Rufus offered a rebuke.

"To label our community as practicing 'shit' is a mockery of the Wicca Creed—and of course, to all of us who hold respected positions in the Coven Council."

Brianna twisted towards the desk. Rufus hadn't changed a bit. He was still tall, dark, and not at all likeable.

"Stow your criticism, Rufus," she stated. "Tommy meant no disrespect." She stepped towards the desk, holding out the Coven Pentagram. "Coven protocol dictates we seek your blessing after evoking the Dispensation Law."

He took the Pentagram, his cool demeanor warming slightly at her apology.

"I suppose you felt compelled to come home after hearing about your mother." He studied the man behind her. "But I must say I'm surprised to see you here, Devlin." A light tug emanated on her jeans pocket, and Brianna looked down.

"Introduce me to this tall fellow behind you, blue eyes." Tommy said. "He looks too urban to be a witch."

"He's Devlin Janus. We grew up together here in Green Sapphire."

Surprise permeated Tommy's face; however, Brianna chose to ignore the look. If she focused attention on Devlin, Tommy would automatically assume they shared some type of intimate relationship.

"You two grew up together? Here?"

Devlin roused behind her, placing his hand on Tommy's shoulder.

"I'm sure Brianna will find time later to bring you up to speed on our relationship. Right now, we have urgent business with Reverend Lord. Give up your seat."

He bolted up and took a seat on a nearby futon. Seeing his puzzled look, Brianna knew his firecracker brain wouldn't stay puzzled for long. He was a master at solving mysteries.

"I suppose Doctor Ellis has briefed you on Sienna's condition," Rufus stated, settling back in his chair. He focused on Brianna's face, and then switched to Devlin's lowering form. His voice took on an amused tone. "I'd like to know how you intend to disrupt the barrier, since neither of you can enter the clearing."

Brianna made a face at him.

"What difference does it make how we do it, as long as we do it?"

His good-naturedness dampened.

"I won't allow you to make a mockery of our ways, Brianna—even if you are Sienna's daughter."

"That's a little high-handed, don't you think?" Brianna asked. "Given the circumstances."

Brianna felt a light pinch on her arm and she snapped her mouth shut. Her bitterness was showing again, and Devlin was warning her of it.

"We've told Francis we have no intention of getting in anyone's way," Devlin interjected. "And we mean it. However, I'm at a loss to see why you would be so dead-set against our taking a look at the circle, especially when the High Priest of this coven has given us his seal of approval."

"I'm not against you entering the clearing. All you have to do is marry Brianna, and I shall gladly walk you both to the clearing myself."

"We have no intention of getting married, just to appease the Sanctity law," Brianna stressed. "But I think you knew that as soon as we entered the room. So, I'll ask you straight out, what is the Council hiding about Mother's collapse?"

"Nothing. It's far too premature to assume anything. Nothing has been ruled out at this point."

"Surely you have some notion," Brianna chided. "An angry elemental, a door left open … "

Rufus cut her off.

"Interference by a stranger? I know all the possibilities, but I would be a poor Third Elder if I centered on the criminal aspect, and ignored the spiritual possibilities first."

"Where does the Council stand on her collapse? We heard of an unsacred circle being constructed."

"Conjecture only. We have inspected the grounds and found no hint of anything dangerous being constructed. There is simply no reason for this energy sickness to be occurring."

"Unless of course, Mother's ritual is still in flux and every patient in the clinic was part of the Intercession ceremony. That could account for their energy sickness."

Rufus frowned.

"If the circle was in flux, wouldn't Francis be suffering the effects? He conducted the ceremony."

"Perhaps he's the carrier of the sickness," Brianna said. "It's not unheard of for a parasite to latch onto the strongest witch's essence during a ceremony."

"It's not the case here, though," Devlin interjected. "I read his aura earlier and it's clean."

Rufus looked relieved by Devlin's words, and Brianna wished she could read auras as well as Devlin. Right now, she needed a gauge to judge everyone by; including Devlin.

"The energy sickness is a priority, of course," Rufus remarked. "If left undiagnosed, it could go beyond our compound walls."

"There is absolutely no indication that this illness is contagious," Brianna spoke up, her gaze switching to Tommy, whose face had suddenly drained of color. "Relax, Tommy, you are perfectly safe." Brianna's focus returned to Rufus. "There is no reason to create a panic by speculating the worst. It might only be a small energy leak. And that can be remedied by the Council easily when we find it."

"If you find it," Rufus stated.

Brianna heard the sarcasm in his tone; however, before she could fling back her own sarcastic retort, Devlin intervened again.

"Is there a way to circumvent the Sanctity law, Rufus? Some dispensation in the Book of Shadows?"

"Absolutely not!" Rufus stated. "The law is straight-forward. For you to aid us in the clearing, Brianna must invoke her rights as High Priestess. Once she does that, she will be required to take a husband." He glanced back and forth between Devlin and Tommy, and then centered back on Devlin. "I'm assuming she'd be forced to choose you, since Mr. Cloisters is an outsider, and not eligible."

Brianna did bristle this time.

"No harm will come to the coven if we examine the circle without being married," Brianna countered. "Desperate times call for desperate measures."

"So we should just abandon our principles, and re-work them every time a crisis occurs?" Rufus asked. He shook his head. "I think not."

Brianna ground her teeth unhappily.

"We won't blemish the Sacred Clearing with our citified hearts. You should look a little closer to home for that sin."

His face shut down completely at the subtle jibe.

"Are you insinuating that a master of dark magic is residing here in the coven?"

"I'm merely questioning the rush to force a marriage between Devlin and I. It's almost as if you hope to pit us against each other. That way, we'll leave before the dispensation runs out." She craned her head. "Or is it that you have an idea of the sinner's identity and hope to sanction them for causing another Dark Time?"

Devlin squeezed her arm, offering Rufus a quick apology.

"Chalk Brianna's rudeness up to a repressed sense of persecution," he muttered. His gaze met Brianna's. "The past is the past, and this is now—and new. You are going to have to invoke your rights as Interim High Priestess."

Brianna ground her teeth with a hiss this time. Invoke her rights when she didn't know whether her Mother was alive or dead? She wouldn't do it. There had to be an alternative solution. Annoyed by Devlin's continuing stare, she shifted in her chair.

"Any damage to the clearing has already been done, and being married won't alter that fact." She glanced out the window and caught sight of Devlin's reflection. Why wasn't he putting up a fight against marrying her? *He'd do anything to save your mother,* her inner voice supplied. *Even marry you.*

"Brianna?" She brought her gaze back to Rufus. "Perhaps if you advised Francis on how to clear the circle, the marriage wouldn't be necessary. He's extremely adept at emceeing Sacred Circles."

Brianna balked at the suggestion.

"No one is going to repair the circle. I forbid it!" She felt a nudge on her wrist and knew Devlin was losing patience with her runaway tongue.

"As good as Francis is," Devlin stated. "He's never been through a busted circle. If he guesses wrong and the clearing is still hot, there will be ramifications not even a marriage can save."

Brianna tuned into the warmth of the fingers lying along her arm, and wondered where Devlin was finding the courage to accept the fact that they might have to marry in order to retrieve her mother's body from the circle. The thought gave her goose bumps, an erratic pulse, and a damnable vision of his naked body claiming hers during The Joining ritual.

"However, given our history with circles," Devlin continued, "I see no reason for Brianna and me to contemplate marriage. Her skills would be better used supporting your leadership role. The congregation will be expecting a certain behavior from her as the next-in-line High Priestess."

Rufus's gaze swung to Brianna, who shifted uncomfortably under his penetrating stare. Why had Devlin brought up her lineage to Rufus? Especially when his aura exuded a questionable energy around his frame? It was clear by his glare that he doubted her ability to follow in the footsteps of her mother. No, that wasn't it, she realized, holding his gaze. He didn't want her to follow in her mother's footsteps.

His careful scrutiny of her placid expression changed suddenly, and Brianna gave a relieved sigh.

"How do you feel about it, Brianna?" he finally asked. "Is it alright for Devlin to risk retrieving your mother by himself, and thus, facing reprisals from the Council?"

"No, it's not alright," Brianna replied, curtly. "We must do it together, or not at all." She heard a fractured hiss. "No, I won't change my mind, Devlin. The illness is contained for the moment, which means if we're lucky enough to find a way to retrieve Mother's body, it's going to take two healthy witches to carry it off."

"She's got a point, Devlin," Rufus agreed.

"Yes, damn her, she does." Devlin turned in his chair, contemplating Brianna's face and posture. A moment later, her hands were engulfed in his strong ones. "Look here; let's be frank with one another. I don't think it's possible for any witch, even a High Priestess, to remain alive after being trapped five days in a circle. Do you?"

A sudden rush of tears welled up and Brianna suppressed a sob.

"If she's wearing her amulet, she could. She might have used it to build a bubble of protection."

Her fingers were squeezed.

"Don't give me the emotional answer. Give me the rational one. Do you believe a witch could stay alive after five days down?"

"N-n-no."

Brianna's voice broke on the word, and her fingers were re-squeezed.

"Right. So let's forget about a loveless marriage that neither of us wants. Instead, let's concentrate on letting me enter the clearing alone. I might get lucky and not go down."

Brianna fell silent, digesting his words. Should she let him sacrifice his life to retrieve her mother's body, when she was already beyond help? As much as she wanted to, she couldn't let him do it. She would have to marry him, and that was that. It was the only logical thing to do.

"Brianna?"

"It's true you are far more versed in Sacred Circle rituals than I am. But I have the power of six generations behind me. And that might be all the edge we need."

"Excuse my ignorance, Brianna," Tommy interrupted from the couch. "But it sounds like you're considering a makeshift marriage to someone you haven't seen in more than a decade." He squinted at Devlin. "I can't allow Brianna to marry you. She's in the middle of a financial buyout that depends on her being in good health and focused."

Brianna's head snapped around and she scrubbed her wet cheeks.

"You've found a buyer for my company already?"

She felt a strong pressure on her arm again, and she snapped her mouth shut.

"This argument is better left till later," Devlin advised. "When we have the privacy to battle it out amongst ourselves."

Brianna flushed at the reprimand.

"Sorry, Tommy. I'm riding on my nerves." The man on the futon nodded as Devlin took up the conversation with Rufus again.

"We will need some time to talk this marriage proposal out between us. We both have a lot to lose *if* we decide to marry."

Brianna heard the emphasis on "if" and winced. He didn't want to marry her; not now, not ever. He was stalling for time. And as much as she agreed with him, she couldn't let him have his way. Too much was riding on their decision.

Tommy's voice cut through the sudden silence.

"There is always a way to circumvent an unbreakable law," he remarked. "I don't see why it can't be done in this instance."

Devlin's sigh was demonstrably loud.

"Because coven law isn't governed by any state or local administrative laws. This particular coven has chosen to abide by Sanctity laws established over a century ago. These laws cannot be circumvented or reworked in any way, no matter the crisis. So, if we are to help the community through this crisis, we must abide by the Sanctity law and marry."

Tired of the subject, Brianna glanced out the window.

"I wish you would stop talking as if we had other options." Her voice turned brittle as she swung back to Devlin. "Mother must be removed from the circle and then buried with honors." She turned towards Rufus. "As coven protocol dictates, I'm invoking my rights as Interim High Priestess. Make note of the time." She shifted back to Devlin. "I'm ready to marry you now." He seemed startled by her words, but Brianna ignored the look. All that mattered was retrieving her mother's body from the circle. "Tommy can serve as our witness," she added.

Devlin threw up his hand.

"Hold on. There are dowries to settle, votes to be taken, and an oath to be administered. The marriage will have to wait a few more hours."

"And leave Mother down another night? Not on your life!"

The room went silent at her declaration, but not for long. Devlin shot to his feet and circled his chair.

"It's already been five days," he chided, gripping the backrest. "One more night won't make a damn bit of difference. Besides, if we are going to have any chance of halting this epidemic, we have to see the sun rise over the circle boundaries and make our judgments at that time. To attempt a retrieval in the middle of the night is just plain idiotic."

"So is getting married," Tommy threw in.

"Shut up, Tommy," Brianna bristled. "You have no say in the matter."

Devlin cut off her indignation.

"Can it—both of you." He began pacing the carpet behind the chairs, and Brianna didn't need to see his face to know he was weighing all their options in his head, looking for one that didn't constitute an insane marriage. Well, let him try. There was no other viable solution. She tapped on her chair arm impatiently.

"Will you, or won't you marry me, Devlin? If the answer is no, I'll be forced to ask Tommy to marry me."

"What!" The man on the futon jerked to life. "Marry me? When pigs fly!"

Brianna's mouth suddenly twitched.

"Thanks for the vote of confidence, Tommy."

He withdrew a hankie from his pocket and wiped his brow.

"Always glad to oblige, blue eyes. Now, stop screwing around and get serious."

Devlin shot them both a glowering stare.

"Shut up—both of you!" He re-circled his chair and studied Brianna's face. "I know that you love your mother more than life itself, but are you truly ready to take on all the responsibilities that go with being a High Priestess? There will be a shift in lifestyle for both of us, not to mention a busted career. And, God knows what we'll find when we go down to the clearing. It could be a replay of Brenda's death."

"There is no other way," Brianna responded. "There just isn't." He sighed and it was clear by the resigned slouch of his shoulders that he agreed.

"Well, then 'so mote it be,'" he stated. He glanced over at Rufus. "You heard Brianna. Note the time and make the necessary wedding arrangements." Brianna gave a small sigh of relief as warm fingers descended on hers again. "We will wait until sunrise to examine the clearing, though … no, this is not up for debate. You may have been blessed with six generations of witches, but I haven't. I will need to be well-rested before we enter the clearing."

Surprised by the backhanded compliment, Brianna could do no more than stare at Devlin's serious countenance. Noting her silence, Rufus hoisted himself from the chair.

"Well, I shall ready the altar in the chapel for the ceremony." He started to exit and then hesitated. "Though it might not seem like it, we are committed to learning what caused Sienna's collapse and fix it." He did exit the room then, leaving an awkward silence behind him. A clearing of a throat finally emerged, and Brianna's gaze followed the sound. She saw Tommy inching towards the door and she sprang from her chair.

"Wait! You can't leave, Tommy, You've been brought to the coven to witness our marriage, and spirit never makes mistakes."

Once again, his expression looked startled.

"I came to comfort you in your time of need. It wasn't to participate in this farce you're concocting."

Devlin sprang to his feet.

"Nevertheless, your sudden decision to follow Brianna may have been orchestrated by spirit. Now, the question becomes, what does spirit intend for you to do here, besides witness our marriage?"

Devlin strode to the door without offering any answer, and Brianna listened as the door slammed shut behind him. She gave a long sigh, glad to have a quiet moment without him. She dropped back into her chair, chewing on her thumbnail. Taking note of her actions, Tommy dropped into the vacated chair beside her, and brought her fingers from her face.

"Why are you marrying this Devlin character without thinking it all through? It's not like you. And what will the marriage accomplish anyway? The chance to perform God-knows what, in a clearing with painted circles on the ground?"

"You don't understand, Tommy, the circle might still be open."

"You've lost me."

Brianna squeezed his fingers.

"Casting a Sacred Circle is like playing with matches. If you're not careful, you could set off a fire that consumes everything it touches, including yourself. One of the worst things that can happen inside a circle is to leave it open when you've finished performing your ritual. It opens a door between two worlds, allowing all kinds of negative energy to seep through and attach its essence to whatever it finds."

"Holy crap! That sounds like a page out of a horror film."

"Don't make fun; this is serious. Great harm could come to the commune if we don't learn what caused Mother's collapse!"

"And what happens if you find the circle has been left open? What then?"

"The Elders will have to close it."

Tommy's face soured.

"Surely the Elders can do that without a marriage. Take Reverend Lord up on his offer. Let this Francis person take the risk."

"You need a healthy witch to examine a circle of this magnitude. The Elders are suffering with energy sickness. Devlin and I aren't."

Tommy bounded up from his chair, dragging his fingers through his hair.

"This is crazy. You could get yourself killed; maybe even get this Janus fellow killed."

"Thanks again for the vote of confidence," Brianna stated, hopping to her feet. It was clear Tommy would never fully understand what it meant to be connected to the world of spirit.

He was far too jaded—and too much of a stickler for organized protocol. "On that bleak note, I think I'll visit the little girl's room and repair my face. I can't get married looking like a drowned rat, you know."

"You shouldn't get married at all."

Brianna sighed.

"Go and keep an eye on Devlin. I wouldn't put it past him to change his mind about the marriage. There's no love-lost between us."

A frown stained Tommy's lips at her confession.

"And that's exactly why you should cancel this farce you're contemplating. Hasty marriages always end unpleasantly—for both parties."

"Not in this case. We will sign divorce papers once this whole debacle is behind us."

Tommy clasped her hands.

"I know you've been thrown for a loop by all this, and I admire your sense of right and wrong, but a makeshift marriage?"

Brianna met his glance, her voice turning brittle again.

"There is no other way, Tommy. The Coven Book of Shadows is specific. No unmarried man or woman may enter a Sacred Circle after they are of age. It's a good law—just inconvenient, at the moment. Besides, if there's any possibility that Mother's collapse wasn't a freak accident of nature, I have to know it and take steps to bring the sinner to justice."

"That smacks of harming someone, blue eyes."

"It certainly does," Brianna stated, spinning on her heel and heading for the door. Reaching it, she flung it open and crossed out into the hall. "Go and find Devlin."

A loud grunt followed her exit, and her lips twitched. In seconds, she was entering the ladies bathroom and studying her appearance. She did look like a drowned rat; her mascara caked and splintered. She brushed the dark streaks from her lower lid, noting her shaking fingers. Could she recite the marriage vows without becoming hysterical? She had to. She had to keep believing spirit would carry her down the right path, with the right tools, with the right person, at the right time. So mote it be, she decided. Everything connected to everything.

CHAPTER EIGHT

A FEW MINUTES LATER

Devlin drew back into the shadows, relieved that Brianna hadn't spotted him lurking behind the fountain rocks. He watched her enter the washroom and exhaled. She was preparing to pull herself together for the wedding ceremony. And he should be doing the same—but first he had to talk to Tommy. His gaze drifted to the hallway. What was keeping the man? It wasn't as if he knew his way around the building, or the commune. Had Brianna given him instructions to stay put until she returned? No, he didn't think Brianna would feel comfortable leaving him on his own. He was simply dawdling in the office, trying to think of a way to short-circuit the marriage. Damn him, he was smart. He might think of a way.

A minute later, Devlin caught sight of his stout figure, and stepped out of the shadows. He crossed the room and pulled Tommy out the front door, and down the sidewalk—to a shady area alongside the building.

"Have you lost your mind coming here?" he asked.

"Me? I'm not the one keeping secrets and telling lies," Tommy accused. "Nor am I pretending to be someone I'm not." He stepped forward. "It's clear that Brianna has no idea that you own D.J. Corp, or that we've met once before."

Devlin returned his scowl.

"No. And you're not to tell her."

Tommy shook his head in disbelief.

"Man-o-man, you *are* a bastard."

Devlin's hands raked his hair in exasperation.

"I'm not being a bastard on purpose. In case you haven't noticed, we're in the middle of a crisis here."

"Well, it's nothing compared to the one you'll be facing when Brianna learns who you really are, and that you've bought her company."

Devlin swung about, focusing his gaze on the park gazebo in the distance.

"You think I haven't thought of that?"

He felt a shadow at his back.

"If I thought that, I wouldn't be bullying you now. Christ, man, she wanted to get on a plane to Texas after I returned with your refusal. She wanted to plead her case to you."

Devlin raked his hands through his hair again.

"I'm stuck between two rocks here, both of them unappetizing. Do I tear her professional life apart? Or do I tear her personal one?"

"If you're that torn, then why the hell did you just agree to marry her?"

"To buy some time," Devlin snarled. "You saw her in there. She was nothing short of a she-bear defending her cubs. The word 'no' was not an option."

"You should've put your foot down more forcibly, right from the start. And why the hell did you buy her company, when, one, you don't need it, and two, you've already torn her life apart once. Do you have some kind of perverted revenge wish against her?"

Devlin fired up, his fists clenching.

"You're lucky I like you, Tommy. Otherwise, you'd be flat on the ground by now."

Tommy fired up as well.

"Screw you! I call a spade a spade when I see it. And this spade reeks of deceit."

A fierce scowl returned to Devlin's face.

"You're really pushing it, Tommy."

"Of course I am!" His tone changed and Devlin knew what was coming. "Now, I'm warning you. Unless you can prove to me that getting married and going into a damaged circle will positively save this commune, I will do everything in my power to stop you and Brianna from attempting it."

Devlin felt his anger rising again.

"That sounded a lot like an ultimatum."

"I don't care if it did." He began scuffing his shoe tip across a clump of grass.

"As Brianna's business partner, I'm advising you to think long and carefully about putting her in harm's way."

Devlin's tone hardened.

"You needn't worry. Neither of us is going into the circle. And for your information, there is a way out of this farce."

Tommy's face split into a grin.

"I'm listening."

"There can be no marriage if a credible witness objects to the marriage. You need to speak up and offer an objection."

Tommy's voice rose in surprise.

"Are you saying you aren't going to marry Brianna?"

Devlin ripped out his words, impatiently.

"I don't intend to marry and divorce, all in a space of a few days. If I can't have Brianna's love for a lifetime, I don't want to have it at all. If you help me by objecting to this marriage, the Council will have to delay the wedding ceremony—until the objection can be sorted out. Brianna will have no option then, but to let me enter the circle alone."

Devlin saw the jerk of Tommy's shoulders. His penetrating gaze bespoke a raw anger.

"You're in love with her—probably always have been," he remarked.

"And always will be," Devlin answered. "So what's your point?"

"I might have to marry Brianna to spite you."

Devlin's growl was ear-splitting.

"You do, and you'll regret it before the vows are even concluded. Brianna needs a husband who can withstand her strong will and viperous tongue. You don't fit that bill."

"Well, she'll certainly get a bastard if she marries you," Tommy scoffed.

"Right, so there's no use in staying silent, is there? Object to the marriage."

Tommy shook his head.

"I won't do it. Suddenly, I like the marriage." He stepped off the grass onto the curbing and away from Devlin, who followed with a vehement growl.

"Dammit, Tommy! The longer you stay here, the sooner Brianna will figure out that we've met before."

"And how is that my problem?" he asked, striding down the sidewalk.

Devlin ground his teeth. It was clear he would have to marry Brianna and hope they didn't kill each other before the sun rose in the morning. He pulled alongside Tommy as they approached the front entrance of the Healing Center. Climbing the steps, he issued a stern warning.

"You have to play by coven rules while you're here. The health of this community depends on it."

A triumphant laugh greeted Devlin.

"You'll marry Brianna?"

"I'll marry her."

"You could make that sound a little less like 'I'll kill her,'" Tommy chided.

"You're pushing again, Tommy."

"Good. Now, do you or do you not suspect foul play in Mrs. Sage's collapse?"

"We won't know the answer to that until we examine the circle."

"Why wait until sunrise, by the way?" Tommy asked.

Devlin lifted his face to study the night sky.

"First impressions are everything, and since energy consists of nothing more than shades of light and dark, it will be to our benefit to judge the energy as the earth shifts from night to day. Until then, you and I need to make an alteration to the marriage certificate—a codicil that will circumvent the Coven Dowry Law."

"Dowry Law?"

"As archaic as it sounds, a High Priestess cannot own property of any kind. She belongs to the earth, dedicating herself to all living things."

"You mean plants, and animals, and shit?"

"Exactly."

Devlin heard a familiar chuckle.

"Does that mean the man she chooses as her husband loses his property, too?"

"On the contrary, her property becomes his."

A gleeful laugh emanated.

"And to think, you could've had Sage Industries for free—if only you had just waited one more day."

"You're pushing again, Tommy."

"I certainly hope so."

Unable to resist his grinning features, Devlin clapped Tommy on the back and pushed him towards the Healing Center door. "Now then, what say we make ourselves presentable for a wedding?"

"You first. You smell like … well, let's just say, it's impolite to marry a woman smelling like a garbage truck."

"She pushed this marriage, not me."

Tommy's lips curled derisively.

"Don't pretend that you aren't thrilled by the turn of events."

"Go to hell, Tommy."

"Not quite yet. I've a wedding to witness."

• • •

Brianna swung her legs over the bed and sat up. It was useless trying to sleep. All she was doing was staring at the ceiling and cursing herself for being the biggest fool in wedding history. She glanced down at the gold wedding band on her finger and shivered. Mrs. Devlin Janus. The words chilled her as nothing else could. And yet, a small part of her insides jangled with excitement.

Her gaze lifted from the ring to the open window across the way. It had been a no-frills wedding, complete with a "you may now kiss the bride" moment that lacked heart or substance. A brief brush along her cheek had been the extent of the kiss, and even Tommy's congratulatory peck had lacked warmth.

The walk to her parent's cottage had been even more ghastly, the trio splitting up as soon as they entered the house. Devlin had hustled Tommy upstairs, into a guest bedroom, while she took refuge in her old room, hoping to catnap until the time came to consummate the marriage.

That had been her plan, but she had been unable to relax. And now here she was, standing in front of her closet, searching for an appropriate item to wear for the Joining. She could go with the sexy trapeze tunic, using it as camouflage for her rattled nerves. Or, she could wear the flannel pajama top plastered with Barbie figurines and endure Devlin's snide remarks when he saw it.

Sighing, she pulled out the tunic. There really was only one choice. She tossed the mini-dress to the lounge chair alongside the closet. She was not going to consummate the marriage while totally naked, and if she could keep the lighting low in the room, she was sure she could maneuver Devlin so that he only saw her figure through vague shadows. *His fingers will be searching for pleasure points, though,* her inner voice chided. *The tunic will be absolutely perfect for that.*

Brianna blushed at the inference. You needn't worry about that, she scolded herself. Our one and only sexual encounter was a disaster, remember? And there's no reason to expect this one will be any different. Frigid—isn't that what Martin called her when they had said their abrupt goodbyes? She had never seen him again; yet the label had shaken her confidence so much, she gave up dating altogether. This time, she'd make sure the sex would be brief—to save both her and Devlin embarrassment.

Her gaze shifted back to the chair. Should she forego wearing panties with the tunic? She blushed again, deciding that the fewer items Devlin had to take off, the better. In seconds, she had shed her blouse, jeans, and underwear and donned the tunic. Letting the fabric slide over her hips, she took a quick peek at her reflection in the door mirror. A quick gasp greeted her. She looked like a lamb being led to slaughter. Her eyes were ringed with dark circles, and her cheeks boasted a pale-white hue.

Pinching her cheeks, she attempted to bring some color back into the skin. How long would she have to wait before Devlin arrived? That would depend on Tommy. He had no idea of the coven's Sanctity law and all it entailed. It was cowardly of her to leave Devlin to settle Tommy down for the night, but she couldn't face her friend—or his pointed questions. And she certainly couldn't face his disappointment if he learned about the Joining ritual.

She glanced at the bed, biting her lower lip. Consummating a loveless marriage to satisfy a Sanctity law was just plain idiotic. Once the deed was done, what would it have accomplished? Nothing. So what was the point? The answer came at once. Without the Joining, her mother's essence would remain trapped between worlds, and the commune would suffer the results of it. It was up to her to get on with the Joining, no matter how humiliating. After all, hadn't she vowed to love Devlin "till death do us part"?

Brianna shivered at the remembrance. How soon would "death do us part" be? She twisted around and studied the open doorway. It might be sooner rather than later—if she couldn't keep a lid on her temper. And of course, once they arrived in the clearing, if they found it was the Guardians trapped in the circle, they would be on the receiving end of a very powerful dose of the Guardians' wrath. She put a brake on that thought, too. She didn't want to think about the power a pissed off elemental could conjure up when provoked.

Brianna heard the floorboards creak above her head, and scurried to the bed. She dove under the covers, tossing the sheet over her bare legs and hoping to God that her body wouldn't betray her during the upcoming Joining. Though the wedding had caused her blood to course through her veins like an awakened river, she didn't know how long that would last.

Was her Invocation the culprit? Her mother had once alluded that a marriage between witches often resulted in a spirit transference during the wedding ceremony—a mating for life that could never be broken. Had that occurred? No, her memories of the ceremony were clear. Devlin's voice was hollow as he recited his vows, a sure sign that no bond was being forged between them.

Scooting back on the bed, she plumped the pillow and then heard the patter of bare feet hitting the wood floor. Angling around, she studied the doorway. A moment later, Devlin appeared in the room barefoot, closed the door, and began unbuttoning his shirt.

Rattled, Brianna bit her lip.

"Tommy's not ... " She couldn't finish the sentence. An amused chuckle came her way.

"Relax, Snow White. The dwarves are all fast asleep in their beds, some snoring much louder than others."

His shirt was tossed to the top of the dresser and Brianna grimaced.

"That isn't funny, you know. Tommy can't help snoring. He broke his nose a few years ago, and it's affected his breathing."

He whirled at her words, gawking at her.

"And you know this, how?"

"What do you mean, how?" Her confusion quickly turned to understanding, and then to outrage. "I have never slept with Tommy! How can you even think that? He's a trusted friend."

"Relax, Goldilocks. I'm only trying to put you at ease."

"Well, you're pissing me off," Brianna huffed, thumping her pillow.

His chuckle came again, but he offered no other comment. Instead, he approached the bed, and then promptly presented his back to her. Sinking down, he shed his jeans and briefs and slid under the sheets. Unhinged by the sight of his naked torso, Brianna lost no time making the first move. She could get through this if she took control of the Joining. She placed her hand on Devlin's forearm before he had even settled himself, and bending over, she sought his lips. A second later, she was flat on her back, staring into his glittering eyes.

"Slow down, Rapunzel," he cautioned. "I know you're used to always being in the driver's seat; however, this is one time you need to let me drive the car." Brianna colored furiously at his words. His grin surfaced and he chucked her chin. "Blushing becomes you, Mrs. Janus." She colored up again, looking anywhere but at his curved lips.

A moment later, the ceiling was blocked out, and Devlin's lips feathered hers—whisper light. The contact had Brianna trembling at the dreamy intimacy. Instinctively, she buried her hands in his hair, shocked to find her senses fluttering in response to his deepening kiss. He certainly knew how to kiss a girl, she realized. The gentle massage was sending currents of desire shooting through her lower limbs. And his hand? It was sweeping the satiny planes of her stomach with light swirls, sledding towards her breasts. How had his hand found its way beneath her tunic so fast? The answer was lost in the splay of his fingers across her left breast. An involuntary tremor began under the caress of his thumb, and Brianna jerked. His mouth lifted from hers.

"Relax. We can get through this, if you just relax."

Relax? How could she relax when he was making her blood pound through her heart, chest, and lungs, like a raging river?

His mouth reclaimed hers, this time more demanding, and all coherent thought fled from Brianna's brain. Before she knew it, his knee had parted her thighs, and she was welcoming him into her body. An intoxicating, manly scent washed over her immediately, but the smell was soon forgotten under the rhythmic flexing of his stomach muscles against hers.

When his thrusts deepened, Brianna moaned aloud, stunned by how pure and explosive raw pleasure could be. A ragged groan sliced her ears, and hearing it, her body melted against Devlin's. In seconds, the world was filled with only him and her quivering limbs. A mutual shudder soon ran along their length, and their bodies settled into a matching tempo of possession.

Swept away, their ardor mounted fast, and Brianna abandoned herself to the whirl of sensations. There was nothing frigid about what she was feeling. There was only a roaring din in her ears and the earth falling away, leaving her belly flexing against Devlin's in persuasion. He brought them to the brink of climax quickly, suspended the moment, and then plunged them over the edge. Time suddenly shattered, exploding in a downpour of fiery sensations, and Brianna couldn't disguise her body's reaction. A moan of ecstasy slipped through her lips, followed by Devlin's hoarse whisper in her ear.

"Te amo, Cernunnos!"

His labored breathing fanned her cheek, and then he took her mouth again, this time with a savage intensity. The white-hot kiss had the real world careening on its axis and Brianna reveling in the tightening coil building again between her thighs. A moment later, she cried out for release, and he gave it, sending her to that place of rapture, utterly consumed.

Somewhere between disbelief and enchantment, time re-started, and Brianna dropped back to earth, feeling like a bird drifting on shafts of air. She lay momentarily paralyzed beneath Devlin, marveling at how exhilarating the Joining had been, and how steamy the sex had become. Spellbound, she listened to Devlin's rapid heartbeat and uneven breathing. Martin had certainly been mistaken in calling her frigid. Devlin had just proved that she was more than capable of sustaining a sexual high.

A salty kiss moistened her lips, and then rolling over, Devlin sat up on the bed. He snatched up his jeans and underwear from the floor and donned them quickly. Zipping his fly, he retrieved his shirt and tossed it on.

"Sleep if you can. Morning will be here before you know it."

He left her without a backward glance, and Brianna lay in silence, holding back tears of disappointment. They had just shared mind-blowing sex and he was leaving? Heat stole into her face. Of course, he was leaving. He had done his duty and consummated the marriage as coven protocol dictated. It didn't matter that he had left her wrecked, and aching to feel him inside her again. What mattered was they view the Joining as token sex—a one-night stand that would guarantee her mother's retrieval from the circle.

She heard the sound of a running shower through the walls and shivered. Devlin wasn't wasting any time washing away the traces of their Joining. *Well, why should he?* her inner voice chided. *The sex meant nothing to him. You mean nothing to him. You're merely a means to a very important end.*

A draft of cool air tickled her legs and she sat up, hauling her tunic back down around her soaked thighs. Tommy was right. A loveless marriage was a sham, and like all shams, it would end unpleasantly—for both parties. She shifted on the bed, inhaling sharply under a back spasm. Great. She had wreaked her back during the Joining. Damn Devlin! He should've powered down the sex a notch.

The shower turned off and Brianna listened for the sound of returning footsteps. When they didn't come, and she heard the faint sound of a door closing, a terrible regret suddenly assailed her. She had just had sex with a sworn enemy, and for what? Nothing. Who would know if the Joining occurred or not? No one.

She covered her face with her hands and fell back on the pillow. It was despicable to have sex in such a callous manner, especially when she had forced Devlin into it. He had offered her a last chance out as they stood at the altar, but she had refused to listen, goading him into the marriage. And now, she was blaming him for that bad choice. A suffocating sensation tightened her throat. When had she become this awful, manipulative person that used people as if she had a right to?

Smothering a sob, Brianna vaulted from the bed. It was despicable what she had done. Not even spirit could look kindly on such arrogant behavior. And, as always, spirit would make sure she paid the price somehow, some way, at some time.

Flinging off the tunic, she entered the bathroom and slammed the door hard. At least there would be no burdensome chains of involvement when she and Devlin met in the morning. Their pride would see to that. She would treat him civilly while urging him to get on with their investigation. Turning on the shower, she buried her self-loathing under the spray of scalding water. By the time she was dressed and falling onto the bed covers, she felt like her old self again.

• • •

A rude shove brought Brianna out of her deep sleep in alarm. She bolted up on the bed, her heart pounding like a runaway horse. Her gaze jumped to the chubby figure standing beside her.

"You scared the hell out of me, Tommy."

"Sorry. I just thought you'd like to know Devlin's on the way to the clearing without you."

Brianna slid to the edge of the bed in a panic.

"Why didn't you stop him?" she hissed. She searched the floor for her shoes.

"I can't go around giving the man orders," Tommy declared. "I barely know him."

"It's never stopped you before," Brianna railed, spotting the shoes and stuffing her toes into them. "Where's my bag? What have I done with my bag?" Spotting it by the dresser, she snatched it up. "We've got to stop Devlin before he reaches the clearing."

"Why?"

Brianna whirled back at the question.

"Because he'll mishandle everything if I'm not there."

"That's not a very charitable thing to say about your husband, blue eyes."

"Sorry. And by the way, he's not my anything."

She swung back around, racing down the hallway and out the back door. Heading for the mulched pathway, she mumbled a heated curse. Damn Devlin! Why had he left the cottage without her? Her brain supplied an answer. *He's intending to boss you around now that you've had sex with him.* She darted around a cul-de-sac of bushes and through a slew of red roses. To hell with that crap, she told her alter-ego.

Behind her, she heard Tommy's sneakers pounding the path. He was keeping up, though he was breathing heavily, and emitting small grunts. She glanced through the shadows and saw the rungs of the footbridge come into view. They were only yards away from finding Devlin. Already, she could feel the power of his aura through the trees. So much for doubting their energies had merged during the wedding. Even out of sight, she knew where he was.

With lightning fast speed, Brianna crashed through the trees.

CHAPTER NINE

THE SACRED CIRCLE

Moonbeams filtered through the shadows, lighting the trees as Devlin reached the oak-carved footbridge. He took a moment to listen to the sounds of the water rushing beneath his feet. It was funny how as much as things changed, they never really did. He could still feel the pull of the past as if it was yesterday. The smell of the trees; the sound of rushing water. All of it shored up memories of what it felt like to be ten again and filled with the adventure of life.

The scent of jasmine teased his nose, and it triggered an image of Brianna's trembling limbs beneath his. He had taken the coldest shower of his life after leaving her bedroom. If he hadn't, he would've made a fool of himself by making love to her again. Even now, he was dying to be inside her, slowly arousing her to a fever-pitch.

He grimaced at the thought. Destiny had played a cruel trick on him fifteen years ago, and now it seemed the Sisters of Fate were bent on doing it again. By forcing the marriage and the Joining, they had made it impossible for him to convince Brianna that he had always loved her. Having incredible sex with her, and then having to leave her behind when this horrible fiasco was over, would make it doubly impossible. She'd never believe that in marrying her, he had finally gotten the only thing he ever wanted.

The sound of pounding feet along the cart path behind him broke his train of thought. What now? Turning, he spied Brianna exiting the shadows into a pool of moonlight, and he drew in his breath. Her aura was glowing with a soft, purple hue, and he could feel the pull of her essence from where he stood. Instinctively, he stepped forward, meeting her at the edge of the bridge, and lowering his head. His lips captured hers in a tantalizing kiss that surprised her, shook him to the core, and garnered a chuckle from behind Brianna. When he lifted his lips, he nuzzled her ear.

"Hello, Mrs. Janus. How does it feel to be an old married lady?"

"As if I was sleepwalking," she answered breathlessly.

He nuzzled her cheekbones, and then found her lips again. This time, she dropped the bag she was carrying, and clung to his shirtfront.

"Ahem. Don't we have somewhere to be?"

The pair broke apart, startled by Tommy's voice. Devlin was the first to recover, releasing Brianna and switching his thoughts to the task at hand.

"*We* have somewhere to be. You need to haul your ass back to the cottage and wait for us."

"Drop the attitude, Janus. Where Brianna goes, I go."

"You can't enter the clearing, Cloisters."

"Why the hell not?"

"Actually, he can," Brianna intervened. She suddenly glanced at the ground around their feet, and Devlin wondered what had caught her attention. She moved off to the left, obviously searching for something. Seconds later, he saw her pick up a small branch from a pile of leaves and return with it. She eyed Devlin as she dusted the branch.

"Tommy's a widower," she told him. "Technically, he's still married." She turned to Tommy, grasping the branch with both hands, and holding it up in front of him. "Clutch the branch and repeat after me … no, use your wedding ring hand."

Devlin watched a startled look cross Tommy's face, but he quickly withdrew his right hand and clasped the twig with his left.

"Earth Dragon, strong and true."

"Earth Dragon, strong and true."

"Send to me, your Magic new."

"Send to me, your Magic new."

"Egg of Protection, we shall see, this is my will, so mote it be."

"Egg of Protection, we shall see, this is my will, so mote it be."

Tommy's words echoed away, as if being carried to the heavens on angel wings, and Devlin could only gape at Brianna in awe. Finally, he broke the silence.

"I like how you think, Rapunzel. Remind me to make love to you before the day is over."

She tugged her blouse into place, and hearing Tommy's amused chuckle, she hauled her duffel bag up from the planks.

"You're an ass," she said, as she passed his shoulder.

Devlin grinned at her rebuke. Being married had obviously mellowed Brianna. She had only called him an ass. He had been expecting a much more vile obscenity. Tommy's chuckle came again and Devlin felt obliged to acknowledge it.

"If you even try to mock me for those kisses you just saw, I'll conjure a curse that'll bite your ass."

Devlin whirled around, giving Tommy no time to mount a comeback to his threat. Instead, he raced down the pathway, eager to catch up to the glowing purple aura disappearing in the tree line.

A minute later, he caught up to Brianna, just as she reached the outer copse of a tree-lined arch. He took the lead from her, leaving Tommy to bring up the rear. In companionable silence, the trio traversed the dirt path at least a hundred yards through the preserve. Coming out of the trees on the north side of the trail, they wound their way to the clearing, pausing when they reached the top of the rise. The change in temperature hit Devlin full-force as he dropped his duffel bag to the ground.

"Do you feel that?" Brianna asked, dropping her bag alongside his.

"Yes. The heat could account for some of the problems occurring." His gaze drifted to the mound lying in the circle, and he felt his pulse take a sudden nose-dive. He had to concentrate on the circle, not the body inside. A moment later, Brianna turned into his shoulder and clung to him.

"I thought I could do this, but I think I'm going to faint."

His arm shot around her.

"Concentrate on the circle, and nothing else. We're a few minutes away from sunrise. If we're lucky, the aura of the circle will still be intact and we'll be able to detect any breaks or leaks in energy."

Her gaze followed his to the horizon, and he heard her voice break.

"That's a big 'if.'" She raised her hand and pointed to the eastern sky. "It will be easier to detect any problems if we position ourselves easterly so the sun is coming over our back and into the circle."

Devlin nodded, striding down the ridge line at a rapid pace. As he strode, he kept his gaze glued to the circle below, and the light suddenly beginning to filter through the trees. A moment later, he saw Tommy settle into a spot a perfect one hundred twenty degrees from him and marveled at how well-balanced they were around the top of the ridge line. Nature had lined them up, he knew, without their even knowing it.

He studied Tommy's position once more and wished he could've had a cup of coffee before beginning. The rush of caffeine would do his frayed nerves a world of good; however, the caffeine would certainly disrupt his metabolism. The purer the body, the better the light-working. A hand suddenly waved in front of his face, startling him.

"Don't space out now," Tommy said, settling beside him. "What comes first? Where do you start?"

"We've already begun." Devlin continued his trek left and joined Brianna who stood with head bowed, studying the area around the exterior of the circle below. Tommy trod the same path as Devlin.

"What are you looking for up here?" he queried.

Devlin lifted his hand, noting the first beams of light heading for the circle.

"Sssh. Give us a moment."

Tommy fell silent as Devlin focused his attention on the ground. Beside him, Brianna did the same. A few moments later, the light began to sparkle along the heat rays and then through it. Finding the barrier, the light punctured the circular veil and crossed the etched markings, revealing the circle's shadows. Devlin let his gaze travel the sketched outline, tracing the sun's rays over Sienna Sage's inert form. How much time had expired between her entry into the circle and her collapse?

There was no sign of any residual energy lingering that he could see, and that didn't bode well for her retrieval. If she had been struck before the actual drawing down of energy, the circle would be cleansed and safe to enter. However, if she had collapsed during the height of the ritual, the build-up of energy would have spiraled inward, creating a series of back-ended loops. If that were the case, they would have more to worry about than the investigation being stalled. Brianna and he would have to break their vow and do a full-scale cleansing, and that meant going into the circle to accomplish it. Had Brianna come to the same conclusion? He turned to ask and was surprised to find her walking down the rise to the painted circle with her shoulder bag. He retrieved his own bag and hurried to catch up, finding Tommy close on his heels.

"Why is it so damn hot?" Tommy asked.

"Runaway energy," Brianna answered for Devlin. "Do you feel the ice laced within the heat?"

"Yes. That's the first positive thing we've encountered."

"Why positive?" Tommy asked, following them while wiping sweat from his brow.

"Ice means frozen in time and place. No deterioration of the organs."

"You're talking cryogenics."

"Nature's way," Brianna replied. She took a step towards the rim of the markings, only to jump back as a black cat launched itself from out of nowhere at her legs. Angered beyond belief, the cat took a swipe at her shoes and then a protective stance of the circle. Deep in its throat, it began to growl loudly at them, arching its back and tail, and spitting its displeasure.

"Good Lord!" Tommy declared, taking two additional steps back as the cat charged forward and swiped at his pants leg. It quickly rushed back to defend the markings again. Devlin and Brianna drew back to join Tommy.

"Well, this complicates things," Devlin stated. "The damn cat is guarding the circle." For the first time since their arrival, Devlin saw a genuine smile stain Brianna's face.

"I know this cat. I mean, I know its cry. It's Mother's cat. Why else would it be reacting this way?" She turned back to the circle and Devlin saw her drop to her haunches and address the cat. "Hello, my sleek friend. My name is Brianna, and I think you've been expecting me." The cat eyed her warily, making no move to attack, but Devlin noticed its hackles didn't drop, nor did its tail stop swishing back and forth as it studied her face. Brianna dropped to her knees, meeting its gaze. "We mean you no harm." As if it understood her words, the cat took a less surly stance, though its ears remained alert.

"Careful," Devlin cautioned. "Cats are notorious for launching unexpected attacks. This creature is not above clawing your face off."

Brianna shushed him, settling down in front of the feline.

"Sit down, both of you," she ordered over her shoulder. "Mother may have cast the cat as one of the Watch Towers. If so, it won't give up its position easily. We must wait it out."

Tommy plopped down on the closest piece of earth at his feet, believing her words without question; however, Devlin backed up the incline and sat at a higher angle on the grass. He'd rather not tempt fate by sitting too close. A cat designated as a spirit guide for a High Priestess had a strength he didn't even want to think about.

The feline suddenly hissed at him, and then a rumbling growl emerged from its throat, aimed directly at Tommy.

"I wish we knew his name," Brianna said, indicating the cat. "I think if I could say his name, he'd give up his guardianship." Brianna shifted on her rump, tossing Tommy a smile over her shoulder. "See, Tommy, I wasn't hallucinating. I did hear a cat that day in the office." She turned back to the animal, unable to see the baffled look that Devlin sent Tommy's way. She spoke quietly to the cat again. "Your job is finished now, my glossy friend. We are here to relieve you of your burden. You must let us examine the circle so that we may retrieve your mistress."

As if the cat understood her words, his growl ceased and his hackles dropped. Brianna reached out her hand, causing Devlin to lean forward and issue a warning.

"Brianna … "

"Sssh! I know what I'm doing."

"Rrrr-ow!"

The cat charged forward, reaching Brianna's hand and sniffing it quickly. Seconds later, to Devlin's astonishment, the cat began to brush its chin and face against her fingertips with a loud purr. Brianna bent forward and stroked his coat.

"We have lots to do, my new friend. It's time for you to relinquish your post to us."

With no further hiss or meow, the feline shot up the incline, and over the rise. Devlin clambered to his feet as Brianna scrambled to hers. He took a fresh look at the figure trapped in the circle and then stopped beside Brianna, surprised when she dropped to her haunches and began feeling the ground with her fingers. She was looking for any displaced energy that might have spilled out. It was a good start to their examination. His gaze tripped left, searching the ground for signs of the same.

"Can you see any doors left open?" Tommy asked.

Devlin studied his face, wondering how he knew to ask that question. A familiar grin came his way.

"Brianna said something about doors being left open; however, all I see is a painted circle on the ground."

"Where you see paint; witches see a protective boundary. Nothing can get in while a ritual is being performed."

"The circle keeps unwanted energy out, and protects you so you can open yourself up psychically," Brianna added, rising and moving off to their right.

"So you're looking for energy," Tommy replied, nodding.

Devlin moved to his left, continuing to study the ground.

"In the physical world, there are four informal laws of ecology."

"Laws of energy," Brianna called back.

Devlin frowned at her interruption.

"Brianna likes the word 'energy' so we'll use it. Law Number One: 'Everything is connected to Everything.' When you enter a Sacred Circle, you awaken that eternal connection within yourself. That ultimately reveals your place in the web of existence."

"I get it," Tommy responded. "The belief that man is not the web of life, only a strand in it."

"Good analogy," Devlin complimented as Brianna rejoined them.

"I wonder if any of the congregation has been taking classes in creating Sacred Circles," she stated. "It's the one question I forgot to ask Rufus last night."

Devlin wondered why they had left such a crucial piece of evidence out of their thinking. That should've been the most important question to have asked. Breaking the developing silence, Tommy spoke up.

"Why is that answer so important?"

"Law Number Two," Devlin answered, shifting left, and wiping beads of sweat from his brow. "'Everything must go somewhere.'" He swept his hand through the air, testing it. "Energy is in constant motion, but it cannot be exerted in one direction indefinitely or it begins to deteriorate."

"Balance is essential." Brianna supplied, moving off around them, this time to their left. Devlin dropped to his haunches, tracing his fingers along the edge of the border.

"When you raise energy during a ritual, you send it out to complete its purpose, and then you ground any energy that may be left over."

"Which means?" Tommy asked, dropping beside him.

"If you sense negative energy around you, rather than deflecting it back to where it came from, which could be from anywhere, you send it to the ground where the earth can neutralize it. The idea is to prevent it from bouncing around and causing harm—which leads us to Law Number Three."

"'Nature knows best.'" Brianna supplied, tracing the other side of the circle.

Devlin peered at Tommy, who was removing his hankie again, and mopping his brow with it.

"The wealth of knowledge that nature knows is so vast that we humans can't even begin to wrap our minds around it."

"It's why we must learn the valuable lesson of 'going with the flow,'" Brianna added, rejoining them and dropping to her knees. "It's about letting nature take its course." Devlin saw her gaze switch between the outer and inner rims of the circle as Tommy dropped beside her.

"And Law Number Four?"

"There's no such thing as a free lunch,'" Brianna stated, rising again and moving away.

Devlin dropped beside Tommy. He lifted a mound of dirt and let it run through his fingers.

"It takes energy to raise energy. You cannot receive without giving. During her ritual—if Sienna made it into the ritual, that is—she would've expended a lot of energy in order to complete any spell she was performing. She would've also had to replenish what she lost by tapping into the universal supply before closing the circle."

"You've lost me," Tommy declared, studying the lifeless form in the circle.

"Every ritual done in the circle has a set structure," Brianna replied, dropping alongside Tommy again. "The circle's opened and it's closed. Creatures called the Guardians of the Watch Tower are called in, and then sent away—politely sent away, of course. Always there is balance. Give and take."

Devlin continued the reasoning.

"Now, we've been told Sienna was performing a ritual called Drawing down the Moon which is one of the most powerful give and takes there is. The energy level raised would have been immense, particularly for a High Priestess. And, if she collapsed before finishing the ritual ... "

"Which unfortunately seems to be more and more likely ... " Brianna offered, rising and stepping away from the pair. Tommy exchanged a glance with Devlin, who ignored Brianna's retreating figure and finished his sentence.

"It's a safe bet that the circle is still open in some way."

"So Mrs. Sage's body cannot be retrieved without it becoming a major undertaking?"

Devlin clambered to his feet, dusting off his hands, and wondering how to answer Tommy's question. There was no sure proof that the circle was still open, yet there was no proof that it was closed either. So it became a stalemate.

"The energy sickness invading the commune would indicate the circle's still open," he finally stated.

"How much worse could it get?"

"If the leak is as tiny as a pinhole, the illness could keep the members down for months."

"Jesus! All that from a circle on the ground?"

"It's not just any circle. And Sienna isn't your average Coven Elder. She is a High Priestess who has worked Sacred Circles for at least three decades, which means her channeling of energy is an awesome thing to behold."

Devlin saw a disapproving look cross Tommy's face as he re-pocketed his handkerchief.

"So what you're saying is, there is no way for anybody to do anything unless you go inside the circle first and neutralize it."

"I'm afraid so," Brianna stated, rejoining them again. She gave a huge sigh. "Let's go give Rufus our thoughts. And let's hope that Francis has what it takes to cleanse the circle, because without a miracle, this calamity is going to go from worse to catastrophic."

"Amen," Devlin agreed, taking Brianna's elbow and spinning her around. Side by the side, the trio began a slow, depressing exit from the clearing and up the incline.

Reaching the crest of the ridge, Devlin turned and surveyed the circle one last time. Francis had better have the skills to back up his position as First Elder, because if he didn't, there was only one person he knew of that had the power to retrieve Sienna's body. And he wasn't about to let her put her life in jeopardy—not when she had just finished promising to love, honor, and obey him for the rest of her life.

CHAPTER TEN

THE REVELATION

"Rrr-oww".

The cat's body exploded onto the path in front of Brianna, and the group came to a sudden halt, drawing back at the frenzied hissing of the animal.

"What now?" Tommy asked.

Brianna heard a fierce scoff.

"The damn creature has lost its mind."

Brianna shivered at the words, wondering why she wasn't agreeing with Devlin's assessment. After all, the cat's behavior was bordering on the psychotic.

"Rrr-rroow."

The cry was tortured, yet Brianna sensed there was a different meaning to the cry. What was the creature trying to relay to them? That they must not leave the clearing? She bent down and addressed the cat, whose tail was now swishing angrily. He spewed out a series of low growls.

"Alright, big guy, we're listening," Brianna stated.

The cat halted its pacing and shot up the incline, braking to a halt at the top of the ridge and looking back at her.

"Rrr-roow."

"What's he saying?" Tommy asked, moving to Brianna's side. "He appears to be talking to you. What did we miss back there?"

Brianna clutched Tommy's sleeve.

"You sensed that too?" She charged back up the incline and joined the cat. "Alright, big guy, I get the message. You need me to look at things from up here instead of down there. But what am I looking for?"

"RRR-owww."

Brianna did a complete spin, scanning all sides of the clearing and back the way she had come. Nothing out of place ... only their discarded duffels. She let her gaze travel on to the circle and its boundaries.

"Merciful heavens!"

She took off rapidly, slipping and sliding down the rise, ignoring the worried shouts from behind her. She hit the bottom of the hill, landing on her rump and gouging the palm of her hand as she reached out to stop her fall. A second later, two pairs of hands hauled her up from the sliding shale, and set her roughly on her feet.

"What the hell's wrong with you?" Devlin asked, dusting clumps of dirt from her jeans.

"Mother's alive!"

"What?!" The men beside her whirled and scanned the circle, studying the crumpled heap within the painted marks.

"She's face up," Brianna urged. "She wasn't face up before."

Brianna felt a clamp on her shoulder.

"Calm down."

"She's alive, Devlin."

"Well, if she is, getting hysterical won't help."

Brianna took a deep breath.

"You're right. I need to keep a level head—and so do you." She watched as Devlin examined the ground around his toes with fierce concentration. And then he was moving off to unzip his duffel bag.

"What are you doing?" she asked in alarm.

He rifled through the bag.

"One of us has to go in the circle and attempt to replace the current ritual with a more powerful one."

"Well, it's not going to be you," Brianna replied.

He ignored her words, pulling vials out from the bag and setting them on the ground alongside it. Brianna's heart plummeted as she watched his fingers. He was going into the circle and would destroy any chance they had of retrieving her mother alive. She had to stop him. Leaning down, she halted his fingers.

"Give me a minute to think, Devlin, please. I know I can work this out without killing Mother. I'm her daughter. I've inherited her genes."

"We don't have time to concoct a plan," Devlin argued. "We have to act now!"

Brianna brushed her foot against the vials, and then crushed them beneath her toes. The crack of glass shattered the air around the trio.

"You will *not* kill my mother! Not without letting me think of a way that won't get you both killed."

A dangerous glint entered Devlin's eyes, and she was sure if Tommy wasn't shadowing her left shoulder, she would've been knocked to the ground.

"You have two minutes to come up with an idea," Devlin barked, "However, if you can't, don't you ever give me another order again!"

Tommy's shadow became a wall as he stepped in front of Brianna and tapped Devlin's chest.

"Here now, back off. If Brianna thinks she can retrieve her mother without injuring anyone, we are going to give her the opportunity to do it."

Brianna stepped around the pair.

"Shush, both of you! I need to think."

She moved off, ignoring Devlin's black scowl and calming her panicked breathing. What magic could she pull from her mother's bag of tricks that had never been tried before, but would work? A trickle of an idea teased her mind but she couldn't quite latch onto its substance. Still, she had to stay open to the answer and trust her skills—no matter how rusty they were.

"Tell me what you're thinking," Devlin said, coming to rest by her right shoulder.

"If we go in, we kill Mother, and if we stay out, she dies. It's a draw all the way around."

"But not if I go in. She's saved and I repay the karmic debt I owe the community. That's a win-win situation."

"That would make sense if you were the only one brought home to solve the crisis. But I got called too, which means I know something that you don't. Something that is vital for her recovery."

She saw Devlin glance at the prone figure in the circle.

"Okay, I'll give you that. We can't go in, so that leaves us with only one viable solution."

"Which is?" Tommy asked, settling alongside Brianna's left shoulder.

"We disrupt the barrier from the outside in," Brianna stated, suddenly.

"Impossible," Devlin replied.

"Maybe not," Brianna stated, stepping back and facing both men. "There are only two scenarios here. Mother was careless, or a sinner bound her in the circle."

"I don't believe the first," Devlin stated.

"Neither do I, so that leaves human intervention, which means the Guardians might still be here, napping and waiting to be released. We might be able to stir them awake."

"Here now, I won't allow either of you to sacrifice your health on a maybe," Tommy stated.

Brianna wasn't going to allow that either, but it would be redundant to say so. Dropping her gaze, she began to trace the outline of the circle and its arc.

"Sometimes electrical energy shows up at night. White against black, red paired with green, shimmering shadows … no one mentioned seeing color bands surrounding the circle, did they?"

She saw Devlin's brows knit together in deep thought.

"No, and nobody said anything about seeing a rope around the circle either."

Brianna continued to think aloud.

"If Mother was conducting a binding spell, she'd use a rope or a piece of string or twine to complete the task. I see no evidence of that anywhere. However, if she was attacked by someone in the commune, the sinner would've had to use rope to bind her from leaving the circle. So, the question becomes, where is the rope?" She began to pace. "I don't see any color wheels steeped within the cone of power, which suggests what? Sleeping elementals, perhaps?"

Devlin picked up on her thought, carrying it forward.

"Or a trapped one."

Brianna held up her hand, shushing Devlin.

"Give me a minute. I'm working it out."

"Well hurry up, the heat in the clearing is escalating."

Brianna's gaze shot to the ground around her feet, studying the shards of glass layered in the dirt, and then moved on to her duffel bag. She had grabbed items from her mother's cabinets last night, unsure of why she was grabbing them and what they could be used for. But she hadn't faltered in her choices, so that must mean the items weren't random, but chosen for a reason. What could she do with sea salt and jasmine oil?

Thinking, she monkeyed with her necklace, surprised when her fingers brushed the gold plating and began to tingle.

"Got it," she said, startling the men who had been watching her thoughtful contemplation with curious expressions. Charging over to her duffel bag, she rummaged through it rapidly. Pulling out two vials, she returned to the circle, popped open the first one, and tossed the contents at the circle.

The veil of energy crackled under the assault, and Brianna felt the disruption in temperature at once. Popping the second vial,

Brianna threw its contents at the veil as well. This time, she felt a distinct shift in the heat waves around the circle. Her idea might just work. To her surprise, a pinwheel of muted colors began to saturate the veil, and Brianna took a step back.

"Well, there are our sleeping elementals," Devlin stated, coming to stand beside her.

"Yes, and as you can see, they're pretty pissed off." The color bands took on a more powerful hue, and Brianna gave a long sigh. "We have no choice now. We have to release the Guardians back to their world."

She heard a matching sigh.

"We're past the point of no return, and that's a fact," Devlin said. "I'll go. I have nothing to lose. You do."

Brianna shook her head.

"I have to conduct the ritual. Only a hereditary witch has the power to pull off the trick I'm going to try. It's out of the box, but mother swears it will work."

"I thought we weren't going to be reckless."

"This trick is risky, but not reckless. It's extremely logical and the best part is it has no dangerous components tied to it ... no, don't argue. It will work if I do it."

Devlin snapped his mouth shut at her words, and Brianna realized she had finally won an argument against him. She had been worried he would be furious over her emphatic "take charge" attitude; however, he appeared to be genuinely in tune with her tackling the situation by herself. Should she show him the Pentagram to relieve his mind? She caressed the smooth surface of a jeweled orb. A soft tingle began tickling the tips of her fingers. Yes, she was on the right track. Outside-in was possible.

Flashing the piece at Devlin, she lifted his hand and dropped the amulet into his palm.

"This is my personal amulet. What do you notice about it? First impressions."

Devlin wrapped his fingers around the piece and closed his eyes. Brianna sensed he was searching for a trace of her essence within the core. His lips twitched unexpectedly, startling her.

"It's free of heat or ice—unlike its owner."

Brianna blushed at once. He was alluding to their heated passion in bed last night, and she had no witty comeback to rail him with. She plucked the necklace from his hand.

"There's no sign of energy displacement anywhere on it, and there should be."

"Which means what?" Tommy asked, joining the conversation.

"That everything we see here has been staged for our benefit. Someone wants us to think Mother's collapse was caused by her own carelessness, when in fact the opposite is true. She had help in going down in this circle."

"That's a giant leap in logic, don't you think?" Tommy asked. "Besides, what does that have to do with the gem?"

Brianna's hand swept the muggy air around them.

"Amulets are worn for psychic protection from negative energy. They are charged and blessed before being worn. And most important, spirit guides use them as healing stones. If we're lucky, I should be able to poke a small hole in the energy field, and make it think I'm a spirit guide."

Devlin's gaze re-scanned the circle and then back to her.

"That's a big if, Brianna."

Her gaze scanned the area around their feet, and then moved on to the painted markings. Dropping down, she sifted the sand with her fingers.

"I wish we had positive proof that a rope once laid here."

"Why does that matter?" Tommy asked, sinking beside her.

"Because we can't accuse anyone of trapping Sienna inside the circle without finding proof of a binding spell," Devlin stated, falling alongside Tommy.

Brianna peered around Tommy's shoulders.

"We can't take any chances. We have to cleanse the space as if there are four elementals sleeping inside, which will be extremely tricky, because if I don't do it right, I could stir unwanted energy like we did before."

"And more lethal energy," Devlin added.

"You see, that's what I'm talking about," Tommy said, as they all clambered to their feet. "Cleaning this circle is just too damn dangerous."

"You've got to trust that I know what I'm doing, Tommy," Brianna stated. "You know me pretty well. I think things out before doing them."

She swung back to the circle, hoping she had impressed Tommy with her confident tone. If he, or even Devlin, suspected that she was having doubts about her ability to tap into the circle, she'd be banned from the clearing faster than a speeding bullet. What was her first step? Clear her mind, or set the grounding?

"Now what?" Devlin asked, his foot beginning an anxious tap in the dirt.

"Unfortunately, the ritual calls for a grounding … no, it can't be you." She stopped him from speaking. "You are essential to the ritual in a different way. I need someone … " her gaze whipped to Tommy. ". . . who was sent here by my spirit guides."

Seeing the stares coming his way, Tommy's face drained of color, and Brianna saw him swallow nervously.

"Who, me?"

"You were sent after me for a reason, Tommy. Now, we know why."

"I came to protect you, not participate in some damn ritual that could get us … " He left the sentence hanging and Brianna pursed her lips in annoyance.

"Will the ritual work without Tommy?" Devlin cut in.

"Under the right circumstances, it can't fail, no matter what's left out. However, I have no way of knowing if these circumstances fit the qualifications."

"Well, I suddenly trust your instincts, so let's do it without him. Just stay mindful of the rule of three, that's all I ask," Devlin added.

"Here now," Tommy asked, his gaze narrowing. "Why are we still talking as if Brianna is actually going to do this?"

Brianna exchanged a glance with Devlin, who caught the slight dip of her head as she crossed to her duffel bag again and rummaged through it.

"It's alright, Tommy," she said. "I was wrong to involve you." Finding the items she was searching for, Brianna stood, and moved to the circle. She placed the two black and white candles she had brought in a straight line, one behind the other. "We'll attempt it without the grounding," she told Devlin.

Popping the top of a small vial, she poured a handful of cinnamon into her right jeans pocket, and then followed it with a handful of sage into her left pocket. Bending again, she doused her hands with Holy Water.

Cupping the amulet in her right hand, she turned to Devlin, who stepped forward quickly. In an instant, she was swept into his arms and kissed with such punishing sweetness that her stomach swirled wildly. To her horror, her senses reeled as if short-circuiting. Currents of desire shook her frame, and she was shocked by a crazy desire to return the kiss. A second later, she was free and stammering in confusion.

"What d-d-did you do that for?"

His grin surfaced.

"I didn't want to die without having kissed you again." Brianna's eyebrows shot up in surprise, but before she could manage a response, he twirled her about to face the circle again. "If you see or feel any breaks in the aura, you pull out, you hear? If you don't, I will add my powers to the mix and let the chips fall where they may."

He took a step back and Brianna was glad he didn't have the ability to read her mind. Thanks to his kiss, it was a cluttered mess. *A definite sawdust factory,* her inner voice nudged. To her surprise, Devlin shook her shoulders lightly.

"Just take a deep breath and go to that quiet place in your mind."

Brianna took his advice and closed her eyes. Thank goodness, she had kept up with her meditation techniques. She felt her shoulders squeezed again and her eyes shot open. She saw Devlin's finger wagging at her.

"Say hello and goodbye to the Guardians, and then get the hell out. And whatever you do, stay calm. Any emotional high on your part could trigger their anger."

Did a burning desire and aching need for one of his soul-melting kisses constitute an emotional high? She tossed the thought away. Better to think of the kiss as a love offering to the Guardians. A gentle shove severed her reverie.

"Get on with it," Devlin urged.

Brianna turned back to the circle, catching sight of her mother's body. The glimpse caused tears to well up and wet her eyelashes. She bit her lower lip to keep a sob from escaping. Get a grip, Brianna. Retrieving your mother's body depends on staying grounded. She took a deep breath, and, a moment later, Tommy's fingers slipped into her left hand.

"Just don't send me to the hospital," he stated, softly.

Brianna flashed him a smile.

"You're the straightest arrow I know, Tommy, and once we start, the spirits will know it too. However, there'll be some tingling … nothing alarming. Don't pull away. The ritual should take no more than three minutes, but I'll try to make it the most interesting three minutes of your life." He took a deep breath and Brianna's gaze shot to Devlin. "I need you to stand directly behind the candles, but not too close. If I release the cone of power wrong …"

"Yeah, I've witnessed that talent already," Devlin interrupted. "Just don't put *me* in the hospital." He counted off the yards, and positioned himself directly behind the black candle.

"Get ready." Brianna stated, centering her torso directly over her hips and knees. She closed her eyes again. Focus. That was the primary thing to remember when doing any ritual. Any loss of focus meant loss of energy. And a loss of energy meant a busted ritual. And a busted ritual meant a catastrophic chain of events.

She tuned into the quiet descending around her, and focused on the feel of Tommy's hand in hers. His palms were dry, his pulse regular. That was a good sign. If he was calm now, he'd stay calm during the ceremony. Perhaps, that was why he had been sent—to keep her calm and focused.

Transferring her attention to her own breathing, she gauged her pulse. Steady and strong—a mirror to Tommy's. In her head, she ticked off the rhythm … five … four … three … two …

• • •

The caped figure studied the figures surrounding the circle and smiled. They were attempting to undo the spell, just as expected. How delightful! Their failure would be a perfect ending to a flawless plan. Not only would Sienna be out of the picture, but in a few minutes, Brianna would be gone too. Maybe even Devlin.

A rustle in the grass had the figure jumping to the side and inspecting the ground. A sleek Moon snake slithered away, crawling under a pile of stacked leaves for cover. The figure smiled again. Seeing a Moon snake during a full Moon was a powerful omen, a sure sign that the leadership of the coven would soon be up for grabs.

The figure turned, studying the trio in the clearing again. They'd never figure the ritual out. It had been too carefully orchestrated and executed. Another rustle of leaves crackled, followed by a black blob streaking past the figure's ankles. Again, the figure jumped aside, hoisting the hem of the black cape up from the ground and draping it over a tattooed arm. The blob stopped and looked back with glittering yellow eyes at the figure. Intimidated, the figure stamped the ground.

"Git, Nicodemus. Or I'll put a curse on you as well."

The figure held up a jeweled Pentagram, swishing it towards the cat. Nicodemus growled low in his throat, and then whirling, bolted from the tree line. The figure watched the feline's retreat, with a smug smile. Not even a magical cat, like Nicodemus, could halt what had been started. In a few hours, the leadership of the coven would go under the Council's vote, and then, thanks to another glorious spell in motion, the leadership would be transferred to a witch with untold powers of magic. No one could stop that from happening. Not Brianna and certainly not Devlin.

The figure snorted. The pair had married, thinking to merge their powers and come out heroes in the Council's eyes. Another arrogant assumption on their part. Well, let them try, the figure gloated. At least for a few minutes. The moment they stepped into the circle, the spiral loop Sienna had built before collapsing would implode on them. They'd be as dead as she was. And, best of all, no one would ever suspect the outcome had been rigged from the start.

CHAPTER ELEVEN

THE CLEANSING

. . . One . . .

Brianna's mind dropped into a quiet darkness full of peace.

"The circle is open, but not unbroken." Devlin's voice urged through the quiet. "Focus on that."

His words sent Brianna's mind winging to thoughts of her mother and the last time she had seen her Draw down the Moon. Her hands had been lifted gracefully upward, and the sight of the blue aura surrounding her had been mesmerizing. She had been so sure of herself that watching her had been a spiritual experience, not only for her, but for the entire congregation.

Spurred by the image, and a sudden influx of emotion, Brianna opened her eyes, cupped three fingers around the amulet, and passed her hand across the boundary of the circle. She felt the ripple of energy at once and knew they had guessed right. There was still lingering energy infused in the circle that needed to be neutralized.

"Gracious Lady, Gracious Lord, strike in me your ancient cord. Aid my quest and approve this spell, magic make for a daughter who fell." Her opening chant sounded foreign to her ears, yet at the same time it sounded right, as if drawn from a page of her mother's Book of Shadows. "From life to death and life again, the spirit wheel turns round. Light to dark, pain to love, all strands of time are bound."

The energy ripple intensified under her words and Brianna felt the first stirring of a tingle in her outstretched hand. She immediately revved up her chant.

"Hail spirits of fire, the air, the land, and the sea. Show me the way that four becomes three. Reveal to this Pentagram, your essence and light. Then depart from this place, with the quickest of flight."

To Brianna's surprise, her fingertips began to glow with a blue aura of energy, and light tingles began to saturate her entire arm. The tingles widened, covering her entire chest, and then slipped down her left arm, into her hand. She felt a slight pull on her wrist and knew Tommy had been doused with a jolt of the energy. Still, he held his course, clinging to her hand, and keeping his composure.

Brianna concentrated on the blue aura, pleased when its essence made itself known to her. A playful water sprite—but not so playful at the moment. She greeted the pulsing aura.

"Spirit of the west, long trapped in this place. Return to your world, with no trace of disgrace. Forgive those who used you, and treated you ill, depart from the place, your next task to fill."

The blue aura dissipated rapidly, leaving a red fire trail swirling along Brianna's fingertips. Again, Brianna recognized the essence. A salamander—aggressive and hot-tempered. She wished it away quickly.

"Spirit of the south, whose anger burns bright, return to your world, bathed in only love's light. Forgive those who used you, and treated you ill, flee from this place, your next task to fill."

The red aura increased its glow, sending a powerful dose of energy into her hand before disappearing from view. In its wake, Brianna saw a double band of green and yellow teasing the amulet in her fingers. Earth and Air—the last of the sleeping giants.

"Spirit of the east, your essence I breathe. Return to your world with your burden relieved. Forgive those who used you, and treated you ill, depart from this place, your next task to fill."

The double band engulfed her fingertips rather than dissipating, and in the center of the circle, a seismic popping noise began.

The air around Brianna's head stirred, and she knew the last two Guardians weren't going to leave the circle without administering some form of punishment. Was their anger for the sacrilege of being left in the circle for five whole days? Or for the sacrilege she was performing with an unclean essence? She had no time to ponder the question as bolts of energy were sent rippling through her thighs, towards her toes.

Brianna sucked in her breath, fighting against being tossed to the ground under the jolt. Quickly, she prayed to keep the energy displacement from jumping to Tommy beside her. She had promised there'd be no harm to him. She had to keep that promise, no matter what. Arm smarting, Brianna realized there was only one way to diffuse the elementals' wrath from reaching him. She would have to release his hand and take the Guardians on face to face by herself.

Shaking off Tommy's fingers, she prepared to step across the boundary line. Her body was jerked back quickly, her fingers re-gripped. Tommy wasn't going to let her go. She had warned him against doing so, and he was standing fast to that promise.

Brianna's outstretched hand jerked under a new assault, and she realized her earlier fear had materialized. The slingshot effect was underway; however, instead of one set of negative energy, she was facing two. She felt movement behind her and realized Devlin was stepping in as he warned. She heard his voice cascade above her head.

"Awesome Sun and shimmering Moon; harken to the Witch's rune. Earth must grow, fire must burn, water must nourish, and air must churn. No other quest can be invoked by your wrath; no other power can disrupt the first path. By the dark of the Moon, and light of the Sun, so mote it be, your task is now done."

The popping in the circle decreased, and Brianna felt an easing in her toes. Devlin's intercession appeared to be working. Brianna picked up the chant.

"We extinguish the full light of this circle at last. We release all evil, both present and past. We thank the blessed Guardians for heeding our call. Go now in love, with blessings for all."

A swoop of air crackled around Brianna's ears, and the color bands around her fingertips vanished with a small "pop-pop." The oppressive heat vanished just as quickly, derailing Tommy's hold on her fingers. In the next instance, she was on her knees, enduring a last jolt of energy, and covering her face with her hands. Her sudden, wracking sobs shocked even her. She heard Devlin's voice to her right.

"No, don't touch her, Tommy. There may still be some lingering energy present."

May be? The set of tremors coursing through her body was solid proof that there was no maybe about it. Her blood was on fire. She hunched over, clutching her fingers.

"Brianna?"

The call was by her left ear.

"Still ... h-h-here," she stuttered through her shivers. "Though I c-c-can't see why I am ... I'm b-blind as a b-b-bat, by the w-way." A welcome heat enveloped her back a second later, and Brianna reveled in the heat of either Devlin or Tommy's jacket.

"Was that the stup ... stupidest thing ... you've ever seen d-d-done?" she asked, with a hiccup. She turned towards the area where she thought Devlin was. "Did it w-work?"

"Do fairy godmothers turn pumpkins into coaches?" Devlin answered, sarcastically.

A warm touch brushed her shoulders.

"That was the craziest—or bravest—thing I've ever seen done, I don't know which," Tommy remarked, sinking beside her. "My hand is stinging like a death adder bit it."

"Now you know how it feels to be bathed in negative energy," Devlin said, dropping to his haunches beside Brianna. "Your vision should clear shortly," he told her. "That is, I hope it will."

Brianna hoped so too. Although she didn't see how he could be comparing this to the Dark Time incident. This one had contained electrical shocks and angry elementals, not much more. It hadn't killed anyone; it hadn't removed another best friend from her life. *At least not yet,* her inner voice chided. She banished that thought, concentrating on the knowledge that she had been as gentle as she could in releasing the Guardians. They had been tossed about under the confusion of energy displacement, but she knew that wasn't the true cause of their anger. No, they were pissed off because they had been left hanging in a confined space for five days.

Off to her left, she heard Tommy's sarcastic tones.

"I thought rainbows only came with the rain."

"The color bands may have been beautiful to watch," Devlin replied, "but trust me, if the Guardians had really wanted Brianna to suffer, we'd be calling the paramedics right about now."

"They couldn't b-battle two witches," Brianna stuttered, the pain in her arm starting to ease. She straightened up and raised her hand to her hair. She had to get control of her flagging energy. Nothing would be right until she did. She scrubbed her wet cheeks with the back of her hand. Her mother! The thought sent her crawling over the markings and into the circle.

"Mother!"

She was dragged back by her legs.

"Stay back. You're in no shape to touch your mother."

The steel in Devlin's voice had Brianna scooting even further backward. What was she thinking? She brushed her eyes again, realizing the residual effects of the cleansing were causing a minor mind meltdown.

"Stay back, all of you!" a terse voice commanded from behind the trio. Brianna turned towards the voice.

"Brad," she sobbed.

She felt a presence slump alongside her.

"Here, drink this. It should vanquish the tremors."

A small glass was shoved into her fingers, and Brianna quickly drained the contents. Hacking coughs had her doubling over.

"What *is* this brew?" she sputtered.

"I'll tell you that when you explain to me how you managed to break the energy barrier."

"I'm afraid I c-c-can't," Brianna stuttered, trying not to gag on the remainder of the liquid burning the back of her throat. "It's a witches' pyramid and it's passed from mother to daughter in secret."

"Well, what you just drank is secret too. It's a mixture that your mother set down in the coven Book of Shadows to ward off tremors and snow-blindness."

"It's working," Brianna remarked. "But how did you guess I would need it?"

"From Rufus. He expected your findings right after sunrise and when you didn't come, he came searching for me. Together, we deduced you had been forced to take drastic actions here. I figured if you were attempting a free-fall ritual, there'd be consequences, so I prepared a little toddy for you."

"I'm grateful," Brianna stated. "But in the future I think I'll skip trying free-fall rituals."

"It's probably for the best. Now, let's see about retrieving your mother's body."

He moved away, and Brianna followed the movement. Her vision was clearing, although the scrim of tears was making it difficult to focus.

"The earth needs time to neutralize the stash of energy, Brad," Devlin stated. "When Brianna's safe to touch, everything else will be too."

Brianna felt a tap on her elbow and jumped under the sensation.

"You're still a live-wire," Devlin admonished, dropping his hand and shaking it.

"It's a fitting punishment for the wicked," Brianna replied, brushing her goose-caked arms.

"What's that supposed to mean?"

"It means I performed an ancient ritual that no solitary witch should've ever tried."

A chuckle sounded in her ears.

"No other witch would've had the power to do it, so your reasoning makes no sense," Devlin muttered. "You're not your mother's daughter for nothing, you know. And just because you don't care to follow in her footsteps, doesn't mean you didn't get some of her abilities passed on via your DNA."

He was right, Brianna knew, and there was a time when she would've considered those abilities a great treasure. But now, too much time had passed and she had traveled too many miles away from the spiritual path of her parents. She gave a huge sigh. If the last few minutes had taught her anything, it was that some roads were dead-ends, and should never be traveled again. Brianna shook off her shivers.

"I can finally feel my toes and fingers again."

Her eye caught the objects scattered around the circle, and she wondered why the little voice in her head was suddenly nagging her to look at her mother's body rather than the desecrated objects.

"Rrr-oww."

The loud cry sounded a second before Brianna felt a black form hop in her lap and take up residence there.

"Go away, Nicodemus," the doctor shooed. The cat growled at the doctor, but held its course. Brianna petted the sleek fur, drawn to the loud purrs now emanating.

"His name is Nicodemus?" she asked, scratching his ears.

"Your Mother's cat," the doctor replied. He glanced at the feline curling into a ball in Brianna's lap. "She loves him, though I don't know why; he's an obnoxious creature."

"I know why," Brianna said, scratching his head. "He's a royal cat; I can feel it." The purrs got louder at her words, and Brianna sensed the cat would not give up her lap, no matter how much coaxing the doctor might try.

"Praise the Lord and Lady. I feel a pulse."

His words had Brianna shoving Nicodemus off her lap. He spat at her angrily, but she ignored the hiss. She watched as the doctor felt along her mother's neck artery and then listened to her heartbeat with his stethoscope. "She's alive, though I can't explain how or why." His gaze skipped to Brianna's. "I don't know what you did, but whatever it was, I think you pulled your mother back from the River of Souls. Her lungs are barely working, but I detect a trace of life still there. You've managed to create a miracle."

Brianna scoffed at his compliment as Devlin dropped beside her.

"There is no possible way I c-could've pulled my mother back from S-summerland with that ritual. If she's still alive, it's because she c-c-chose to be. Whatever happened to her, she was not willing to let the sin stand."

"Either way, you've managed to help us avert a catastrophe."

He raised his hand and gave a frantic wave. Brianna heard the sound of rushing footsteps and scooted out of the way as two tall teens with dark hair, dropped to their knees. In a matter of seconds, the boys had lifted her mother's listless body to a stretcher, hoisted it up, and left the clearing with Brad calling out instructions to a third youth, who met them when they reached the crest of the hill.

Brianna scrambled to her feet, feeling a brush along her ankle, and a loud meow. She glanced down at the form rubbing his chin along her lower leg and smiled. Nicodemus—ever vigilant, she mused, a true Priestess' familiar. She felt a tug on her arm, and the cat bounded a few yards away.

"How are the shakes?" Devlin asked.

"Gone, and my vision's back."

A long sigh emanated.

"It's a good thing the elementals wanted to leave the circle more than they wanted to exact punishment for being trapped."

Brianna's brain shot to attention at his words.

"What did you just say?"

"You heard me."

"That's it. I couldn't imagine why the elementals were so furious at being released. They should've been elated to leave, but they weren't. I could sense it." She turned to Tommy. "How long would it take to file charges against the coven, Tommy?"

She felt a touch on her arm and jumped under the shock wave. Devlin's scowl was fierce.

"You're not filing charges against anyone. Not without proof."

"I have proof." Brianna ticked off the reasons on her fingers. "The circle was closed; there was no leakage of energy anywhere, and the quarters were left inside the circle on purpose."

"You're sure?"

"I'm sure. And you know I'm right because Mother's still alive. It isn't possible to be alive after five days comatose—unless you're a High Priestess with the skills to thwart an attack."

"Which means one of the Elders is behind the collapse?" Tommy asked, from their right.

Devlin's scowl deepened.

"We do not know that. We only have Brianna's hunch to go by, and I don't think we can rely on that at this stage. She's not fully recovered from the cleansing."

Anger suffused Brianna's cheeks.

"I'll pit my intuition against yours any day, Devlin Janus, and if you remember, you told me to pay attention as I dispatched the Guardians. Well, I did, and now I'm going to do something about it."

Brianna's elbow was snatched roughly, and her body propelled towards the rise.

"Before I let my wife make a complete mockery of her heritage by accusing a coven member of an evil deed, you and I are going to have a little chat. And this time, you're not going to invoke any of that High Priestess crap with me." He flashed a wave at Tommy. "Stay and take notes on the items in the circle, Tommy. Rufus will want to claim them, and I want a complete inventory before he does."

Tommy nodded his head and Brianna wondered why Tommy agreed to follow Devlin's orders; however, Devlin's tight hold on her arm propelled her up and over the rise so fast that all she could do was attempt to catch her breath and stay on her feet. In less than thirty seconds, they were entering the wooded path and approaching the standing footbridge.

CHAPTER TWELVE

THE FOOTBRIDGE

Reaching the shade, Devlin swung Brianna to face him.

"Did you lose all your senses during the ritual? Or is it that you hate this commune so much that you would jeopardize its existence by formally accusing a member of the congregation of a sacrilegious practice?"

Brianna pulled from his grasp.

"I don't see why you are accusing me of what you should be doing. After all, you don't owe them anything. They turned their backs on you, so why do you care what I accuse them of?"

"Because it matters, deep in my soul, what you do," Devlin stated, giving her an airy wave. His voice suddenly turned brittle. "Now that the crisis has been averted, Mrs. Janus, we're leaving."

Obviously stunned, Brianna took a step back.

"Leaving?"

"We've done what we came to do, and now it's time to let the Elder Council handle the rest."

"Are you insane?" she croaked at him. "The Council will mark this incident down as an incident the Ancients decreed."

"Let them. We won't be here to challenge it."

Dismissing his words, Brianna skirted his shoulders.

"I'm not going home until the sinner is found and brought to justice before the Council."

Stepping forward, Devlin yanked Brianna back around.

"The Council's more than capable of finding the sinner without your help."

Brianna shook her head.

"They won't punish the sinner without a push from me, though."

"And just how do you intend to push them?"

"By reminding them that I am the current High Priestess of this coven."

Her words stunned him, but he recovered quickly. Snatching her shoulders, he shook them.

"Invoking rights that you have no intention of honoring isn't the game you want to play here. It's unfair to use your status against the Council."

"It's the only leverage I have," Brianna responded. "You've seen how we've been treated so far. Nothing but half-truths—or outright lies."

He frowned at her words.

"So we respond to their bad manners by lying to them?"

"If that's what it takes, yes," Brianna replied. She whirled about, continuing towards the footbridge. "We're finally making headway, and I'm not going to start going backwards at this point."

Devlin re-grasped her shoulders and spun her around again.

"Suppose you do bully the Council into sanctioning the sinner, what then?"

"I leave here knowing that I've atoned for Brenda's death."

Devlin's gargled croak rent the air.

"My God, you earned that forgiveness ten minutes ago—when you saved your Mother."

"And when she's well, I'll recant the invocation and leave."

Devlin glowered at her, his tone turning surly.

"We don't belong here anymore, Brianna. I know you've sensed it, because I've sensed it through you. There's no further reason to stay, but at least when we leave, it's our choice this time—not theirs."

Her eyes suddenly ringed with tears, but Devlin hardened his heart to them. Her tears were not going to sway his decision. If she wasn't going to think of her own safety, he would. Her voice broke through his thoughts.

"Why can't you understand that I owe it to Mother not to leave here with things unfinished?" she asked.

He pounded his forehead.

"How can you be so smart, and yet so blind? Have you not noticed the damn cat?"

A startled expression crossed her face at the question.

"Nicodemus?" Devlin's hand waved impatiently, to a spot behind her. Brianna turned, spotting the cat sitting just beyond the footbridge, staring at her. "What does he have to do with anything?" she queried, swinging back.

"He has everything to do with it. If you weren't so focused on hammering out justice, you'd notice that since we cleansed the circle, he is continually skirting the fabric of your aura, attempting to cement the Binding."

"Binding?"

Devlin gave a fractured growl this time.

"Have you forgotten your studies?" He ticked off on his fingers. "The Hand-fasting, the Joining, the Binding, the Crowning." His signaled the cat again. "Nicodemus is a royal cat, and like his ancestors, he can only bond with a High Priestess."

"An old witch's tale," Brianna scoffed. "Nicodemus belongs to Mother, and always will. When she's herself again, he'll resume his allegiance to her."

"Your mother will never resume her position as High Priestess," Devlin exclaimed. "You saw to that when you invoked your rights. Can you not see that your mother knew if she transferred her powers to you, Nicodemus would transfer his allegiance to you too? She knew that by using his powers, and hers, plus your own, the spell could be fractured and then reversed."

Intense astonishment touched Brianna's face, and Devlin realized she had never once considered the possibility that her mother had made an incredible sacrifice that couldn't be undone. The thought must've made her heart flutter though, because he saw her clutch the front of her blouse. A ring of tears surfaced again.

"You're saying Mother chose to die? That she lost all hope of survival?"

Devlin leaned into her, tilting his head towards hers.

"I'm saying that she initiated a change of power in the hopes that you would find a way to keep her alive. Though we didn't know it then, your invocation was what she was banking on. With you as High Priestess, your powers will be hard to thwart. It's clear your mother recognized the sinner, and knew the only way to stop him, or her, was to make you as powerful as possible. Now, you've managed to pass the first two evocations—with flying colors, I might add," he told her, softly. She colored up fiercely, and he squelched a desire to kiss her soundly. "The Binding is now in motion," he stated, grasping her shoulders. "Nicodemus will continue to attempt to merge with your essence, and once he does, there will be no going back, no chance to change your mind. Is that what you want? To give up all you own, and take responsibility for the coven?"

Brianna shrugged from his grasp, and Devlin knew she was dissecting his question. Was she ready to throw her current life away? Perhaps, days ago, she might've been. But now? He saw her suppress a sob as Nicodemus inched closer to the footbridge.

"You're right," she finally stated. "Nicodemus is skirting my aura." She fell silent and Devlin wished she hadn't. When she went quiet, her energy pulled away from him, and it took a lot more of his energy to cross the distance and re-merge with hers. He stepped closer, and his words held a degree of warmth and concern.

"Tell me what you're thinking. It unnerves me when you go all quiet like this. Do you want to stay and hope that you can evade Nicodemus long enough for us to push the congregation for answers?"

She whirled, her eyes widening in surprise.

"And if I say yes?"

His lips twitched.

"I'd have to stay and push with you. That's a no-brainer."

Brianna made a face at him.

"There's no need for sarcasm."

He made a face back at her.

"Don't tell me my insults have finally managed to prick that tough hide of yours, Mrs. Janus?"

"Stop calling me Mrs. Janus in that condescending way. And yes, your insults have worked. You've shamed me into seeing the big picture."

Devlin's fingers raked through his hair.

"I know I'm going to be sorry I asked this, but what is the big picture?"

She leaned against the bridge railing, surveying his face.

"If I leave, I betray Mother's faith in me, and her unconditional love for this community, especially if I don't consent to the Binding. Any continued refusal to bind with Nicodemus will cause him harm, and if that occurs, I will lose my soul." She straightened from the rail with a sigh and frivolous wave. "Besides, I can't have the Ancients condemning you for what are clearly my Karmic debts."

Devlin's wave dismissed hers.

"Slow down, Rapunzel. You aren't living in that ivory tower of yours alone, you know. I have sins of my own to atone for here."

Brianna held up her hand.

"I think we're way past that argument now, especially since you sensed Mother had a premonition of all this and I didn't."

"It's a hunch, nothing more."

"But it makes perfect sense—and that's why we're staying."

An amused grin came her way.

"You're one hell of a she-bear, Mrs. Janus."

"And you're an incredible ass," she stated, whirling. Devlin chuckled again, tracing her footsteps. Hearing the laugh, she spun on her toes, walking backward as she railed him. "If you don't stop calling me Mrs. Janus, or Cinderella, or Rapunzel, I'll be forced to place a curse on your head that not even you can reverse."

"I'm not that brave, Sleeping Beauty," he muttered, as she swiveled and headed towards the distant trees. His footsteps soon dogged hers on the mulched path, and then, taking charge, he snatched her fingers, passed her, and pulled her along behind him. When they reached the intersection to the cottage, he slowed their steps.

"We'll make a pit stop at the cottage first, then go and check on your mother, and then after that, we'll start pushing for answers."

"And if there's time," Brianna interrupted. "We'll visit Papa and tell him we're not leaving."

Devlin clasped her fingers, and lifting them, he kissed the digits.

"Your father will hit the ceiling when he learns we're married," he stated. Brianna pulled her fingers from his.

"He'll be fine when we sign and present the annulment papers to him."

"*If* we sign the papers," Devlin emphasized. "Right now, I'm enjoying having a powerful High Priestess in my life. And, as my wife." He winked at her, and then whirling her about, he pushed her towards the driveway ahead. "Get a move on, Cinderella. I need to use the bathroom—stat."

"You can use the little boy's room without me. I'll meet you at the clinic," she said, pulling away. He snatched her elbow back, holding her in place.

"We need to stay together. Now that you've cleansed the circle, you will be our sinner's next target."

"He'll have to go through Nicodemus first," Brianna retorted, signaling the cat traversing the road behind them.

"Damn cat!"

"Be nice," Brianna warned, "Or I might have to unleash his powers on you."

"Is that a threat?"

"I don't believe in threats," Brianna answered, "I prefer the real thing."

"I'm not your pet mouse, Cinderella."

"No, you're just a sex toy I can dispose of when I choose," she shot back. A black silence followed the taunt and, obviously seeing the dangerous glitter of his eyes, Brianna took a hasty step back from him. "I was kidding. I'd never use Nicodemus to terrorize you."

"You really are an infuriating brat." Devlin stated, studying her posture. "And while we're on the subject of sex, I intend to make love to you tonight—all night."

He didn't wait for her reaction, just turned and headed towards the rooftop now peeping between the trees.

• • •

Watching him go, Brianna's cheeks became warm. Merciful heavens! He wanted another sexual interlude with her—twice in one day. *And what do we think about that?* her inner voice asked. She grinned amiably. That the Joining was extremely pleasurable—in its entirety. Her alter ego sent up another thought. *What if he just wants a little sex to curtail his frustration with the turn of events?* Her shoulders sagged suddenly. Her mother's investigation would be sacked, that's what. And it would be written up in the Coven Book of Shadows as "one of those things." The thought depressed her so much that she gave a choked sob. A moment later, strong fingers shook her frame.

"Dammit! Don't look so unhappy or I shall have to make love to you right here in the middle of the street." His words had Brianna stiffening, and his laughter bubbled up and out. "There now, that's the prickly woman I know. Hankering to claw my eyes out, eh?" To her surprise, Brianna laughed at his jibe. Grinning, he pulled her past him, and then pushed her towards the driveway only a hundred yards ahead of them. "Get a move on, Snow White," he stated.

She went, but not before giving him one of her haughtiest sniffs.

"If you don't stop calling me those ridiculous fairy tale names, I shall stir the Earth Dragons awake, and let them do their worst to you." A deep chuckle greeted her, but Brianna chose to ignore it. Now was not the time to trade insults; they had to get to the clinic and monitor her Mother's health.

Reaching the outskirts of the cottage several minutes later, the pair wound around a massive cat-claw tree and stepped onto the stone walkway next to the driveway. Passing the standing Jeep, Devlin slowed his steps.

"Uh-oh. Looks like trouble."

Brianna followed his gaze, giving a mumbled curse when she caught sight of Francis' tall figure loitering on the porch.

"Damn. Just what I need. Another scolding from Francis."

Devlin patted her arm.

"Play nice now, Goldilocks, or he might stir the Earth Dragons to do their worst on *you*."

Brianna's heart skittered at the thought. Francis was certainly capable of stirring an elemental, but by the stern look on his face, he had something more pronounced in mind—like stirring her anger. She heard a wizened grunt as Devlin laced his fingers with hers and stepped onto the walkway.

"He can't possibly object to my being pushy—now that I'm your husband."

Brianna studied their meshed fingers.

"I suppose I shall have to say polite things about you if he asks."

"It's a requirement. Do you need a list of my good qualities?" he teased.

"Not a list, just one," she stated.

He grinned boyishly at her.

"Tell him I'm great in bed."

"You're not that great."

He laughed outright.

"Liar." Brianna opened her mouth to call him a horse's ass, but he forestalled her by placing his finger over her mouth. "Ah-ah, be a good girl and mind your manners. Francis is watching." He dropped his fingers, greeting Francis as they reached the porch steps. "Good morning, Francis," he said, "You're up early. No morning vespers on the schedule?" He hopped the steps, forcing Francis to take a step back. Brianna saw Francis's smirk.

"So, it's true. Brianna has invoked her rights as High Priestess and you've married?"

"Word travels fast," Brianna said, with a sigh.

"Not as fast as my bladder … you'll excuse me." Devlin flicked open the door and leaving the pair staring at the closing door, and then each other. Brianna was the first to move. She stepped to her left, onto a stone path that led to the side of the cottage. In seconds, she was entering a beautifully landscaped meditation garden. The overpowering peace and quiet of the garden calmed her rattled nerves at once. Spirit Falls, she mused. Were there any spirits languishing about today?

She heard the sound of water trickling over rocks, and headed for it. Seconds later, she was plopping down on a stone bench, wondering if it was wrong to think of using her heritage against Francis. Spirit wouldn't like it. And what spirit didn't like, it took care of. *You should've never come home,* her inner voice nudged. She straightened her spine. I had to come; the Ancients decreed it. *And now?* her alter-ego prodded. I need to prove that we were sent here for a much larger reason.

Footsteps sounded, and Brianna quickly shored up her courage. She mustn't let Francis goad her into losing her temper. He would try; he always tried. Plastering a smile on her face, she studied Francis' slumped shoulders and then, out of the blue, she sensed he needed a friend. Could she be that friend for once in her life? It would be hard, since their relationship had always consisted of slammed doors and sarcastic name-calling. Still, she had to attempt to heal the rift that had grown between them.

Striking a casual pose, she waited for Francis to take a seat on an adjacent bench. Craning his head, he gave her his undivided attention. She lost no time in getting right to the point with him.

"I assure you, Francis, it was never my intention to invoke my rights when I came—or marry Devlin."

Surprised by her words, his demeanor changed.

"There's still time to change your mind. You can recant the invocation and appoint another in your place."

Brianna's breath caught in her lungs.

"And who do you suggest I choose?" she asked. "You?"

"I *am* the most capable," he answered.

Brianna gave a brief laugh. Francis had changed. In the old days, he would've never had the courage to brag about his character in such a brazen manner.

"I'm sorry, Francis. You will just have to wait your turn. I have no intention of recanting the oath I took—at least, not at this time. Mother's going to be well enough to resume her position as High Priestess when this crisis is over. And when she is, I'll do the right thing and sign whatever papers are needed to restore harmony to the community."

His body shot to attention.

"You must recant now—before the power has shifted so far, it can't be reversed."

Brianna laughed.

"I appreciate your concern, Francis, but until Mother is well, and the sinner who harmed her is found, I must hold true to the invocation."

"Another mockery to add to your growing list," he replied, with a grimace.

"Mockery? I've done everything by the book. Rufus made note of the time and date of the Invocation."

"And you think that makes it right?" Francis muttered. His expression turned to dismay. "At least you didn't have time to indulge in The Joining ritual. If you had, the congregation would be *forced* to accept you as their High Priestess."

A warm flush stole into Brianna's cheeks. Now why had he brought up the Joining? It wasn't a subject for public discussion. *He'd want to know—if he's the sinner,* her inner voice advised. Brianna bit her lip. Yes, quizzing her would be a must—if he was the sinner. He seemed not to notice her reddened cheeks as he continued his thoughts.

"I'm sure when we study the Coven Book of Shadows, we will find that you are not eligible to hold the office—thanks to your careless handling of Sacred Circles."

Brianna tossed her head. Here it was. Condemnation for Brenda's death. She should tell Francis to go to hell, but what purpose would it serve? It would brand her worse than the sinner they were looking for. She looked up through the sun-shot tree branches.

"Have you been sent to warn me that might happen, Francis?"

"No, of course not. That would make me somebody's puppet. Do I look like I'm being controlled by anyone here?"

Brianna started at the question.

"You've always gone your own way, Francis. No one will ever control what you say or do. I know because I tried hard enough to control you when we were kids and I couldn't do it."

He frowned at the criticism.

"No one is immune from the power of spirit, Brianna—not me, not you—which is why I'm unsure of your motives for returning home—given all that's happened. And now that you've invoked your rights, there is plenty of reason to worry."

Brianna's gaze impaled Francis.

"If you want a motive, Francis, ask the former High Priest of this coven for it. He called me with the news of Mother's collapse."

"Your father was ill, his mind clouded. Plus, he made the call without consulting the Council first."

"His mind wasn't clouded at all. He's read the Coven Book of Shadows. He knows who succeeds whom in a time of crisis."

Francis' face remained mulish, and Brianna wished she had the ability to read his mind. Though he was being upfront with her, she had the feeling that he was also holding something back.

"Why did you have to bring Devlin into this?"

"I didn't. I had no idea he was coming until we met in the airport. Papa called him."

"And you say your father's mind isn't clouded? He brought an outsider into what is clearly a coven matter."

"He's paid his dues, Francis. I think you can cut him a little slack."

"He got off scot-free, you mean. And now there's a rumor that you allowed him, as well as another outsider, to witness a healing ritual designated for a hereditary witch's eyes only. Why would you do such a thing? This friend of yours might divulge the ritual when he leaves here."

"Tommy won't divulge a thing. And as for Devlin, he can't. His marriage to me prevents him from doing so."

"Another mockery to add to the Book of Shadows."

"This crisis called for drastic measures in the clearing. I needed a back-up witch in case the pyramid didn't work. As my husband, Devlin was the logical choice."

"I would've cleansed the circle, if you had only asked."

"I couldn't take the chance. Though you have shown no symptoms of the illness so far, I couldn't be sure that the energy wasn't lying dormant in your system. And as for Devlin revealing what he saw, he's a grown man, and I can't control what he says or does."

"As High Priestess, you must *order* him to stay silent."

Brianna shifted on the bench, this time unable to hide her annoyance.

"Be careful, Francis. You're starting to tell me what to do—just like you did when we were kids. You know how I reacted then. I cast a perfectly nasty spell on you." He looked startled by her admission, and Brianna wished she could pinpoint why she was being so ugly towards him. It no longer mattered what had been said between them fifteen years ago. What mattered now was that they should treat each other civilly. Her expression softened.

"I promise you, I will find out who is behind this nightmare, Francis."

"And Devlin?"

"He feels the same," Brianna stated, rubbing her thigh. "Please don't condemn him for marrying me. I forced him into it, and out of love for Mother, he agreed."

"And he got what he's always wanted because of it: you."

Brianna flushed at the insinuation, but she recovered quickly.

"If you want to know if Devlin and I have had sex, why don't you just ask? No, wait, don't bother, I'll tell you. Devlin invoked the Joining last night, and it was marvelous—from start to finish." He flushed at her words, and Brianna felt compelled to take another dig. "You're free to report back to the Council that Devlin and I have consummated our marriage. And while you're talking to them, please let them know I intend to evoke The Weaving after lunch."

His face registered shock.

"You intend to interrogate the congregation?"

"As soon as possible; that is, if the Council doesn't throw up an objection."

"Of course we'll object. There's been no discussion, no logical reason for such action."

"Well, you've had my warning. It's all in the hands of spirit now."

"You're speaking for Devlin, too?"

"Absolutely. As High Priest, he wants what I want."

"Then you won't mind if I ask him to tell me that himself?"

"Of course, I mind. He's been put through enough since he's arrived. He's been saddled with a wife he doesn't want, and browbeaten by the Elders for caring what happens to this community." She saw his frown. "Don't worry, Francis. Neither of us intends to make a permanent place for ourselves here in the Coven. Our hypocrisy only goes so far." Her tone hardened. "The cleansing has made it clear that Mother was attacked and left to die in the circle on purpose. The sinner must be found and brought before the Council for sanctioning."

Her words brought an instant reaction from Francis, who sprang to his feet and took a defensive stance over her.

"Calling up a Weaving at this point is spiritual suicide. I won't let you do it."

"*You* won't? Brianna replied, leaning back from his towering frame. "Be careful, Francis. That threat puts you at the top of the list as the possible sinner."

He took a quick step back, a look of pure horror staining his face.

"You think that I could hurt your mother?" He took a step towards Brianna again, his fists clenching. "A sin against her is a sin against the Ancients," he declared. "To imply that I would ever betray her, or this commune, proves just how unfit you are to govern us. The Council will find the sinner in their own way—without your help."

"I see you still can't tell when you've lost an argument against Brianna, Francis," Devlin stated, startling the pair with his quiet arrival. He handed Brianna a cup of coffee, and quickly slid on the bench beside her. Brianna took a noisy slurp. The caffeine rush was delicious, a perfect antidote to Francis's accusations. *And so is the sinewy body sitting next to you,* her inner voice commented. *He smells delicious, looks delicious, and probably even tastes …* Briana stifled the voice. Keep your mind off his muscled thighs. *Right. Concentrate on getting answers, and then think about his muscled thighs.*

Frowning at her sarcastic mind rambling, Brianna studied the stand-off between the two men as Francis resumed his seat and assumed his former mask of judge and jury. Turning to the tote bag Devlin was setting next to her, Brianna peeked inside. A moment later, she withdrew a nutrition bar, juggling it and the coffee cup she held in her hand. Seeing the balancing act, Devlin took the bar from her fingers and tore the wrapper off, handing it back to her. She nodded her thanks, and breaking the silence, picked up the threads of her conversation, ignoring the fact that she was talking with her mouth full.

"I don't relish accusing anyone of Mother's collapse, but we must at least talk to the members and see if we can trace a timeline for her actions. She must've talked to someone, been seen by someone, before she decided to conduct a ritual in secret."

"And if the last person to see her was a visitor in one of our shops? What will you do then? Interrogate the whole state?" His scoff was followed by an airy wave. "This commune is open to visitors daily, and like any other town, we can catch the flu and suffer from it."

"I might agree with that, if I hadn't cleansed the circle and felt the energy shifts."

His expression lazily appraised her, and Brianna had the fleeting impression that he was hiding something. Could he be the sinner after all? She studied his now stern expression while popping the last of the chocolate bar into her mouth and brushing the crumbs from her lap. If he was, she was giving him plenty of fuel to come at her with. If only she had Nicodemus here. She could use him to probe Francis' mind. She banished that thought at once. She needed to stay away from Nicodemus and his powers.

"What pyramid did you use to cleanse the circle, if I may be so bold as to ask?"

The question was so unexpected that Brianna almost gagged on the last morsel of chocolate in her mouth.

"She can't tell you that, Francis," Devlin intervened, hearing her wracking cough and slapping her on the back. "And even if she could, I wouldn't let her."

A flash of humor finally crossed Francis' face.

"Still taking her side, I see. Even after all these years." He laughed outright. "I can't wait to see your face when she signs the annulment papers and you realize that you've been nothing but a means to an end for her."

Brianna saw Devlin stiffen and placed her hand on his thigh. She mustn't let Devlin be goaded by Francis' smarmy remarks. It was just what Francis wanted. It was what the entire community wanted. He studied the fingers on his thigh, and then covered them with his own. The glimpse of his strong fingers on hers made Brianna's heart beat more rapidly, and she was startled by how good his touch made her feel.

Wisely, she turned her attention to the sandwich bag next to her. Reaching in, she offered him a nutrition bar. He shook his head, surprised when she took the wrapper off and stuffed the bar into his hands. Taking a bite, he changed the subject.

"When we spoke with Charles last night, he hinted that before this incident, Sienna suspected someone in the congregation was misusing the Sacred Clearing. Did she say anything to you on the subject?"

The tension in Francis's face eased.

"Actually, she did. She asked me to quiz the students and see if any of them were experimenting in the clearing."

"And were any of them?" Brianna asked.

"No. They hold the greatest esteem for their mentors, and of course, your mother." He shook his head. "If there is a sinner, it's in the adult section of the congregation."

"Which is what I have been saying for the last ten minutes," Brianna remarked.

"None of that matters now," Devlin cut in. "We need to concentrate on formulating a solid plan for outing the sinner in the quickest way possible."

"Brianna has already concocted a plan. She's evoking The Weaving," Francis exclaimed.

Devlin's head whipped around and Brianna shifted on the bench, unnerved by his piercing glare. She pinched her lower lip with her teeth, praying he wouldn't shred her character in front of Francis. She had been wrong not to discuss the Weaving with him first, but as always, when she was around Francis, her tongue had no censorship.

"Let's just hope, the Weaving doesn't splice off, and backfire on us," Devlin finally retorted.

"You should've thought of that before conducting magic without a solid base to work from," Francis chided. "The cleansing was just plain dangerous."

"You will be doing the commune a great disservice if you offer that perspective to the Council. Because I will be forced to point out that the former High Priest of this Coven conducted magic without a solid base to work from long before I got here." To her surprise, Francis seemed at a loss for words at her statement. Did he think she would exonerate her father's behavior just because they were related? Beside her, Devlin didn't seem surprised at all by her words. He simply crushed his coffee cup and tossed it in the tote bag.

"Love can make a grown man do a lot of things he shouldn't—even abuse a law he has sworn to uphold."

Brianna winced. Was that statement directed at her, rather than Francis? It sounded like it. She raised her eyes and found Devlin watching her. What law had he abused? *The marriage vow, you ninny,* her inner voice chided. An image of their hands feathering over each other's body, burned her memory and she blushed immediately.

He chucked her chin, as if to say "you're blushing, Mrs. Janus", and she colored up even more fiercely. Seeing her discomfort, he brought his attention back to Francis.

"It is ridiculous to continue trading insults when we haven't even spoken to one congregation member yet," he said. "We could get lucky right off the bat and learn the identity of Sienna's attacker."

Brianna saw Francis's scowl reappear.

"You're wasting your time, but then it's your time to waste. You're dispensation will be up in just a few hours."

A half-smile crossed Brianna's face.

"Leaving is not an option. The Invocation has seen to that and Mother's retrieval from the circle ensures that there will be a prayer vigil tonight." Her gaze returned to Devlin. "We won't have a better time to speak with the members than during the vigil."

"You cannot interrogate the congregation under the guise of mourning," Francis huffed. "Proper protocols must be followed."

"Damn Coven protocol!"

Francis glowered at her curse, but was cut off from replying by Devlin's curt tone.

"Stow your anger, you two. We've got a more pressing problem." His gaze darted to Brianna's face. "We have to tell your father about our marriage. He won't be surprised, of course, knowing how fast gossip travels here, but we have to attempt an explanation."

Brianna blanched at the thought. She'd rather eat a bag of nails than face her father's wrath. Across the way, Francis laughed.

"Good luck with that," he said, with a flippant wave. "I only wish I could be there to see his reaction." He strode from the garden, his long legs moving rapidly across the stone tiles. When he disappeared around the side of the cottage, Brianna heaved a sigh of relief. Devlin picked up on the sound.

"You were pretty hard on him, don't you think?" he asked.

Brianna's lips puckered in annoyance.

"I'm hard on everybody, according to Tommy. And, why are you defending him? He said some pretty rotten things about you before you arrived."

"Well, he appears to have the confidence to carry it off. And besides, sticks and stones … " He left the ditty hanging and rose. "Relax, Mrs. Janus. Everything's under control—except for your father." He snatched her arm and pushed her towards the garden gate. "Get a move on. We're late." She hissed at him; however, when she reached the side of the house, she slowed her steps and then came to a complete stop.

"There he is again," she said.

"Who? Francis?"

"No, Nicodemus." Devlin's eyebrow rose as he studied the black cat sitting directly in the center of the walkway. He stamped his foot at the creature.

"Git!"

The cat scampered away, diving for cover beneath a nearby rose bush and growling low in his throat. Devlin turned back to Brianna, who was staring at him with a look of bafflement.

"What have I done now, Cinderella?"

"Nothing. I was just wondering if Nicodemus is for or against our marriage."

"He's for it."

"How can you tell?"

"He hasn't clawed my face off yet."

Brianna made a face at him and, then seeing his boyish grin, she rounded the cottage and onto the sidewalk again. His amused chuckle followed her exit. To her dismay, a warning voice whispered in her head. *Watch out. You're losing your heart to him.* She tossed the thought away, switching her thoughts to her mother.

"Next stop, holy hell," Devlin stated, pushing her around the front end of the Jeep.

"That's not funny," she responded, as he held the passenger door open for her. She slipped inside.

"Neither is walking barefoot on a bed of glass," Devlin said, slamming the car door. He circled the Jeep and climbed into the driver's seat, tossing Brianna an amused grin as they caught sight of Nicodemus bolting past the front bumper of the Jeep. Devlin fired the engine.

"Damn cat's off again. He'll be at the clinic long before we are."

"So mote it be," Brianna responded, clutching the amulet around her neck and caressing the jewels.

•••

The hooded figure finished drawing the circle on the floor. Damn Brianna. She had more lives than her mother's pet cat. But she wouldn't be so lucky this time. A large book was snatched up from the library desk, and deposited into the middle of the circle. The figure stepped back, pleased by the sight of Sienna's Book of Shadows lying there. Sienna had been careless in her trust of witches for once. And now, the book would cement Brianna's fate as well.

The figure raised a jeweled hand, palm facing up. With nimble fingers, a silver cord was laced through the digits, its ends left dangling. Seconds later, an excited chant split the air.

"From you to me, this spell I make; this was not right for you to break. Its path I will abruptly bend, and back to you the spell I send."

The figure waited for a moment, and then breathed a sigh of relief as in the middle of the raised palm, a pinwheel of red hues appeared and started to spin.

"Element of Fire, burning bright; I call you here with me tonight. Fulfill this desire sent to thee; work this magic just for me."

The pinwheel glowed brighter and then, with a flick of the wrist, the figure hurled the red energy into the circle and atop the book. The sound of crackling rent the air and then with a heated "whoosh," the pinwheel vanished into the book, out of sight.

The figure smiled at the disappearance and then spun. All that was left now was to set the circle in motion, and trick Brianna into coming to the library.

CHAPTER THIRTEEN

THE REUNION

Shutting out the raised voices, Devlin closed the door and grinned. Brianna had been polite at first, withstanding the shredding of her character by her father, obviously deeming it appropriate. However, when the attack turned to Devlin and Brenda Carver's death, she had immediately fired up and ordered him out of the room. He hadn't wanted to go, but her venomous glare had said "go or else." He chose correctly.

And now, lounging against the wall, listening to the raised voices, he felt elated. The more her father pressured Brianna to recant the Invocation and annul the marriage, the longer she would stay married to him. And that fit in perfectly with his plans for a future with her. Of course, she would be furious when she discovered the marriage certificate had been altered with a small caveat.

Would the secret purchase of her company jeopardize his chances of getting her into bed with him again? *Probably. But don't let that stop you,* his inner voice prompted. *Keep kissing her—until she has no other option but to fall into bed with you.* An increase in his heartbeat had him remembering his hard body atop hers. It would take more than a few kisses to make Brianna stay committed to the vows she took. His thoughts turned sour. How did you tame a she-bear bent on destroying you? He was sure he'd find out—when this damn situation was over.

Hearing the light sounds of Troika coming through an open doorway, Devlin abandoned his spot on the wall. The argument between father and daughter appeared to be dying down in intensity. And since the door hadn't reopened, inviting him back in, he felt confident leaving Brianna to defend herself without him. Besides, he needed to visit the ailing patients and get their take on Sienna's collapse.

Hearing feminine voices drifting out of an open doorway, Devlin followed the sound. Would the unknown women be receptive to speaking with him? He hoped so, because if they weren't able to locate some shred of evidence soon, they might never learn who was holding a grudge against Sienna.

Spotting the bickering pair as he reached the door, Devlin smiled with pleasure. The room contained two patients, rather than the standard three. In the far bed, he recognized the wrinkled face, fiery red hair, and plump body of Margaret Lord. The last time he had seen that face, it had been steeped in anger and reciting reasons why covens should never adopt orphans and educate them. He could still remember her shrill lecture as if it were yesterday.

He winced at the remembrance and then witnessed the pointed gestures of her fingers as she made an emphatic point of some kind. Her voice still held a shrill quality, and she appeared to have packed on an extra ten or twenty pounds.

His gaze shifted to the closer bed. This had to be Eileen O'Connor; however, judging by the sleek line of her profile, she had changed drastically since childhood. Back then she had been a wiry teen, constantly in motion. Now, she had filled out, and her voice had softened to a husky bass. Her hair, like Margaret's, was worn cropped short; however, the color was a deep, jet black. The aura surrounding her frame revealed the same vibrant personality he remembered, and he was relieved that she didn't appear to have aged beyond her years.

"Devlin? Devlin Janus?" The question hung in the air, and Devlin swung his gaze to the older woman scrambling to a more dignified sitting position on her bed. Devlin hid a smile at the frantic wave beckoning him forward. He crossed the tiles and rounded the first bed, taking Margaret's offered hands. To his surprise, she tugged on his fingers, forcing him to bend over and receive a welcoming kiss. Releasing his fingers, she fell back on her pillows. "Rufus said you and Brianna were here, but I thought he was joking." Her gaze swung to the closed door as if expecting another visitor. And then her face scrunched up. "I suppose Charles couldn't help himself. After all, Sienna is Brianna's mother, but I am surprised he called you, Devlin. I haven't quite forgiven you for Brenda, you know." Her gaze shot to the closed door again, and Devlin wondered who she was so anxious to see come through it.

"For heaven's sake, Margaret, stop quizzing Devlin as if he was still sixteen and stealing cookies from your cookie jar," Eileen reprimanded. "I think it was brave of him to return, especially after all the horrible things that were said to him."

Margaret's eyes widened at the rebuke.

"You can't possibly know what was said to him. You were lying on death's doorstep for weeks—thanks to him."

"Margaret!" The word was said with such horror that Devlin laughed. Margaret hadn't really changed at all. She was still fond of speaking her mind with no censorship. It was clear her focus was on being sure he knew how badly he had erred all those years ago. The question was why. He felt a touch on his sleeve and turned to find a pair of sea-green eyes studying his face. "I'm very glad to see you here." She shifted her body to make room for him on the side of the bed. "Sit here, where I can see you." She leaned back on her pillows, and Devlin did as she suggested, hiking his leg up and sliding onto the edge of the bed. "I'm Eileen O'Connor, in case you didn't remember. I used to have a terrible crush on you."

Devlin grinned.

"Did you? I wish I had known that sooner."

She laughed at his jibe.

"I was six, and you were ten. You doused my clothes with water because I had set myself on fire. You cursed at me loudly—a naughty thing to do to a six-year-old girl."

Devlin laughed, wagging his finger at her.

"And you made me promise to buy you a new ceremonial dress or you'd tell my parents that I had set your dress on fire on purpose."

The twinkle in her eye wasn't lost on Devlin as she followed his playful scolding with a bright laugh.

"It worked though, didn't it? You bought me a new dress a few months later." Her gaze suddenly turned sad. "Charles says you called every day for weeks after the Dark Time—for an update on my health. I can't thank you enough for that." Her expression clouded over and Devlin knew her mind had traveled back to Brenda's death.

"It was awful about Brenda, such a waste." Her gaze drifted to a spot on the wall over Devlin's shoulder. "Sally seems to have made her peace with that awful time, but I can't seem to get past it. And now, to succumb to another illness almost as bad as the first … well, I suppose I will have night sweats for months after this terrible ordeal is over. It will make it almost impossible for me to ever erect a Sacred Circle again." She turned her head, covering her mouth as she gave into a husky cough.

Devlin patted her legs.

"My careless handling of Brianna caused the Dark Time, but I knew what I was doing when I sealed the circle to ward off any repercussions."

"But could you have done it without Brianna's help?" Eileen asked. "Sally has always maintained that you couldn't."

"What do you think?" Devlin asked, eyeing her curiously.

"I think you could've sealed it with your eyes shut, and your hands tied behind your back."

Devlin laughed at the preposterous statement.

"It's nice to know somebody that day was in my corner."

"Oh, don't get me wrong, I disliked you for years for what you did. But then I read in an old magazine how your restoration of a natural habitat in Wyoming has guaranteed a new lease on life for the wolves residing there. I knew then that you had atoned for that awful day, and that it was foolish of me to dislike you any longer, so I forgave you."

"Just like that?"

"Don't make fun. I'm serious."

"Sorry. I didn't mean to make fun. I'm grateful for your forgiveness."

She stifled a cough, and lowered her voice to a near whisper.

"We heard voices in the hallway earlier, but haven't been able to find out what's occurred. Has a new patient been brought in?"

"Actually, it's good news," Devlin said. "Sienna's body has been recovered from the clearing."

"What!"

"Thank the Goddesses!"

The exclamations were simultaneous as both women bolted up in bed and nailed him with a suspicious stare. To his surprise, Eileen was the first to challenge the news.

"You reversed the spell? When none of us could?" She sank back on the pillows, chewing on her lower lip thoughtfully. "I don't know how I feel about that."

"I know how I feel," Margaret snorted, her face as glum as Eileen's. "You are still a foolish boy, Devlin Janus, and you are lucky you aren't being laid out in the chapel for funeral services right now."

Devlin studied her face. Why was Margaret assuming that he had cleansed the circle without help?

"Brianna and I examined the circle together, Margaret."

"How could you? Are you married?" Her gaze dropped to his hand. "Oh, yes, I see that you are. Well, I suppose that's why Rufus had to agree to let you attempt a cleansing."

"Margaret!" Eileen's tone was disapproving as her gaze surveyed Devlin's hand. "I had no idea that you were married, Devlin. The magazine I read said nothing about a wife."

"It was spur of the moment on both our parts." Devlin replied.

"Well, whoever did this to Sienna has lost all sense of decency," Margaret remarked, with a huff. "We've always prided ourselves as an honest community. I don't understand why the person responsible hasn't come forward."

"Could you tell if Sienna was purposely harmed?" Eileen asked, changing the subject.

"Too soon to tell," Devlin answered. He studied Eileen's face, surprised that she had asked the question instead of Margaret Lord. His instincts told him that Margaret knew much more than she was saying.

"Perhaps, one of the young teens is responsible for what happened." Margaret sniffed. "They are always begging to cast their own circles. Francis has his hands full as their mentor."

"It's far too early to think of outing the teens," Devlin remarked. "We will know more when the Council conducts an investigation."

Margaret's mouth snapped shut; however, Eileen came out of her stupor with an airy wave.

"We'll find it was a horrible accident, nothing more," she stated.

"An accident caused by displaced energy," Devlin corrected.

"Which has been neutralized, or we wouldn't be starting to feel better," Eileen replied. She placed a hand on Devlin's knee. "Why are you really here, Devlin? In our room, I mean."

He considered fudging his answer, but thought better of it.

"If we are to solve this ominous mystery, we must trace Sienna's whereabouts before she entered the circle."

"So you've come to interrogate us?" Margaret grumbled. "Shame on you!"

"Hush, Margaret. Devlin's right. Someone must remember seeing her."

"You, Margaret? When did you last see or speak with her?" Devlin queried. She wrinkled her brow, attempting to recall.

"We attended vespers on Sunday evening together. She stayed to help me mop up the kitchen … "

"Did she confide in you?" Devlin asked. "Mention that an un-Sacred circle had been cast?" Margaret's face paled at the question.

"Heaven's, no! Has there been a black circle cast?"

"It appears so."

Fear, stark and vivid, glittered in her eyes. She shuffled her feet from under the covers and slid to the edge of the bed.

"I must find Rufus at once. The congregation must be gathered together for a protection blessing."

"You're not going anywhere," Eileen touted, "Stop her, Devlin. Brad has given strict instructions for her to stay in bed and recuperate."

Devlin hopped from the bed, barring Margaret's way.

"You must do as the doctor says, Margaret. Until your symptoms subside, you cannot participate in, or emcee a blessing."

She frowned at his words, but slipped back into the bed and stuffed her feet under the sheets. Eileen banged the metal frame of her bed.

"I saw Sienna Sunday at the vigil, and then again at morning vespers on Monday. She seemed herself, asked no suspicious questions, never commented on anything amiss."

"Was Francis at the vigil?"

"Yes, of course. He conducts Sunday vespers."

"And Sally?"

Eileen's brow furrowed.

"No, I don't remember seeing her there. But then Danny attends the junior services on Sunday. Sally shadows him like a mother hen, so I can only assume that is where she was."

Another sniff rocked the air.

"Sally is a loving, devoted mother. It is cruel of you to hint that she may have had something to do with Sienna's collapse. Next, you'll be spouting Francis is involved."

Devlin saw a dangerous glint light Eileen's eyes.

"I am making no such accusation. It is my responsibility as Second Elder to discover the truth of Sienna's collapse. No stone can be unturned in accomplishing that task; if a member of the congregation is at fault, the Council must identify the person and sanction them immediately."

"It is Rufus's responsibility as Third Elder to head up any interviews. Yours is to set up those interviews and nothing more."

Devlin cut in, bent on warding off another barrage of insults.

"Actually, it's the Interim High Priestess' responsibility to oversee things," he said.

Eileen's head whipped around.

"Did you say Interim High Priestess?"

"Yes, Brianna invoked her rights as High Priestess last night."

Eileen's face drained of color, while a screech from the far bed echoed shrilly.

"She did what?!" Margaret shot up as if to leave the bed again, and Devlin derailed her escape. Seeing his gesture, she slid back under the covers and gave him a nasty glare. Seeing it, Devlin knew what question would be next. Had a marriage taken place after the invocation? Eileen came to life on the bed.

"She married you, didn't she? She invoked her rights, and then took a husband. That's how it's done. That's how you were able to disrupt the barrier of the circle so quickly. What a brilliant move on her part, and what a lucky break for you, huh? Finally getting to marry her after all these years?"

Devlin heard the dripping sarcasm as he re-took his seat on the bed, but before he could offer a retort, Margaret intervened.

"You're saying Brianna married you to halt this despicable illness? I don't believe it."

"I think it was extremely smart on her part," Eileen countered. "I always knew she had Sienna's powers, but to short-circuit a circle when it might harbor a spell within a spell. Oh, I wish I had been well enough to see how she did it."

Devlin heard a hiss from his left and turned.

"You've something to add, Margaret?" he asked.

"Of course I do," she stated firmly. "I intend to condemn this bogus wedding the first moment I see Rufus. You and Brianna have upset the balance of the community by returning and mocking our creed. If Rufus agrees, I will have plenty to say to you—none of it good." Her gaze shifted to Eileen. "We shall devote our prayers tonight for protection and healing." Her gaze shot back to Devlin. "You and Brianna will join us here for the prayers—to atone for causing such an imbalance in our spirits."

"I don't attend prayer meetings anymore," Devlin stated, "And I'm quite sure Brianna has no intention of leaving her mother's side this evening."

"You will attend this one." Margaret railed at him. "Brianna has set herself as a High Priestess, and she must act like one. She must lead us in prayer for her mother. And if there's any possibility that her foolish stab at cleansing the circle has caused this horrendous illness to re-ignite—inadvertent or not—she must ask the congregation for forgiveness."

Devlin frowned at her censure. The congregation would have a long wait if they expected an apology from Brianna. It was clear that he would have to reveal Sienna's condition to the women. But how to do it tactfully?

"Sienna would never approve of unfocused prayers, you know," Eileen interjected, attempting to break the sudden silence in the room. "She didn't believe in random spell-making or a reckless stirring of the Guardians."

Devlin's hand sliced the air, cutting off any further criticism.

"Sienna is not dead. We found her alive in the circle."

"Alive? Impossible!" Margaret exclaimed, shifting her feet beneath the covers.

"Five days down, and still alive?" Eileen marveled. "It's unheard of."

"It can't happen," Margaret continued to snuffle. "Francis says so. And he is certainly well-versed in performing the most elaborate of rituals. He's as good as Sienna in my estimation."

Devlin heard the edge in her voice and responded.

"Was Sienna having problems with Francis?" he asked. "Something that might tie into her collapse?"

"Good heavens, no!" Margaret responded, snapping her mouth shut and giving Devlin a forbidding glare. "Francis wouldn't hurt a fly. Ask anyone."

Devlin's gaze shot to Eileen, who glanced at the wall over his shoulder.

"If you know something, Eileen … "

"I suppose you'll find out anyway from Charles or Rufus," she stated, bringing her gaze back to him. "Sienna didn't approve of Francis's fast rise within the Elder ranks. She thought his motives lacked clarity, especially since Rufus fought against his being initiated as an Elder."

"She told you that?"

"Of course, Sienna has always been honest with the Council regarding any pending appointment. She'd be a poor High Priestess if she didn't." She broke off speaking and Devlin saw a light flush stain her cheeks as she glanced at Margaret. "That came out as an insult to Francis, and I didn't mean it to, Margaret."

Margaret glowered at her.

"You owe Francis the apology, not me."

"Honestly, Margaret, your devotion to Francis is admirable, but even you must admit that his circle skills can't hold a candle to Sally's."

Devlin's gaze shot to Eileen. Now here was a piece of information to be stuffed in the "suspect" category. Along with Eileen, Sally had the power to emcee a Sacred Circle.

Devlin heard a fractured wheeze.

"Francis can emcee rings around Sally. I don't know why you've chosen to insult Francis instead of supporting him. And why aren't you offering me sympathy?" she stressed, her voice beginning to crack. "Sienna was my dearest friend, and I'm unable to leave this room to offer any kind of consolation to Charles." She sought a tissue from a Kleenex box and wiped her eyes. "Oh, I wish Rufus was here." The bed under Devlin's rump jiggled, and he saw Eileen's rash movement to leave her bed. Devlin signaled her back. Hopping from the bed again, he flung an arm around Margaret's sagging shoulders.

"Rely on your faith to get you through this, Margaret."

"I suppose you think I'm a foolish old woman for crying instead of daring to leave this room," she remarked. "I suppose nothing ever rattles you."

Devlin's smile was tired as he squeezed her shoulders.

"You're mistaken. Sienna's collapse has knocked me for a loop."

Eileen tapped the bed frame with her fingers again.

"I don't mean to nag, Devlin. But the Council will need proof that the cleansing was successful. An entry must be logged in the Coven Book of Shadows, and the Council must give their blessing on its use."

"The ritual is out of the box and not for public noting." Devlin stated.

"She must give up the ritual—no matter how secret. It is the law." Margaret huffed.

"As Interim High Priest of this coven, I won't allow her to reveal the spell until we have brought this master of dark magic to trial."

"You have no say in this matter," Margaret muttered. "You gave up that right when you killed Brenda Carver."

"Margaret!"

Devlin didn't let Eileen smooth the way this time.

"I may have given up all rights to the Wicca faith when I left," Devlin argued. "But my marriage to Brianna keeps me safe now. You can't toss either of us out."

"Well, of all the nerve!"

The door handle rattled, startling the trio from their conversation.

"What now?" Eileen asked, seeing Tommy's rotund figure lounging on the doorframe of the open door. "Good heavens, Devlin, how many outsiders have you and Brianna brought with you?"

"Only one," Devlin replied. "This is Brianna's attorney and business partner, Tommy Cloisters. Tommy, this is Eileen O'Connor, Second Elder of the Council. And this feisty lady in the other bed is Margaret Lord."

A grin crossed Tommy's face as he moved forward with an outstretched hand.

"Good to meet you, Miss O'Connor. I hope you are feeling better. You too, Mrs. Lord," he stated, swinging his gaze to the far bed.

A rare frown crossed Eileen's forehead as she dropped Tommy's hand.

"Why has Brianna brought an attorney with her? Is she intending to make allegations against us for Sienna's collapse?"

Devlin heard a light cluck from Tommy.

"I'm not here in any kind of legal capacity, Miss O'Connor. I'm Brianna's friend, besides her attorney." His gaze bounced to

Devlin. "I don't mean to cut your visit short," he stated. "But the doctor is looking for you."

Devlin hopped from the bed and circled the rails. He gave a small wave to the women, which prompted another husky plea from Eileen.

"Please convince Brianna to come to the vespers this evening, Devlin—as a sign of good faith. It will prove that neither of you has an ulterior motive for being here."

Devlin's right eyebrow rose in surprise and, though Eileen blushed, she snuggled deeper under the covers and dismissed Devlin. "That didn't come out right. I'm sure you've atoned for your sins in many ways since leaving us."

Amused by her accentuated coughs, Devlin hid a smile and headed for the door.

"I'll have Brianna stop in to visit—as a sign of her good faith in atoning for my sins."

"Don't be gnarly," Eileen stated. "And by the way, congratulations on your marriage."

Sketching a wave over his shoulder, Devlin exited the room with Tommy on his heels. Once in the hallway, he shook off the room's negative energy. It wouldn't do to have his aura saturated with streaks of grey shadows, like those surrounding the women's frames. He felt a light tap on his shoulder and turned his head.

"What was that all about?"

Devlin lowered his voice.

"Things have gotten dicey since we left you."

"Good God, what now?"

"Brianna is hell-bent on evoking an ancient ritual called The Weaving."

"The what?"

"A formal hearing," Devlin answered. "Like a town hall meeting—only it's really a polite interrogation of the entire congregation."

He saw Tommy's nod.

"Should I be prepared for fire to rain down on both your heads?"

Devlin wagged his fingers at Tommy.

"It can rain on my head, but I'm not about to let the firestorm hit Brianna."

"Why am I not surprised?" Tommy chided, following Devlin down the hall. Reaching the end of the corridor, Devlin paused and took a deep breath before rounding the doorframe. His back ached, and his muscles screamed, and he had increasingly uneasy feeling that something sinister was stalking him.

CHAPTER FOURTEEN

THE PLAN

Studying the comatose woman in the bed, Devlin realized he didn't need to protect Brianna from anything. Since the marriage, he could feel her aura, no matter where she was. If someone wanted to harm her, he'd sense it long before she did. It was clear their marriage had fused them together somehow, like rain and springtime. *Like satin sheets and naked bodies,* his inner voice added. Like mind-blowing sex and roaming hands, he shot back. Now, if he could just find a way to convince Brianna that the Sisters of Fate wanted her to give herself to him, totally and unconditionally.

He surveyed the room, relieved to see the doctor hadn't allowed the room to take on the feel of a funeral. No candles were lit, no flowers of bereavement were displayed, and the New Age music playing through the speakers had a peaceful quality to it. However, he still felt a flicker of something not quite right in the room.

Brushing the nape of his neck, he realized they should've followed Sienna directly from the clearing to the clinic, pressuring Brad into formulating a healing plan for her. Hell, they needed a healing plan for the entire community. A light touch on his sleeve had Devlin spinning on his heels with a ferocious curse.

"Dammit, Tommy! I forgot you were following me."

"Sorry. I thought all you warlocks had second sight." A cheeky grin surfaced as he stopped alongside Devlin and studied the heart monitors.

"You've been watching too many horror films," Devlin told him. "In Wicca life, a witch is a witch—male or female. There's no distinction."

Tommy emitted a half-grunt.

"May I ask what you're looking for? Do you suspect that some negative residue has followed Mrs. Sage into her coma?"

"No, she assigned the Guardians to prevent that. However, she's beyond healing washes and herbal medicines. You have only to look at her to see that."

Tommy dipped his head.

"It's too bad you can't tap into her thoughts. If you could, you'd know who is behind this tragedy."

"And we wouldn't have to wait on the Weaving. The interviews are going to take a full day and a half."

"Does Mrs. Sage have days?"

"Yesterday I would've said no, but today it's clear that her essence is so powerful that not even five days of obvious suffering could end her life."

"It sounds like you're saying she holds the power of God in her hands," Tommy scoffed.

"She holds the power of the earth in her heart, and that makes her extraordinary. Spirit, or whatever you want to call the Creator, has seen fit to bless her with the good side of the power of three."

Devlin's gaze re-scanned Sienna's serene features. What other task had Sienna assigned the Guardians to do? A frown skirted his lips. That secret would probably never be unearthed. Reaching out, he seized her wrist, detecting a faint thrumming beneath his fingers. Her essence appeared to have split in two, leaving her susceptible to permanent physical damage.

"Something's wrong. You're scowling," Tommy stated, studying the woman in the bed. "I refuse to believe things are as hopeless as everyone says."

"So do I," a deep voice stated from behind the pair.

Devlin and Tommy whirled in unison, startled to find the doctor joining them at the bed. They watched his contemplation of her tranquil features.

"Sienna's essence has been thoroughly damaged, though I can't pinpoint whether it was damaged five days ago, or five hours ago." He shooed the pair back, and Devlin realized he was a man suffering from a torn conscience. If the damage had occurred five days ago, then the blame centered in the commune. If five hours ago? He didn't intend to speculate on that.

Giving way to the doctor's second wave, Devlin moved from the bed to find Brianna hovering in the doorway. Her meeting with her father had ended badly. She looked totally wrecked. And she had been crying. Her make-up was smeared and her lips devoid of their usual cherry lipstick. Tracking her thoughts, he crossed the room to her side.

"How bad was it after I left?"

Her hand flew to her cheeks, brushing away the caked streaks.

"Pretty awful. Papa says I've ruined your life, and condemned the commune to another Dark Time. And you don't want to know what he thinks about using the marriage to cleanse the clearing."

"Not if you value your sanity," Charles said, eyeing Devlin while skirting Brianna's form. He crossed the space and stopped alongside the doctor.

"As the Interim High Priestess, Brianna has evoked the ancient law of Weaving," he stated. "I see no other recourse, but to suggest that the Elder Council abide by her decision."

Brad frowned at the suggestion.

"Are you sure you want to put the congregation through that? They're bound to bring up Brenda's name."

A sudden silence descended in the room, and Devlin watched Brianna drop into a chair alongside the bed.

"I can take it." she declared. "At least, I think I can."

Seeing the nervous bite of her lower lip, Devlin was relieved by her words. For a moment, he had thought she would play the anger card, regardless of how hopeless it might be. Twisting his head, he gauged her expression as thoughtful rather than resigned.

Clearing his throat, Brad flung his stethoscope around his neck. Beside him, Charles stalled whatever he was about to say.

"I will contact Rufus and set the ceremony for two." His gaze landed on Devlin. "That should give you enough time to relearn the creed and decide on the appropriate ritual."

Devlin frowned at the barb, remembering Brianna's earlier remark about half-truths. The doctor wisely changed the subject, addressing Brianna.

"You mother's vital signs are stable at the moment; however, if they begin to fail, I will have no choice but to have her air-lifted to Tucson. If that occurs, the police will automatically become involved—whether we want them to or not." Seeing Brianna's mouth open, he held up his hand. "I'm not saying we're at that point yet."

Devlin saw Brianna's glance trip to her father.

"So, we're just writing Mother's soul off as irretrievable?"

A pained look crossed her father's features, and Devlin heard a long sigh.

"Unfortunately, no one in this congregation has the power to raise the prayers your mother needs to heal. Not even my skills are enough. It's simply beyond us all."

"It's not as hopeless as you think," Brianna interrupted, "Mother's essence could be restored—if we know what spell was used to take her down."

A discreet cough had the pair glancing at the doctor again.

"There is no full-proof way to restore her essence. I know. I've searched the Book of Shadows."

A shocked look crossed Brianna's face.

"You have Mother's personal journal?"

"No, of course not. That's a sacred text—for her eyes only."

Devlin managed to hide a smile. The group had no idea what Brianna was hinting at. But he did. She was thinking ahead to a binding with Nicodemus. He studied her face. He'd be damned if he'd let her merge her essence with Nicodemus without discussing it with him first. If she was going to take over the reins of the coven, and alter his life as well as her own, he wanted some say in it.

"Without her journal to guide me," Brianna finally asserted. "The congregation is never going to accept me as their High Priestess, especially when they learn how I obtained the title."

"Unfortunately, your birth makes that an idiotic excuse at best."

Her gaze turned from ice to fire at his statement.

"I have already committed the worst of sins by declaring myself Mother's successor. I certainly won't usurp her magic when I know full well that I don't have the spiritual purity to do it."

"Well, I for one believe in your magical skills, so that's a moot point as well," Brad countered.

"We are not at the end of the road here," Devlin jumped in. "We still have a few avenues to explore before resorting to last-ditch efforts."

"Such as?" Brad asked.

Brianna stirred in her chair.

"Examining the amulet Mother was wearing at the time of her collapse. Its energy will still be intact."

The doctor's face paled, and his gaze shot to the bed.

"She wasn't wearing any jewelry when we brought her from the circle."

"She never goes without her amulet—at least I've never seen her without it." Brianna's gaze shot to her father and then to Devlin, who saw the fear written in her eyes.

"Don't panic. We'll find it," he stated.

"Unless, of course, her personal journal was burned as part of the spell." Brianna added. She sprang to her feet, obviously worried by her own words. "It's crucial we inspect the clothes Mother was wearing at the time of the collapse."

"They're in the infirmary," Brad replied, moving from the bed. Charles' voice stopped him in mid-stride.

"I'd prefer the congregation not get wind of what you're doing—at least, not until the Council has energized the Weaving ritual. Can I count on everyone's discretion?"

"No one will say a word," Brianna stated. Her gaze found Devlin's and then Tommy's. "That's an order."

Devlin's mouth twitched. The she-bear was back.

"Sounded like an ultimatum to me, blue eyes," Tommy remarked, before Devlin could spit out a retort.

"Yes, well. It seems I'm a High Priestess now, and my loyalty is to the Coven."

"And it's my duty as your trusted advisor to let you know that your potion has worked on Danny and the other patients. I've released all but Danny. What coughs and stomach ailments there are can be treated at home." An uneasy silence descended which the doctor broke at once. "Well, we all have some place to be, don't we?" He headed for the doorway again, this time Charles dogging his heels. Their voices faded away and a long sigh reverberated.

"Let's hope that's the last time we're treated like lepers," Brianna remarked.

"Let's hope you know what you're doing—and that you keep a civil tongue in your head while you're doing it." Devlin chided.

"What can I do?" Tommy asked.

"You must go back to the clearing with Devlin and see if Mother's amulet is buried there," Brianna replied. "The negative energy spawned in a Sacred Circle leaves an energy trail to follow—if one is smart enough to look for it."

"I won't leave you to fend for yourself," Tommy stated, placing his hand on her shoulder. "You might be the sinner's next target." Devlin frowned at his words, and the touch. Tommy was taking an awful lot on himself by giving them orders. "The members will be ambulatory again which means if they see me digging holes in the clearing, they will start asking questions you can't afford to answer. No, I'll stay and let Devlin go."

Devlin pondered his words. Was it best to let Tommy continue to be regarded as a welcome visitor in the commune? He glanced down, studying the linoleum floor speckled with dirt trails. Tommy wouldn't know what to look for in the clearing; but he needed another strong back for the digging. They had to go together. He glanced at his watch. Would there be time for scrounging before evoking the Weaving with the Elders? It didn't matter. Sienna's recovery depended on their finding her amulet. Their continuing silence finally sparked him to comment.

"Tommy's not as conspicuous as he thinks, and I need his help. You don't."

"Is the clearing safe?" Tommy asked, a moment later.

"It's safe," Devlin interjected. "Any latent energy flux would be from Mother Nature recycling herself."

"Or from a hidden back-up spell," Brianna threw in.

Devlin gave her an impatient wave.

"You halted the original spell. The damn cat proved it. You need to focus on finding your mother's Book of Shadows. It will contain her thoughts and possible counter rituals."

"Her amulet is more important," Brianna argued.

"We can't do everything together. We must use our time efficiently. Splitting up is the only logical way to accomplish that."

"I'll go with Brianna," Tommy advised, again. "Her safety is questionable at this point."

"Brianna already has a bodyguard."

"Good God, you aren't talking about that black creature that's always following her around?" Tommy croaked.

"He'll keep her safe," Devlin stated. His glance strayed to Brianna. "If we find Sienna's amulet buried near the circle, we'll come find you. We won't bait the sinner without you."

Tommy stepped forward, grabbing Brianna's hands.

"Is the Circle safe?"

"Yes, I think so."

Tommy dropped her hands and sketched a wave as he headed for the door.

"Then I have just the thing in the trunk of my car. It's small, but it's a top of the line metal detector." He started for the door, and then paused when Devlin didn't move. "Well, aren't you coming?"

"I'll meet you at the Jeep," Devlin replied. Tommy's left eyebrow lifted, but he didn't push, just whirled and disappeared out the door.

"You do know that if the Elders find out that we allowed a stranger to dig in their Sacred Clearing, they'll hang us from the nearest tree," Brianna stated.

"We won't get caught," Devlin stated. "He's resourceful; I'm resourceful."

"In that case, I'll take a look at Mother's clothes in the infirmary by myself. If nothing's amiss, I'll head to the cottage and hunt for the journal."

Devlin glanced at his watch again.

"Keep track of the time. We can't miss the ceremony at two."

"I have no intention of missing it," Brianna stated. "Francis will be conducting the introductory prayer and I will have plenty to say if he mucks it up."

"And you will say it politely, of course?"

"Oh, I shall be extremely polite," Brianna replied, heading for the door. Devlin smiled at the curious tilt to her lips. Was she teasing him, or was she totally serious? The next couple of hours would tell that story. God forbid, if he had to admonish for making accusations they couldn't back up.

"Earth to Devlin … hello … "

His head shot up.

"Sorry. I was trying to visualize you being extremely polite."

"Ha-ha. Very funny."

She left him then, skirting the door and disappearing from view. Very funny, she had said. Well, there wasn't anything funny about the mess they were in. And the sooner they proved it to everyone, the better.

CHAPTER FIFTEEN

THE CLEARING

Devlin tamped the dirt with his shovel and then gave it an extra pat. They had been digging for over an hour and all they had to show for it was strained muscles and pouring sweat. He gave the earth around the circle another swift whack, and then swinging around, he studied the ground behind him. At least they were leaving the clearing the way they found it. It would take an eagle eye to see the pockets of earth they had disturbed, and he didn't think the Council had developed that rare quality yet.

He swung back around to see Tommy filling in the last of his open holes. His shovel whacks echoed in the air, and hearing a fractured wheeze, Devlin realized they both needed a break, and some water. The burnished sun was deadly at this time of the year; at noon, the heat was relentless. Already, he could see Tommy's cheeks stained with a bright red hue.

Devlin tossed his shovel to the ground with a grunt.

"Give it up, Tommy. We've done all we can do. The amulet's not here."

Tommy leaned on his shovel.

"We could widen our search with the detector again."

"It will do no good. We've guessed wrong." Devlin rubbed his hand across his bare chest, flicking off a string of sweat beads. "At least, we've saved Brianna from roasting in the blistering sun."

Tommy pulled his hankie from his pocket and wiped his drenched brow.

"I could do with a drink of water."

"It's next on the list. However, you should be thanking God for the heat. It has allowed us to have the clearing all to ourselves."

"Yes—us and the cat."

"Cat?"

Tommy tossed his head towards the rise.

"The creature arrived about thirty minutes ago. It's been sitting there watching us ever since."

Devlin's gaze lifted to the crest of the ridge, spotting the cat at once.

"He's persistent, I'll give him that," he stated. "Any other time, I'd … wait … " He slammed the tip of the shovel into the ground. "I'm such an idiot … take a seat, Tommy." Devlin gestured at the ground. "It's time to let someone who was here and knows what happened, show us."

Tommy glanced at the ridge, and then back to Devlin.

"Rely on a cat?"

Devlin lowered himself onto his discarded shirt.

"He's not just any cat; he's royalty."

Tommy hunkered beside him.

"Is that another one of those way-out-there spiritual truths?"

"You should have a little more faith, Tommy."

"I'm a man of science. I work with facts and what I can tangibly see. And those facts don't include a magical cat." He looked to the ridge again. "See there, the cat's gone off again. A cat is a cat."

Devlin's gaze flew to the ridge. Leave it to Nicodemus to prove him a liar.

"Rrr-owww."

The pair jumped at the meow, their heads swiveling. Devlin was the first to spy Nicodemus sitting in the middle of the circle, his large yellow eyes staring directly at him.

"He seems focused on you," Tommy remarked.

"A part of him recognizes my aura as belonging to Brianna. The other part of him senses I might want to hurt her. Without the binding, he can't be sure."

"What binding?"

"The one … Good Lord!" Devlin shot to his feet. "It never dawned on me that Sienna might've buried the amulet *inside* the circle."

Startled by his hasty rise, Nicodemus' hackles rose and he hissed at the pair. Seeing his swishing tail, Devlin addressed the cat.

"I'm grateful to you, you obnoxious pest. Now, get out of the circle and let us dig."

As if understanding his words, the cat dashed out of the circle and up the ridge. Devlin lost no time in taking his place. Dropping to his knees, he began digging in the dirt where Nicodemus had just sat. In seconds, he uncovered the hidden amulet. Holding it up, he flashed it at Tommy.

"How's your sense of faith now, Tommy?"

"It's eight on a scale of ten," he answered.

Devlin hopped to his feet, glancing at the circle markings.

"Now to find the buried rope."

"You're sure there's a rope?"

Devlin gave him a thin-lipped smile.

"Oh, ye of little faith … of course there's a rope. And Sienna's amulet is going to locate it for us." Devlin held the crystal aloft and began walking the perimeter of the circle. As he walked, the crystal flashed a series of colors. Red, yellow, blue, green. "When the energy spectrum reaches black, we will have found our rope," Devlin stated. He heard a doubtful grunt, but ignored it. Amulets never lied and Brianna was right. There is always a trail to follow if you are smart enough to look for it.

Halfway around the circle, the crystal began to darken, and by the time it had changed to a full, black hue, Devlin was dropping to his haunches again. He ran his finger along the ground, close to the painted markings. Was there a small seam around the paint? He chipped at the markings with his fingers. The paint fell away in small pieces and his nails were soon digging at the seam in earnest. In less than a minute, he had found the small piece of twine and was pulling it up and away from the markings.

"Son of a bitch!"

Tommy's curse matched his own thoughts, but he didn't stop to agree. He continued pulling the twine up and out. When the last of it unraveled, he held the twine up.

"How's your faith now, Tommy?" he asked, dangling the twine in front of him.

"It's off the Richter scale."

Devlin nodded, studying the length of the twine, and then studying the ground.

"You're scowling," Tommy stated.

"Not scowling; thinking." He studied the small length of twine in his fingers. "I think our attacker might be a woman."

"What!?"

Devlin signaled the disturbed area and then flashed the rope.

"Though I've been away from the practice a long time, I can feel a feminine energy on the rope. And I sense that it's been buried for months, not days. This attack has been a long time coming, carefully plotted and executed."

Tommy's hankie found his sweating brow.

"If I hadn't seen in person how powerful a necklace could be, I'd tell you to go to hell with your theory."

Devlin stuffed the twine and amulet in his jeans pocket with a grunt, and then bending, snatched up his shovel.

"Let's put this circle back to its original state and go find Brianna. Hopefully, she has had success in finding her mother's journal. If we have that, and the amulet, we can start making progress on solving this mystery."

The pair set to work immediately, and in less than fifteen minutes, they were climbing the rise and heading for the center of town.

•••

Brianna glanced at her watch. 1:00 P.M., and still no sign of her mother's journal. She had torn the cottage apart, searching for secret panels and hidden drawers for over an hour, with no luck. And now she was hot, frustrated, and just plain tired. She heard the steeple chime toll, and glanced down the sidewalk. The coven was showing signs of coming to life. Members were walking the streets again, and peals of laughter filled the air at sporadic intervals.

Brianna felt a brush against her pant leg and jumped. Glancing down, she spotted Nicodemus, and quickly stamped her foot at him. He scampered away, but not very far. He hugged the building, peering back around the corner at her. It was getting harder and harder to fend off the binding with Nicodemus. His persistence was eroding her nerves. And so was the heat. If only her search had been successful. If only … her thoughts derailed suddenly. What if her mother had given her journal to one of the members for safekeeping? They would be screwed if she did. There were at least seventy members in the congregation, and any one of them could be hiding it.

Brianna's gaze found the clinic dome. Had she entrusted it to an Elder instead? She hoped not; they would keep it hidden from her—at least until they had deemed her magical skills suitable. A bead of sweat trickled down the front of her bra, and she grimaced. She needed to find a cool place to hibernate until Devlin and Tommy returned from the clearing. She heard the tinkle of a shop bell, and saw a couple entering the Tea Room Cafe a few storefronts ahead. Her stomach rumbled at the thought of food, and she headed for the door.

Not to her surprise, the cafe was half empty when she stepped inside. She let the glass door slide into place behind her, spotting an empty table at the rear of the diner. Maneuvering past the front register and three occupied tables, she gave only a brief glance towards the hovering cashier at the counter. She hadn't realized how hungry she was until she caught the appetizing smells emanating from the small kitchen.

Reaching the rear area, Brianna plopped down and crossed her arms on the table. It felt good to be indoors and out of the stifling heat. In less than fifteen seconds, the female cashier was alongside her chair, pencil and pad in hand. Her greeting was friendly.

"Hello, Brianna."

Brianna glanced up, attempting to put a name to the face.

"My God, Marla, is that you?" She sprang to her feet, embracing the woman with a warm bear hug. Surprised by the overture, the plump woman pulled back, giving Brianna a bright smile.

"It's me alright—all one hundred and sixty pounds of me." She patted her round midriff. "There's more of me than when you last saw me, huh?"

"And it's a good thing," Brianna stated, slipping back into her seat. She scanned Marla's face. "I'm glad to see you suffered no lasting effects from the Dark Time. You do know Devlin and I are extremely sorry about what happened that day."

"Hey, you don't have to tell me that. Prior to the bad part, I was having the time of my life. I never felt as alive as in that circle. Everything around us was brighter; colors more vivid, smells more memorable, and my energy was definitely off the chart. There are moments when I long to feel that way again, but … " She shrugged leaving the rest of the sentence hanging. "Now, what can I get you to drink? You must be famished in this desert heat."

"Do you still serve that terrific strawberry cooler?"

"It's the best seller on the menu."

"And those great veggie pitas?"

"Still on the menu, too."

"I'll have one of each."

Marla scribbled the order on her pad, and then scrutinized Brianna's face.

"I'm sorry about your mother. If there's anything I can do to help, you must tell me. I owe a debt of gratitude to her."

"There *is* something," Brianna said. "Mother didn't happen to give you a package to keep for her, did she? A package that might've been square, like a book?"

"Why, no, but isn't she more likely to give one of the Elders a package like that?"

"I suppose," Brianna answered, biting her lip.

"I wish I could help," Marla murmured. "Your mother was instrumental in my taking over the management of the Tea Room. Without her belief in my abilities, I might have left the commune the same as you, and wound up alone and miserable … oh dear, that didn't come out right." She glanced down at Brianna's left hand. "Besides, your wedding ring proves that you are certainly not alone … or miserable."

Brianna's fingers found the band and spun it absently.

"I am truly sorry for not staying in touch with you. I have no excuse to offer except that I was in a bad place for such a long time after I left."

"Hey, I'm not mad at you. Sienna has told me all of the wonderful things she's read about you over the years, and I'm as proud of you as she is. I wish she had told me you were married though. I would've sent you a wedding gift."

"There's still time." Brianna smiled. "I haven't been married all that long. I'll give you my address in Washington."

"It's a done deal," she grinned. She flashed her notepad at Brianna. "I'll be back shortly with the drink."

She moved away, leaving Brianna to her own shadowed thoughts. The Dark Time had ruined so many lives. And all because of one careless, stupid mistake … she banished the thought. Better to think on the mistakes she might be making now.

Propping her elbows on the table, she rested her chin on her raised hands. She hoped Devlin and Tommy were having better luck with their search than she was. If they found no trace of the amulet, she would be forced to focus on Rufus Lord as the sinner. As Third Elder, he would have the knowledge and skills to conjure a debilitating spell and hide it under a title. Brianna glanced at her watch. One fifteen. What was keeping Devlin and Tommy?

"Here you go," Marla said, arriving at the table with her drink. She placed the glass in front of Brianna. "Your sandwich will be out soon."

"We'll have what Brianna's having," Devlin declared, plopping into an empty seat at the table, and flashing Marla a smile. The woman looked startled at his familiar greeting, but held off replying as Tommy's rotund figure dropped into the second empty chair with a grunt.

"That drink looks positively refreshing. Can you bring me *two* glasses? I'm overheated."

There was a trace of laughter in Brianna's voice as she addressed Marla.

"It's alright, Marla. They're with me." She lifted her hand in Devlin's direction. "In case you haven't guessed, that's Devlin Janus."

"Devlin?" Her glance trailed across his face, studying the contours. "Why, it *is* you. How are you?"

He flashed her one of his boyish grins, and Brianna wondered what Marla's reaction would be if she mentioned the wedding ring on her finger had been placed there by Devlin. Tommy's apology drove the thought away.

"We're running late. So sorry for putting you out. Are we forgiven?"

Marla smiled at his toothy apology and nodded, rushing off again towards the counter. Brianna waited a moment before addressing the pair.

"Well?"

Pulling his cell phone from his shirt pocket, Tommy called up several photos, and handed the phone off to Brianna.

"The amulet was buried inside the circle," Devlin stated, as she clicked through the images.

Brianna's head shot up.

"Inside? That means Mother buried it, not her attacker."

"Which also means she shielded the amulet so its energy wouldn't go underground and be neutralized."

"And that's not all we found," Tommy added. "We found a piece of twine threaded within the circle border—across the front portion. If Devlin hadn't used your mother's amulet as a dowsing rod, we'd still be sweating our balls off down there." He flushed immediately. "Sorry. That was rude."

Brianna swept his apology away, her anger overriding her sensibility.

"They have lied to us," she exclaimed. She slammed the phone down on the tablecloth and caught Devlin's gaze. "Someone on the Council knows exactly what happened in that circle and is attempting to cover it up." She bolted to her feet, and Devlin snatched her wrist, keeping her in place.

"Sit down," he ordered. "And lower your voice. We need time to adjust our thinking."

Brianna pulled her wrist from his grasp, rubbing the area where his fingers had clamped.

"I mean it, Devlin, one of the Council members is behind this." Her eyes flashed with outrage. "Mark my words, in less than an hour the Elders are going to feel the wrath of a very pissed off High Priestess."

"Sit down and stop making a spectacle of yourself. You're drawing attention to the table."

Brianna glanced around, noting the surprised expression of the other diners as they sat studying her awkward posture of flight. She sank back down, lowering her voice and leaning in to the two men.

"As soon as I invoke the Weaving, I'm going to browbeat every single member of the Council until one of them confesses their sin."

Devlin's mood veered sharply.

"What you're going to do is soften your image," he stressed. Her mouth opened and he held up a finger. "I'm not talking as your husband now, but as your High Priest. You need to lose the shirt and jeans and don a traditional coven gown. You cannot direct the ceremony dressed like a modern-day business woman. The Weaving will take finesse on your part, not bold accusations."

"And let whoever is responsible continue to pull the wool over our eyes?" Brianna groused.

"If that's what it takes, yes."

"I don't like it."

"But as the current High Priestess of this Coven, you will take the sage advice of your High Priest, and do it anyway. I cannot allow you to browbeat any member of the coven just because you've seen a damned photo. Now, start acting like the High Priestess your mother raised you to be, and come up with a sensible plan that doesn't get any of us killed in the next hour."

"Here now," Tommy intervened. "The children don't like it when Mom and Dad fight."

"That's not funny, Tommy," Brianna groused.

"And neither are the insults you two are trading. Besides, we all want the same thing here." He looked back and forth between the pair. "Don't we?"

"Of course," Brianna answered. Her fingers found Tommy's. "Mom and Dad are finished fighting now." Her gaze found Devlin's. "Any problems in the clearing?"

"We left the place as we found it."

"You're sure? The Elders will notice any suspicious clumps in the ground."

"Relax. It was just us, and the damn cat."

"Nicodemus was there?"

"Yes. That precious cat of yours pointed the way … now, why are you frowning?"

"Because you're asking me to wear a ceremonial gown for the Weaving when I no longer own one."

Devlin flicked his fingers at her.

"Borrow one from your mother, and do something with your hair—something magical. If you remember your lessons in spell making, clothes make the Priestess. Besides, I've waited a long time to see you decked out like a Fairy Queen. You wouldn't want to disappoint your husband, now would you?"

"Certainly not," Brianna said, gritting her teeth. "I've been waiting a long time to cast a spell on him that can't be reversed, and this seems like the perfect opportunity for that."

She heard Tommy's familiar chuckle, followed by Devlin's boyish laugh.

"You're years too late, Rapunzel. You've already cast a spell on me that can't be reversed."

Brianna sensed that odd pull of her energy again. Devlin's eyes were boldly appraising her and she felt her heart ache under her breast. Or was it Nicodemus, who was close by; she could feel the pull of his aura as well. She shook off both magnetisms.

"If I had been able to find mother's journal—which I didn't, by the way," she said, "thanks for asking. I could reconstruct her spell. I'd be able to manifest the same conditions that took her down."

A heated growl sliced the air.

"Don't make me cast a binding spell on you."

She flashed her hand in front of Devlin's face.

"Stop! I was only joking. Besides, there is simply no time to construct a proper counter spell." Her eyebrows rose. "I thought you wanted me to act more docile and unassuming, and now that I am trying to be, you're against it."

"That's because there is no possible way for you to be docile and unassuming for very long. We'll think of something else." Devlin pointed to her glass. "Now drink your fizzy and cool off."

"Yes, dear," Brianna replied, picking up her glass, and taking a swig. Devlin's mumble was barely audible.

"Give me the strength not to hex her, Tommy."

His chuckle came, along with Marla and their sandwiches. Before long, the only discernible sound at the table was a series of long, contented sighs.

CHAPTER SIXTEEN

A FEW MINUTES LATER

Devlin popped the last morsel of pita into his mouth and gave one final sigh. The sandwich had restored his energy completely. He glanced at his table companions and noticed the change in their expressions as they finished the final crumbs of their sandwiches. Funny, how food tended to satisfy all forms of hunger—mental as well as physical.

His gaze focused on Brianna, surprised to find her studying the wall hangings as she nursed a second strawberry cooler. Was she attempting to restore old memories of the place? He glanced around. Little changes had been made here and there, and the room exuded a more homey essence than it used to. Devlin was sure the transformation was due to Marla's charming skills with needle and thread.

An over-loud sigh emanated from beside him, and Devlin turned his head.

"Now, that's what I call a sandwich," Tommy remarked, patting his stomach.

"Better than ten tacos and a margarita?" Devlin asked, amused by his childish gesture.

"Much better. And what is in this red drink that makes it so friggin' good?"

"We could tell you, but then we'd have to kill you," Devlin remarked, reaching back and digging into his jeans pocket. He whipped out his wallet, hearing a pleased chuckle greet his sarcasm.

"This commune does have shades of the gangster lifestyle, if you think about it," Tommy stated. "No alcohol served anywhere,

Elders who hold the power of Godfathers, gang rivalry. Shall I go on?"

Across the table, Brianna shivered in disgust.

"No, the comparison is too real." She picked up their earlier conversation. "What have you done with the amulet and twine?"

"They're perfectly safe," Devlin replied. He saw her mouth open. "No, I'm not telling you where we've stashed them. I know you. If you have the amulet, you'll use it. You'll design some counter-spell in secret with it. And then you'll hunt Nicodemus down and merge your powers with his. I can't allow that—without a discussion first."

She bit down on a curse, and Devlin sensed she recognized the steel in his voice. She knew he was past intimidation.

"Very well." She glanced at her watch. "It's almost two."

Marla met Devlin at the register, giving him a warm smile as she took his money.

"I see by your wedding ring you're married, Devlin." Her gaze raked his face as she hit the register keys.

"Yes. It was love at first sight."

"How romantic!" Marla cooed. "You must miss being away from her very much."

His cynical inner voice chose that moment to throw up a taunt. *Why don't you tell her that you dream of having sex with your wife every minute, of every hour?* He banished the thought at once. Craving sex with Brianna was nothing more than the pull of the Joining ceremony. It'll taper off as the hours go by. *You just keep thinking that,* his inner voice baited.

Marla's voice swam back into his hearing.

"Where did you settle after you left here, Devlin?" She handed him his change, and taking it, he pocketed it in his wallet.

"Texas," he stated, quietly. He tucked the wallet into his back pocket a moment later. "I have my own eco-corporation."

She flashed him another smile.

"I can see by your features that you still belong to the land. It's nice to know that you kept true to your upbringing."

"Some things never change," he quipped. He gave her a nod and then headed for the door. Exiting, he bumped into the pair waiting for him on the sidewalk. He gave Tommy a cursory glance.

"Go check on Sienna while we're conducting the Weaving ceremony with the Council. And don't forget to make those calls we talked about."

"What calls?" Brianna wanted to know. Devlin's gaze transferred to Brianna.

"Tommy's agreed to make some business calls for me." He saw her lips twitch slightly. "No, I'm not stealing him from you now that we're married. He offered to help, and I'm letting him."

He took Brianna's arm as Tommy strode away from them.

"You're making a habit of giving people orders," Brianna scolded as they traversed the sidewalk. "You probably should stop."

"I will—right after you agree to make love with me again."

A black blob flashed by their toes, derailing Brianna's outraged screech to one of fright. Seeing the cat, she stamped her foot at him. He darted away, down the sidewalk, and behind the building.

"He's becoming an awful nuisance, Devlin."

"He can't help it, so stop trying to provoke him."

The taunt had Brianna halting abruptly, pulling from his grasp.

"My God, that's it. I had it all wrong."

"What are you yammering about now?" Devlin asked, taking her arm back again, and prodding her forward. She pulled from his grasp.

"I sent the Guardians away from the circle, not realizing that Mother had instructed them to stay and guard her essence. Oh, why didn't I pick up on that warning sooner? If I had, Mother's essence would never have been left unattended. Part of her lingering coma belongs to my sheer stupidity. I have to make it right."

Devlin snatched her arm and swung her about.

"Don't even think of bonding with Nicodemus to make it right. You're going to focus on evoking the Weaving, and that's all you're going to think about."

She broke his hold on her arm.

"Stop freaking out every two seconds, will you? You're making it impossible for me to think good thoughts, and I need to think good thoughts—if I want to secure the Council's blessing."

Something cautioned him not to ask her to embellish on that, so he sighed loudly instead.

"You're trying my patience to the max, Goldilocks."

"Good. That means you'll give up being my conscience, and find something better to do with your time."

"I have something better to do with my time. You're just not agreeable to doing it with me."

Her glance sharpened.

"You're an incredible ass, you know that?"

Obviously not wanting to hear his answer, she flounced away, heading for the Healing Center on her own. He followed her path slowly, recalling the smoldering passion they had shared only hours ago. Their bodies had been in exquisite harmony with one another then. And now? She was locked in his mind and heart permanently. Her essence was worming deep into his soul, and he was sure the haunting meant he was on a collision course with the Sisters of Fate once again.

•••

The glittering cape swung up and over the masked features of the figure's face. It was dangerous to be hanging about the Sage cottage in broad daylight. Anyone could take notice. However, Nicodemus had to be found and disposed of. He had been trailing

Brianna for hours, and each time, he was getting closer to bonding with her essence.

The figure grimaced. It was a dreadful fact that Nicodemus had the power to sabotage any spell a witch constructed. Cats could literally skirt the fabric of spells, and often did, when their Mistresses were threatened. The cat had done it in the clearing five days ago, and now that he had a new Mistress, he was attempting to protect her with the same tenacity as his former Mistress.

"RRR-owww."

The cat's cry had the figure rearing back in fright. Cats were also sneaky. Nicodemus was proving it by appearing out of nowhere and growling his dislike. The figure swished the end of the cape at the feline.

"I'm not afraid of your power, Nicodemus. I have plenty of my own."

"Rrrr-Owww."

The figure dismissed the meow, raising a hand and chanting boldly.

"From you to me, this spell I make; this is not your power to break. The path you take will abruptly end; and back to you, the spell I bend."

A red fire cone appeared in the palm of the figure's hand, spinning wildly. Seeing it, the cat growled low in his throat and then arched his back with a fevered hiss. Not at all intimidated this time, the figure flicked the energy at the cat, who attempted to dodge it with a quick jump upward. He was two seconds too late. The bolt of energy slammed into his backside, and then catching hold, it rippled up his back and down his front paws. His painful scream set off a chain reaction in the earth beneath his paws. Startled insects broke off their scurrying and fled to a safe haven further underground. The birds in the nearby trees fell silent, and a small wind eddy spiraled up and over the cottage. The cat stiffened suddenly, and then collapsed to the ground, motionless.

Feeling the change in energy shifts, even the caped figure backed up quickly and fled the scene. In seconds, the waterfall in the meditation garden stopped flowing, and a colorful desert iguana toppled over, off the top rock and into the darkening pool of swirling water.

CHAPTER SEVENTEEN

THE WEAVING

Brianna stepped back from the mirror and drew in her breath. She had turned into her mother in the last few minutes, and it was an eerie transformation. She studied the netted hairpiece awash with sparkling moons and stars. She had wound the netting through her blonde ringlets in a most tantalizing way and had been thrilled with the result. It had been years since she had taken so much care with her appearance and it felt heavenly—a true feminine delight. In fact, since she had donned one of her Mother's svelte blue gowns, she had felt a refreshing energy, as if she had just been bathed by one of the Ancients' healing washes.

Dropping into a chair in front of the dressing table, she began retouching her make-up. The Council would be floored to see her in coven attire; probably even rendered speechless. What would Devlin think? *That you're gor-ge-ous,* her inner voice complimented. *He'll make love to you on the spot.* Brianna grinned at her reflection. One can only hope, she mused, dropping her lipstick tube. He will definitely be shocked to see how well she cleaned up; she was shocked herself. And how would Nicodemus take the transformation when he saw her? Would he be confused by how much she resembled her mother? The watch on her dressing table buzzed the top of the hour. Two o'clock, and she was late!

Brianna rushed up from the chair, stopping to slip her toes into a pair of sparkly heels, before giving a last glance into the mirror. Pleased by the voluptuous woman staring back at her, she whirled about and dashed out of the cottage.

Six minutes later, she arrived at the Assembly Hall, out of breath, and cursing her choice of footwear. She had nearly broken her ankle twice during the run from the cottage. Reaching the outer door, she paused and took a deep breath. *It's now or never,* her inner voice coaxed. *Success or failure.* She flung open the door and stepped inside.

The six figures standing in the center of the room turned, startled by the door banging against the wall. She recognized Rufus, Sally, and her father at once, and even though she hadn't set eyes on Eileen O'Connor in fifteen years, she recognized her robust figure and bobbed hair-do. Francis was conspicuously absent from the group, and the two figures standing by her father were total strangers.

She felt a touch on her arm and turned.

"God, you are breath-taking." The words were barely out of his mouth when she was swept into Devlin's arms and kissed with a hunger that belied his outward calm. Her heart jolted at the ravishment of her mouth and her heart began pounding like a runaway train. The moment her legs began to tremble, she broke the kiss and backed out of Devlin's arms.

"You're smearing my lipstick," she said, breathlessly.

"I'd like to do more than that," he retorted. "But the Council's waiting."

Her glance switched to Doctor Ellis, standing off to the left of the group. He was staring at her as if he had seen a ghost. Well, wasn't he? She was wearing her Mother's gown, so technically, at the moment she was her Mother.

"Do you remember the proper chant?" Devlin whispered from beside her. "You must not, because I can feel your heightened energy as if it were my own."

Brianna twisted her head and met his penetrating gaze. Did he not realize that their marriage had made it possible for him to actually do that? She certainly was able to feel his energy through walls. Obviously, her senses were more attuned than his, because he continued to stare at her with a strange look that belied any recognition of her energy.

"I remember," she finally remarked, dismissing his concern.

"We're ready for you, Brianna," a deep voice beckoned from her left. Brianna jumped at the sudden appearance of Rufus Lord. "I assume you remember all the Council protocols?"

Brianna sent him an annoyed glance.

"I can recite them by heart, if you'd like." She felt a squeeze on her arm and softened her tone. "I know all the chants, and I promise not to demean the ceremony."

The Elder looked doubtful, but he didn't push the issue.

"Very well. We're ready when you are."

He spun on his heel, leaving the pair to follow him to the center of the room. Watching him go, Brianna knew he was playing his role as Third Elder to the hilt.

"Keep your cool when we get there," Devlin warned. "I'm getting tired of squeezing your arm all the time."

Brianna stumbled, surprised by his sarcastic tone.

"That's easy for you to say. You aren't wearing three inch high heels and a push up bra."

"But I *am* wearing a clean shirt and coven trousers."

"I noticed. You look like … " She left the sentence hanging.

"What? Ridiculous?"

"No, dashing—like a Victorian rake."

"Careful, Mrs. Janus. That sounded a lot like a compliment."

"You're an ass." Brianna said, slipping away from him. She joined the group circle, addressing Rufus as she took her place in the center.

"It's Coven protocol for only the Elder Council to be part of the Weaving ceremony," she said, eyeing Sally to her right. "Has Francis chosen not to participate in it?"

She met with silence, and sensed no one wanted to be the bearer of bad tidings. Finally, Sally stepped forward.

"Francis has chosen not to participate. He feels that this ritual will do more harm than good. As First Elder, he has invoked his right to substitute another witch in his place."

"And you got the luck of the runes?" Brianna asked.

"I was flattered he thought of me. However, I promise you I am quite capable of channeling spirit. I shall not let you down."

Brianna studied Sally's face. Why in the world had Francis chosen Sally as his replacement? Her recent illness made her an iffy candidate. *He did it to piss you off,* her inner voice chided. *He lives to piss you off.*

Waiting for Devlin to join the circle, Brianna took a moment to judge the rest of the Council assembled around her. They were dressed in their ceremonial best, staring at her like terriers waiting for attention. Their glances were shifting between her and Devlin, and then back to her again. Brianna sensed immediately she was being scrutinized for flaws. Well, that was better than being intimidated by dark, angry expressions, wasn't it? She took a breath and adjusted her smile. Now, if only she could ignore Rufus's critical squint. He seemed to be the only one in the circle with enough courage to wear his feelings on his face. His next words proved it.

"We are ready whenever you are, Brianna. We will try to do you proud—even though evoking an Ancient Power without having undergone the Crowning is an insult to the Coven."

Brianna's eyes darkened with emotion.

"Your objection is noted, Rufus; however, I can't imagine Papa phoned me about Mother without realizing that I might have to invoke my rights as Interim High Priestess if I came. Surely it dawned on you that I would follow Coven protocol to the letter once I arrived?"

"Evoking the Weaving is highly premature, though," Sally responded. "And not at all proper—given your questionable history with us."

"Forgive me, Sally, but I was under the impression that this Coven excelled in not judging others. I thought we were all about forgiveness as well. It seems I was wrong. Now, it looks as though the Coven forgives some, but not others."

It had been a cruel thing to say, and Brianna didn't know why she had felt compelled to twist Sally's words. After all, they were standing in a sacred place, intending to summon the goodness of spirit, not trade in silly, childish taunts.

"Enter the Land of Spirit, through any open door; and drink from the Grail of Life for one day more. It is there you will find the cauldron of love, as it is in the below, so it is in the above."

Devlin's strong chant had Brianna's mind switching gears. She centered her body and, lifting her arms, she addressed the heavens.

"Before time was, there was the no-thingness. And the no-thingness was the One; and the no-thingness was the All. And the no-thingness felt a gentle stir, and the stir became a breath of life. And the breath of life expanded, splitting into two forms, equal but opposite. And the no-thingness named the forms God and Goddesses. And the Gods and Goddesses stretched out and became energy. And the energy became gases, and suns, and planets, and moons. And the whirling globes were alone, solitary, except for the no-thingness. And the no-thingness saw it was good and showered the forms with light. And the light formed union. And the union formed seeds. And the seeds sprinkled the heavens above and the earth below. And all were blessed by the Gods and Goddesses, in homage to the no-thingness. And the Goddess chose the Moon as her symbol to remind the seeds all are born, live, and die, and are reborn again. And the God chose the sun as his symbol to remind the seeds, that all things come to pass under its light. That has been the way of existence before time was.

And with the blessings of the no-thingness, the nothingness into nothingness is the whole journey. So mote it be."

The group clasped hands.

"So mote it be."

Sally's voice washed over the group's heads, loud and confident.

"In the realm of magic, this Coven shall reside, no one but the chosen shall view what's inside. If life be to Earth, as Water to emotions, let harm come to none, this is our devotion."

Rufus' voice picked up the chant.

"Our magic's our passion; the spirit's our guide. The love for the Goddess we hold deep inside."

Devlin carried on the chant.

"We stand on the threshold of guardian light, to empower the Priestess with heavenly might. Protection from harm is all that we seek, this is our will, so mote it be."

His words drifted away, and Brianna felt the stirring of an energy shift. It was now or never, she knew. Success or failure. She lifted her right hand, focusing her attention on her palm.

"Gifts I bring, and respect I'll show. Fly all around me to and fro." An energy shift occurred again and Brianna felt it immediately. She revved up the chant. "Help me with my magical quest; make it strong, and then you can rest." A purple cone of light appeared in the middle of her palm and began to swirl slowly. "A weaving of truth is an honor not broken, to all who are asked, no lie can be spoken." The purple hue began to whirl faster, and Brianna revved her chant up another decibel. "Through spirit, body, and mind, water the seed and watch it grow. For what you send out, will return to you times three; this is our will, so mote it be." The colorful cone darkened to a deeper hue of purple and rose from the center of Brianna's palm. The group raised their arms to the whirling dervish, echoing Brianna's last words.

"This is our will, so mote it be."

The cone vanished abruptly, as if sucked through a straw, and the air in the room turned suddenly cold, and then suddenly hot. And then, reclaiming its normal state of flux, the air became unnoticeable again.

Brianna dropped her hands, suddenly drained by the ritual—or the touch of Devlin's hand on her back. She was in need of fresh air—the outdoors kind. Her palm was still smarting from the pinwheel, and she longed to cool it off.

"Well done, Brianna," her father complimented. He threw an arm around her shoulders and gave them a squeeze. "It's nice to know you still know how to honor your heritage. Your mother will be extremely proud of you when she wakes."

"From your mouth to God's ear," she told him, returning the hug. She felt a familiar presence by her side and turned. "Well, how did I do, Mr. Janus? Any flubs or mistakes?"

"You were sensational," he said. His voice lowered. "Remind me to tell you how sensational you were when we're in bed tonight." He saw her mouth open and gave an airy wave. "I know, I know. I'm an incredible ass."

He moved away before she could agree. Her father studied her face and then said the obvious.

"It's clear you still have the man's heart after all these years."

Brianna frowned.

"I don't want it, Papa. Why can't he see that?" His eyebrow rose, and Brianna blushed. "That didn't come out right. I don't hate Devlin anymore, but I can barely manage my own heart, let alone his."

"Leave it all in the hands of spirit, my dear," her father remarked. "They will sort it out."

Brianna brushed back a stray tendril of hair.

"How long before the interviews start?" she asked.

Her father dipped his head.

"We have sent the junior elders out with messages. We should see the first of the members arrive sometime around four."

"I'm sorry it's come to this, Papa. I know how upsetting this process will be for everyone." She shook her head. "I only hope it works."

"It'll work." Eileen said, overhearing her words and joining the conversation. She studied Brianna's attire. "You look smashing in that get-up, by the way. And the hairpiece is to die for."

Brianna laughed at her focus on style, brushing her hands down the front of her gown.

"This dress was always Mother's favorite. I'm surprised I had the audacity to wear it." Her hand lifted. "And the hairpiece was a last minute concoction."

"And the Pentagram you're wearing?" Sally asked, settling beside her. "Is it your personal amulet?"

Brianna wrapped her fingers around the piece.

"Umm, I bought it a New Age Fair a long time ago," Brianna said. "It's been a trusted friend ever since."

"Speaking of friends," Sally said, "I like the one you brought with you. I met him in the Square this morning, and he seemed genuinely interested in discussing the Wicca creed."

Brianna hid a smile. Tommy could care less about spiritual creeds. He was simply flexing his legal muscles—quizzing the Elders with the same boyish charm he used in the boardroom. It had obviously worked on Sally. Who else had he tried his charm on?

"Rufus has requested we vacate the center so they can prepare the room for the interviews." Devlin said, joining the women.

"Don't you mean he has ordered us to vacate the room?" Brianna asked.

"He did say please, I think." Devlin replied, taking her arm and then Sally's. He guided the women to the front door, continuing his thoughts. "Just remember, you've won his blessing on the

Weaving, and knowing that, you should cut him some slack." His words had Brianna's jaw clenching, but she held her tongue. She had won Rufus's blessing, but only time would tell if she kept it.

Coming into the sunlight, Brianna shaded her eyes. A sudden feeling of dread assailed her and she glanced about. *Nicodemus.* The name echoed on the wind and she caught her breath.

"Did you hear it?" she asked.

"Hear what?" Sally queried.

"N-n-nothing," Brianna stammered. "I thought I heard someone calling my name."

"It must be the excitement of casting your first real spell." Sally murmured. "You were fabulous, by the way." She stepped off the curb, heading towards the clinic. "See you at the celebration later," she called back.

Brianna watched her stride across the roadway and towards the Main Street Fountain. She breathed a sigh of relief, wondering why she should be glad to see the last of Sally. She knew why. For a moment, during the ceremony, she had felt the pull of an odd energy outside the cone of power. She had dismissed it as nerves, but now she wasn't so sure she should have. She glanced around the area again.

"What is it?" Devlin asked, noticing her preoccupation with the tree-lined shrubs.

"I don't see Nicodemus," she said. "I haven't since lunch."

"He's probably taken the hint and found something else to occupy his time."

"You're right. I'm obsessing." She was hit by another feeling of dread and, following her instincts, she switched direction and angled towards the cottage. She had to find Tommy at once and convince him to tell her where her mother's amulet was stashed. Now that the Weaving was in place, she could use the amulet to find her mother's Book of Shadows.

Strong fingers suddenly clamped her wrist, and swung her about.

"Slow down. Where are you going in such a rush?"

Brianna dismissed the concern simmering behind the question. "To talk to Tommy."

"I wish you'd talk to me instead. We're in this together—for better or worse."

"Till death do us part?"

"That, too."

Brianna dropped her gaze to the sidewalk, a new anguish searing her heart. She'd not have Devlin's death on her conscience, not if she could help it. Of course, there was a sure way to end this tragedy, but she wasn't sure she had the courage to take it. The thought triggered a growing lump in her throat. Did she have the courage to use Nicodemus's powers for her own personal gain? It would be despicable, if she used him. He was a royal cat, and as such, he deserved to be treated with the utmost respect.

Strong fingers gripped her chin and raised it, cutting into her thoughts. Devlin's mouth twitched in amusement as her eyes widened in surprise.

"It's useless for you to try to outfox me, Brianna. Remember, I can almost read your thoughts. I forbid you to merge your essence with Nicodemus without telling me, and that is an order."

She used her wide-eyed, innocent look as a smoke screen.

"I have personal business to discuss with Tommy. Not everything is about you and me."

"If you think that, you're not the smart corporate business woman I know you to be. It is about us—your mother saw to that. And as your High Priest, a status you willed on me, by the way—I will not let you risk your life for this coven any more than it already has been."

A long, brittle silence followed his words, leaving Brianna's stomach churning in alarm. There it was again. That tangible bond between their thoughts. He sensed she was thinking of merging her essence with Nicodemus and he was condemning her for it. Breaking the silence, she said lightly.

"Yes, your majesty."

"Don't use that tone with me, Brianna. I'm not kidding."

"Then stop being a braying ass," Brianna muttered. "I've gotten the message. I'm not to do anything reckless that could get us both killed."

Devlin grinned.

"Dump the doubts, Rapunzel. No one takes you out without taking me out first. That's the way it has to be, period."

Brianna bit her lower lip. Dump her doubts? She wished she could. *Another reason why you should forge a bond with Nicodemus,* her inner voice urged. *You can't have Devlin sacrificing his life for you.* She felt a warm wave of breath on her mouth, and realized Devlin's head had lowered. It was a light kiss that lasted no more than ten seconds, but Brianna's senses trembled. When he raised his head, his eyes clung to hers, analyzing her reaction. And then he spoke, his voice thick and unsteady.

"I'll give you two hours to finish your business with Tommy. After that, we must prepare a set of questions for the congregation to answer." He let go of her chin, and turning on his heels, he strode down the sidewalk. He took the same path as Sally to the Main Street Fountain, but angled left from there.

Brianna watched his measured gait until he disappeared through the door of the Tea Room Café. Her fingers brushed her mouth absently. Just like the pull of Nicodemus' essence, Devlin's kisses were becoming harder to resist. The kiss sang in her veins, making her wish his tongue was blazing a liquid trail of fire a little lower down.

She felt a breeze brush the hem of her gown and glanced down. Nicodemus, she smiled. When she caught sight of only the sidewalk cement, she felt another unexpected ripple tease the hem. Where was Nicodemus? It wasn't like him to give up his task of staying by her side. In fact, he couldn't give it up. He was committed to the Binding and it was time for her to think seriously of merging with him. To continue to shut him out of her essence would result in the loss of his powers.

The thought of his essence floating in some unseen limbo for eternity made Brianna come to a sudden decision. She must convince Tommy to give her the amulet, and once she had it in her possession, she had to use Nicodemus to find her mother's Books of Shadows in the quickest way possible.

CHAPTER EIGHTEEN

THE COTTAGE

Brianna studied the figure immersed in paperwork at the kitchen table.

"Any luck with the business calls?" she asked, startling Tommy. His blue eyes pierced the distance between them as she seated herself. He shuffled the notes in front of him.

"All good news," he answered. "On our front too. I've sold your company."

"What? To whom?"

"D.J. Corp."

"But I thought they weren't interested."

"They looked at the paradigm again, saw something financially feasible in it, and made a counter offer. I just got off the phone with Jake Rogers. We'll cement the deal when I get back to Washington."

Brianna leaned forward, settling her hands atop Tommy's wrist.

"I can't thank you enough for all you've done, Tommy. You've been a true friend, through all of this."

He studied her thoughtfully for a moment.

"You're buttering me up for something. What is it?"

Brianna didn't waste time.

"I need Mother's amulet."

"What for?"

"To stimulate Nicodemus's powers. He can read essences."

"And this will help us, how?"

"He can locate Mother's Book of Shadows, which will list her thoughts and impressions over the past few months. I believe the journal will also name the sinner we are looking for."

He shifted in his chair.

"How dangerous is stimulating this cat for answers?"

Brianna's answer froze on her lips. There was no physical danger in the binding with Nicodemus; however, the ramifications would be sizeable. Her life in Washington would come to an end, and the Coven would be the only solid reality in a shifted world. But she couldn't tell Tommy that. At least not right now. She had to convince him there was no danger. Her fingers squeezed the top of his knuckles.

"You've got to trust me, Tommy. This is my chance to relive a moment, and be the solution rather than the problem."

His pudgy face rearranged itself into a grin.

"I know I'm going to regret this … " He stood and walked to a cookie jar atop the kitchen counter. Lifting the top, he hauled out the amulet. Returning to the table, he dangled the crystal in front of Brianna. "Your husband is going to be mighty mad," he remarked, dropping the amulet into her upraised palm.

"He'll be furious—but not for the reasons you think," Brianna replied.

"Where is he, by the way?" Tommy asked, reseating himself.

"At the Tea Shop, arranging for the celebration that will follow the interviews." She rose from her chair. "We're setting the first of several traps by quizzing the members. And if I'm lucky enough to have found Mother's Book of Shadows before then, we will bring our sinner to justice not long after." She pocketed the amulet. "I need a short nap, though. You should do the same while we have a few loose hours. Devlin will be along shortly."

Brianna whirled from the table, hearing a rapid movement behind her.

"Tell me you know what you're doing."

She halted in mid-stride and spun back. Her laughter floated up from her throat.

"When have you ever known me to not know what I'm doing, Tommy?"

"Since never. But you've never been a High Priestess before. The power might be going to your head. Power corrupts, you know."

Brianna's laughter floated again.

"Relax. It's a title, nothing more. It's the ongoing practice of the title that creates the Priestess. And the Crowning, of course." She saw his baffled look. "We won't be here long enough for the Crowning, so you can stop worrying."

His expression softened at her words.

"Life sure is a bitch. You think you've got it all figured out and wham! Something totally different enters the picture."

Brianna's mouth twitched.

"Amen to that. Now, go get some sleep. I need you at the top of your game tonight."

"Yes, ma'am." He skirted her shoulders and then took the staircase two steps at a time. When he disappeared into the hallway, Brianna headed for her room and, hopefully, for a productive binding with Nicodemus.

• • •

Brianna rounded the doorway, spotting the black form lying in the center of her bed.

"Well, there you are, you naughty creature. Got tired of chasing after me, eh?" The shape didn't move, or acknowledge her greeting. That same feeling of dread stole over Brianna again and she bolted to the bed. "Nicodemus?" She shook his inert body, horrified when she felt how cold it was. "Oh, no," she mumbled. "Not you."

Energized by fear, she whirled from the bed, frantically searching for her Pentagram on the dresser. Who had been so mean as to harm Nicodemus? *A deranged mind,* her inner voice prompted. Well, she'd make that deranged mind pay—in spades. Locating the crystal, she rushed back to the bed, and holding it over the cat's body, she improvised a chant.

"Into this crystal before my eyes, I bless thee and charge thee, my power to rise. The love for this cat, I hold deep inside; let magic return him to his spiritual light. Swift is the magic that will make it so; send high above and down below. The no-thingness is all; the no-thingness is none. This is my will, and let it be done."

The dangling amulet began to pulse with a rainbow of colors, surprising Brianna with its cascading light. To her delight, the prism began to radiate with a swirling white mist, which showered out of the crystal, and onto Nicodemus's inert body. His paws soon twitched, followed by his tail, and then his fur began to ripple, as if being combed luxuriously. He sneezed abruptly, and then opening his eyes, he stared at Brianna. She felt a tremendous surge of energy roll through her body, and realized he was merging their essences. In seconds, she was on her knees by the bed, encased in an amazing feeling of completeness. The feeling lasted only a few more seconds, before the cat bounded up and purred loudly at her. Brianna studied his posture.

"You're welcome," she said suddenly. "Good Lord, I'm conversing with a cat." Brianna bolted up. "I'm awake and dreaming." She pinched her arm. A loud chuff echoed from the bed and she glared down at the cat. "No, I am not always this suspicious …"

Her hand came to her mouth as she realized she had understood the cat's thoughts perfectly. Her mother had never said a word about High Priestesses being able to converse with their Guardians. A series of stuttered purrs began to vibrate from Nicodemus's throat, but this time the thoughts were so jumbled, she couldn't decipher them. Sinking onto the bed, she studied the yellow eyes now reflecting glimmers of light.

"Slow down. Just because you can understand my thoughts easily, doesn't mean I can read yours." A stuttered sneeze rocked the bed. "Very well, get on with it then. We both know what has to be done." Brianna crossed her legs and signaled for Nicodemus to crawl into her lap. When he continued to sit purring at her and not moving, she frowned. "This is no time to be difficult. Mother's life is at stake."

The cat rose and stretched its front legs out, and then took its time extending its back legs. Brianna's lips twitched as she watched his slow movements. He had a sense of humor, she'd give him that. He was making it clear which of them was really in charge.

A series of sneezes swam from his nose and Brianna closed her eyes, attempting to focus on reading his aura. To her surprise, their auras merged, and a moment later, she was astonished at the sense of fulfillment he passed to her.

"Everything connected to Everything," she mumbled, softly. Nicodemus moved then, crawling into her lap and sitting in readiness, his back to her. Brianna scratched his nape and then brushed it. "Let just hope I'm the awesome witch Mother believes me to be."

"Rrr-oww."

"Yes, I'm ready. Stop your scolding." Forcing her mind to concentrate, she wrapped her fingers around Nicodemus's neck and closed her eyes. "'And ye shall say these words. I will love and harm none, I will live, love, and live again. I will meet, remember, know, and embrace once more. For the free will of all, And with harm to none; As I will, It now is done. So mote it be.'"

Her thoughts filtered back to her, and she wondered why she didn't feel some guilt over the relief she was feeling. She had just altered her life with a series of words and it felt—well, freeing.

A door slammed in the distance, and her eyes flew open.

"Rrr-owww."

"Oh my God, Devlin! He'll kill me when he learns what I've done." The cat sprang to the floor, heading for the door. "Stop!" Her call had Nicodemus whirling back with a stuttered growl. Brianna scooted to the edge of the bed, dangling over the side and meeting his glittering gaze. "You cannot tell him what I've done; he gave strict orders for me not to bind with you without telling him first." The cat meowed its disgust. "And you are not to converse with him until I say it's alright. Do you understand?" A chuff came her way. "I don't care if it's not proper to withhold the Binding from him. You will do as I say, and that is that!" A louder growl emanated, but the cat remained in place. Slipping from the bed, Brianna stuffed her toes into her shoes rapidly. "Stay in this room until I come back for you. If our sinner sees you alive … who is our sinner, by the way? You have to know." He didn't answer and she stamped her foot impatiently. "This is no time for power plays." He ignored her words, bolting for the open window and jumping through.

Watching his tail disappear, Brianna scrambled to the window.

"Come back here. You're not safe." She hung out the window, watching his body disappear into a set of rose bushes and emitted a curse. Blasted creature! He was up to no good, and there wasn't a thing she could do about.

Hearing voices beyond the doorway, Brianna scrambled from the bed and headed for the kitchen. She had to keep Devlin from sensing the binding. She had promised she wouldn't commit to it without discussing it with him first. But how to do it? He was a master at reading auras, and she was sure that her aura was now stained with Nicodemus's—for good or ill.

Frowning, she slowed her steps. *Focus his mind on the upcoming interviews,* her inner voice prodded. *Keep him busy on that and he'll never notice the shift in your aura.* Right. Got it. Charm him first, then hit him with the truth.

CHAPTER NINETEEN

THE GATHERING

The Weaving started with an energized prayer, but quickly fizzled to a polite and subdued inquisition. Four hours and ten minutes later, the interviews stopped at the Council's insistence. And now Brianna stood juggling a plate in her hand while pouring a strawberry cooler from an ice pitcher into a thermal container. She had been circulating for two hours, making apologies and accepting sympathetic condolences on her Mother, and through it all, she had kept her wits about her and portrayed the loving daughter of a Coven High Priestess. The afternoon interviews had been grueling; all thirty of them, sapping her energy as she did her best to be subtle in her questioning. Luckily, the members had been subtle as well. Though curious, they had maintained the proper perspective and answered each question honestly.

Replacing the pitcher in the cooler, she glanced across the grass to a gathering of bodies. She hoped Devlin had gleaned more from his questions. Her interviews had garnered nothing concrete concerning her mother's collapse. And if Devlin's brought the same, she would have to admit that the sinner was far more devious than she imagined.

She let her gaze drift to the woman standing beside Devlin and felt a sudden tug on her heartstrings. Was the stress of keeping the Binding from Devlin finally taking its toll on her heart? She rubbed the sore spot. *Nonsense, you're just jealous. Eileen O'Connor is showing a lot of interest in your very handsome husband.* Make-believe husband, you mean, she chided her inner voice. *Until his mouth closes softly over your breast,* her inner voice taunted.

Her gaze studied the conversing pair. Eileen was certainly monopolizing Devlin's time, though. Her face was animated, with frequent taps on his arm as if emphasizing a point, and Devlin appeared to be enthralled with whatever she was saying. *Go over and tell Eileen he's your man.* Stop, she told her runaway thoughts. We are divorcing Devlin Janus the first chance we get.

Craning her head, she listened to the angelic music playing overhead, and heard a stuttered purr around her ankles. She glanced down to find Nicodemus rubbing his chin against her bare leg. Yes, the Elders do have great taste in New Age Music, she told him. The soothing harps certainly make the food more appetizing. Her gaze lifted to the standing group. Yes, Devlin appears to be far better equipped to quiz the congregation than I am, she continued. Now, get away from me before he notices you hanging about my ankles.

"Hello, Brianna."

The greeting startled Brianna, and sent Nicodemus flying for cover. Brianna brought her gaze to the edge of the buffet table. She studied Sally's features, noticing the large gold pentagram, hanging in the center of her black dress. No one else could wear such gaudy jewelry and make it look stylish except for Sally. Brianna dropped her plate on the edge of the table, and exchanged a warm hug with the woman.

"Are you sure you should be talking to me?" she asked. "Francis looks as if he's ready to bite my head off."

She glanced over her shoulder.

"He doesn't take defeat well. He was sure he would find a potion that would cure the Coven illness and heal Danny, but you beat him to it."

Brianna felt the hair on the back of her neck prickle at Sally's words, and she raised her hand to rub the area. Funny, if she didn't know better she'd swear she was being warned about something. But what? She glanced at Sally more closely. Was the warning about her? No, the aura surrounding her figure was pathetic, sheathed with a silver and grey luster, but that only spoke volumes about her current snobbery towards her husband. Feeling a tight knot starting at the back of her throat, Brianna gestured towards the table.

"Sit down, Sally. You look ready to drop."

Sally sank onto a folding chair, and Brianna picked up her plate from the buffet table and joined her. As she sat, she noticed Sally's vacant stare into space. Where had her mind gone to so rapidly? And what was she thinking?

"Are you sure this gathering isn't too much for you, Sally? You've done a remarkable job on pulling it all together at the last minute, but you've barely recovered from your respiratory illness."

The energy around Sally's aura fizzled to an even more gray shade, and once again, Brianna felt that odd prickling on the back of her neck. What was spirit trying to tell her?

"I promised Francis that if Danny got well, I would see to it that I returned the favor in whatever way I could." Her gaze swept Brianna's face. "Danny's the reason I get up each day, you see." Her hand fanned the air. "I can't thank you enough for giving him back to me."

Brianna placed her hand over Sally's.

"It was a joint effort, Sally. And you mustn't be so hard on Francis. It's clear he loves you a lot."

Her gaze dropped to the ring on Brianna's left finger.

"You were always first in his heart though."

"In Francis's heart? No way. It was always Brenda."

"I meant Devlin, silly." She removed her hand from beneath Brianna's, and Brianna wondered where that observation had been dredged from. "I always thought in the end, you and Devlin would be together."

"Did you? I always thought it would be Jordy Skyler." Brianna gave a long sigh. "He sure knew how to kiss a girl." *Are we on the same page?* her inner voice suddenly mocked. *Jordy Skyler's lips never made blood pound in your brain, leap from your heart, or make your legs tremble when he kissed you. Not the way Devlin's do.*

Brianna changed thoughts abruptly, stifling any thought of Devlin's mouth on hers. Her gaze found Sally's.

"Do you remember when we were nine, and Jordy stood in the recess yard, and yelled, 'Sally Carver has buck teeth and cootie legs'?" Brianna saw a hesitant nod. "You were devastated by his insults, and when you started to cry, Francis marched across the yard and bloodied Jordy's nose so bad he couldn't talk for a week. Francis never once stood up for me like that."

"He didn't need to. You fought your own battles."

"Yes, and look where it got me—separated from parents who love me, and the loss of my three best friends." Sally's face softened at her words, and Brianna covered her hands lying on the table once more. "I'm so sorry about Brenda, Sally. I know it's a painful subject, but I don't want to leave here not having said how sorry I am. I have no excuse to offer—what I did was despicable."

"Devlin said the same thing to me only hours ago."

"He did?" Brianna quizzed. Her glance shifted to the tall man now engaged in listening to Rufus' chatter, and she drew in her breath. Even from far away, she could feel Devlin's sexual magnetism pulsating. It radiated with a vitality that was raw and turbulent.

"What do you suppose he did after he left Green Sapphire?" Sally asked.

"He found his own life—away from Sacred Circles and rock gardens."

"Don't you miss the way it used to be?" Sally asked, her gaze swinging back to Brianna. "Growing herbs and making candles? Don't you miss the way we were?"

Brianna took a bite of her fruit salad and chewed thoughtfully.

"I do miss the birthday celebrations," she stated. She changed the subject abruptly, focusing on the morsel in her mouth. "Why do I recognize this taste?"

"We ate it for the first time on your tenth birthday."

Brianna dropped her fork.

"Oh my God, that's right. We placed dishes of it in the four corners as a gift for the Guardians."

"Along with the four sandalwood candles I made."

"That's right," Brianna remembered, with a grin. "We wanted to please the Guardians on all levels. Fire, earth, air, and water …"

". . . which was working fine until the hem of Eileen's skirt caught fire, and she started jumping around and screaming like a banshee."

"And you started giggling," Brianna remembered.

"You giggled first, and then Brenda got going."

"And then Marla joined in."

"But only because you were giggling," Sally reminded. "We always giggled when you did. I miss those moments, don't you?"

Brianna thought back. Funny, how time could distort a memory. The only thing she remembered now was how much Sally had copied her actions back then. She had liked what Brianna liked, aped all her school assignments, and generally, had no opinions of her own. Sally's lips lifted suddenly. "Devlin stepped in, whipped my cape from my neck, and wrapped Eileen with it before she went up in smoke." She gave a long sigh. "He became our hero at that moment, didn't he?"

Brianna tried to think back to that moment too, and realized the memory was nowhere in her mind's storehouse. Had everything fun that occurred in the commune been stricken from her memories because of the Dark Time?

"I know Eileen fell madly in love with Devlin that day," Sally finished.

"She was six years old." Brianna laughed. "Much too young for him."

Sally sighed and glanced to her left again.

"Her crush soon turned to the real thing, though. She was devastated when he left the commune. So was Marla."

Brianna's interest perked up.

"He had two admirers? I never knew."

"Of course you didn't. Eileen never told anyone but me about her feelings."

"And now Devlin says she's an Elder on the Council," Brianna stated. "I'm so proud of her."

"Are you? I think she's much too young for the position, don't you?"

Brianna's head whipped around. Once again, she felt that uncommon prickling on the back of her neck. What was she being warned about? Sally's revelation about Eileen's crush on Devlin? Or Sally's obvious dislike of Eileen's appointment to the Council? She was sure now that she was being warned to pay attention to Sally's words.

"Was the congregation against Eileen's appointment, Sally?"

"Heavens, no. Eileen's loved by everyone. Why, two years ago, when we all came down with the flu, she was the only one to figure out that the hatchery had been contaminated in some way. We stopped using the clearing in Green Glen after that, and built a new clearing down in the Hollow."

"Green Glen?" Brianna repeated. A picture of the old woods flashed into her head. "Do you mean the clearing along the outer boundaries of the property? Why ever would that clearing be used for ceremonies? It's old-school."

"Well, we couldn't very well continue to use the clearing after what happened to Brenda. Sienna felt the circle might still be contaminated and chose to switch our Sabbat ceremonies to the hatchery—until the earth had a chance to renew itself. We began using the clearing in Hollow Creek again, not long after Francis was appointed First Elder."

Pleased by the change in topic, Brianna quizzed Sally on Francis.

"Did Francis happen to mention a conversation he had with Mother about someone abusing the Sacred Clearing?"

"He certainly did. I convinced him it was pure nonsense."

"Why would it be nonsense?"

"Because no one here would be so bold as to cast a dark spell against a revered High Priestess."

"Perhaps, the spell was meant for someone else," Brianna remarked.

A loud sniff emanated.

"We don't cast spells on people for our own gain. Besides, who could possibly be the target, if not your mother?"

"Me. Or Devlin, perhaps. Someone in the congregation may still hold a grudge for the havoc we caused."

Sally's lips pursed.

"Yet, here you are—back in our good graces. I suppose living outside the commune has made you suspicious of every little thing."

"I'm afraid so," Brianna stated, picking up her fork again and pushing her food around her plate. So much for quizzing Sally about anything pertaining to her Mother. She was clearly a die-hard advocate of the Wicca lifestyle, and obviously devoted to it, heart and soul.

"I suppose Devlin has become as jaded as you," Sally remarked. Her gaze skidded off to the other side of the clearing, and Brianna glanced that way as well. Devlin was now engaged in an animated conversation with both Marla and Eileen. She heard Sally's haughty sniff a second later. "Your marriage to Devlin has devastated Marla. She cast a spell on him years ago, trying to bring him back to the commune, but as you can see, it didn't work. He stayed single—until recently." Another sniff rocked the air. "Marla never could keep a proper Book of Shadows. Not like you and Eileen could. Do you still keep a journal, Brianna?"

The change in subject had Brianna's head spinning.

"I'm afraid not. There's no call for rituals in my line of work." She slipped a cauliflower floret into her mouth, and chewed it lazily. She wished Sally would go away. All the reminiscing was giving her a headache. Her entire energy field was fizzling all of a sudden. What was causing the rift? Sally's close proximity to her shoulders or the fact that the woman beside her no longer resembled the gay, fun-loving girlfriend she remembered? Either way, she'd check with Devlin to see if he had detected anything amiss with her aura. For her part, she could only detect a sad, distressed grey.

"Francis says you travel quite a bit in your work."

"Yes, I'm afraid so."

"And Devlin?"

"I really couldn't say. Yesterday was the first time I've seen him in fifteen years." Brianna's gaze shifted to Devlin again, and found him settled amongst another group of church members. He appeared to be making headway in his contacts while she appeared to be losing all interest in quizzing anyone about anything.

Brianna heard movement beside her and glanced at Sally who was popping up and greeting Eileen with a brief hug and kiss as she joined them. Brianna saw a sly wink come her way.

"Have you been talking girl-talk about rock gardens and herb stews?" Eileen asked.

"We've been trying to put some closure on our childhood," Brianna answered. "However, it's a little hard to do when the only thing we can remember is your dress on fire, and Devlin beating it out before you went up in flames."

Brianna heard a light cluck.

"It hurt like hell. I still have the burn scar to prove it."

The girls fell silent at her words, and then Sally rallied.

"Francis says I need to live more in the moment, although it is hard to do when you have a thirteen-year-old son demanding your attention. Did you know Brianna's become fabulously wealthy?"

Brianna flushed at the compliment, and seeing her discomfort, Eileen sighed.

"She looks more tired than anything, Sally."

Brianna heard a familiar sniff.

"You always were jealous of my friendship with Brianna."

"You're deluded if you think that. I was jealous of Brenda's friendship with Brianna. They were inseparable."

Brianna felt a distinct rise in the energy level around her, and realized that the two women beside her had become bitter rivals over the years. What had caused the rift? It wasn't like Eileen to hold a grudge, and it certainly wasn't part of the Wicca philosophy to wish harm on another human being.

Scooping a last morsel of fruit salad into her mouth, Brianna studied the women staring daggers at each other. She'd discuss their behavior with Devlin when she saw him. Perhaps, they had been barking up the wrong tree all along. Perhaps her mother's collapse was simply the result of two bitter women working at cross-purposes.

"I'm sorry to interrupt your time with Brianna, but Francis is asking to see you. He won't say why, but then he never does."

She gestured to the other side of the clearing, and Brianna caught sight of Rufus and Francis sketching a wave in their direction. Brianna acknowledged the wave as Sally strode from the table. Tuning into the sudden silence, Eileen dropped into Sally's vacated chair.

"She's pretty hard to take, isn't she? She's not at all the girl we used to know when we were kids."

"She almost lost her son," Brianna stated, pushing her plate away, and realizing her appetite had gone south, along with her energy. She glanced across the way, watching Francis drape his arm around Sally's shoulder as she reached him. The gesture had Brianna rubbing her chest area. "She seems to love Francis a lot," she stated.

"She's mad about him."

"You sound as if that's a bad thing," Brianna remarked, wiping her mouth with her napkin.

"Not bad, just odd. Francis dated Marla after you left, and it was pretty much agreed that they would marry. And then out of the blue, he married Sally. Marla was devastated."

"Is that when mother stepped in and gave the management of the café to her?"

Eileen's head snapped around.

"Marla told you about that?"

"Not in so many words. She mentioned going through a bad patch while we were having lunch in the Tea Room earlier. Your comments just seemed to strike a chord."

"It was a very bad time—on an emotional level—almost as bad as that day in the circle."

"Sally mentioned something about having to use the hatchery for ceremonies after that day."

Eileen propped her elbows on the table, giving Brianna her full attention.

"Your mother thought it best at the time. We used it for years as our primary clearing, until the ground there became contaminated."

"Another contamination? What caused it, do you know?"

Eileen craned her head, her countenance turning thoughtful.

"You're thinking that someone might have abused the hatchery clearing on purpose, aren't you? In order to force us to go back to Hollow Creek for our ceremonies."

"I thought you didn't believe anyone abused the Sacred Clearing."

"I didn't until you and Devlin arrived and cleansed the circle. I can't speak for Rufus or the other Elders, but I take trapped Guardians in a circle as serious business. It means that your mother came face to face with her attacker and recognized him or her. And because she did, she invoked the Guardians to stay and protect the circle."

Brianna suppressed a gasp. Eileen had drawn the same conclusion as she about the Guardians. Did that insight place her at the top of her suspect list?

"You don't think she was invoking them to keep watch on her essence, instead of protecting the circle?" Brianna asked.

"Her essence? I never thought of that." Her expression turned thoughtful again. She shook her head a moment later. "No, if she was protecting herself it would mean that the same mandala she was performing could be recreated to restore her health, and Brad has assured us that he has found no such ritual in the Community Book of Shadows."

"But suppose the ritual could be found?" Brianna asked, shifting in her chair. "What then?"

"It would take a pretty powerful witch to carry it off," Eileen stated. "And as good as we are at ceremony, not one of us Elders holds that much power."

"I might."

"Good heavens! You're not really thinking of recreating your mother's ritual? It would be suicide."

"Maybe not. With Mother's inherited skills, and Devlin as my consort, it could be done."

Eileen's hands came down on Brianna's folded ones, and Brianna saw her gaze soften.

"We both know that your marriage to Devlin is a sham." Brianna blushed at the bald statement; however, Eileen seemed not to notice. "Though we hold no animosity towards you or him any longer, our forgiveness doesn't extend to allowing either of you to slander our heritage. And as for performing a ritual to restore your mother's health, well, you must never mention such a thing to Rufus or Francis."

"Why?"

"Because they have already discussed the idea with Brad, and he has assured them the attempt would be futile."

Brianna's pulse took a nosedive, but she offered no further comment out loud. Brad may have searched the Coven's standing Book of Shadows but she was sure her mother's personal journal would offer a much more hopeful outcome to restoring fractured essences. Brianna felt a light pat on the back of her hands and looked up.

"By the way, I like your friend Tommy. He's funny and smart."

"He means the world to me," Brianna stated, picking up her fork and weaving circles on the tablecloth with it. "He was there when I had nobody else. He saw me through some really dark days."

"It's hard to believe that he and Devlin are friends, though. They seem such polar opposites. How did they meet?"

"I introduced them to each other last night."

Eileen's head whipped around.

"Are you positive? I was sure I heard Tommy tell Marla that they had met in Texas recently, during a business deal."

Brianna's fork clattered to the table.

"Did you say Devlin lives in Texas?"

"No, I don't know where he lives. However, Marla said he told her he owns some big environmental firm—D.J. something."

"D.J. Corporation," Brianna stated, a sudden shiver lacing her spine.

"Yes, that's it. I understand from Marla, he owns three silver mines, a wildlife refuge, and an underwater habitat off the coast of Italy." Her glance bounced off Brianna to the far side of the clearing. "He doesn't look like a millionaire, does he?"

No, just an arrogant bastard, Brianna thought, following Eileen's gaze. She studied the tall figure inching closer to their table, and then began to inspect the tablecloth beneath her fingers. Devlin Janus was D.J. Corporation. Why hadn't she seen it before? Hadn't he said he had rearranged a NASA meeting when they first met? And hadn't Tommy said earlier that Jake Rogers was in Florida for a NASA meeting? And now, here he was, being "outed" as a liar who had refused to do business with her. Why had he withheld his identity from her? Because he was an arrogant coward, that's why.

Her gaze flew to the chubby figure now standing alongside Devlin. Tommy had lied to her as well. He had kept Devlin's secret. Her heart lurched suddenly. My God, Tommy sold her company to Devlin. She bolted to her feet.

"What's wrong, Brianna? You've gone completely white."

Brianna glanced down and inspected the tablecloth.

"Just tired. It's been a long day."

Brianna heard another long sigh, and saw Eileen hop to her feet.

"I suppose I should apologize to Sally. It's not her fault I can't stomach her childish taunts. How about having breakfast with me in the Tea Room in the morning? We can catch up on the old days, and your life in Washington."

Brianna nodded, watching as she strode from the table and began weaving in and out of bodies towards the Elders gathered on the far side of the grass. Reaching the group, she flung her arms around Sally and whispered something in her ear. Sally promptly returned the hug with a kiss on the cheek.

A plate suddenly swam in front of Brianna's face, and she recognized the smell immediately. Pumpkin. She pushed the plate away and sank back down in her chair. Devlin dropped the plate on the table, and sank down alongside her. *A bribe from the Gods?* her inner voice chided. Yum. A gift from Satan, you mean.

Devlin suddenly noticed her apathy.

"What's wrong? It's pumpkin pie—your favorite." He signaled the plate, and Brianna felt the table jiggle as he settled his legs beneath it. "I'm famished. I'll eat and then we'll talk." He ignored her silence and began slicing into a large wrapped crepe filled with red berries. "I forgot how good coven food is," he stated. "This cranberry soufflé is top-notch. Marla is one hell of a cook."

He popped another large chunk of the crepe in his mouth, and it took all of Brianna's will power not to snatch the plate, and fling it to the ground. She heard a brief purr from behind her chair and grimaced. He would eat, and then they would talk, she told Nicodemus. She intended to throw his lies in his face at the first possible moment, and then leave the clearing. And if her curses gave him indigestion, it was just what he deserved for lying to her. She heard a brief sneeze.

"Scat, you pesky cat!"

Devlin's frantic swing at Nicodemus had the cat diving away, and Brianna swallowing the lump in her throat. Was she about to cry over the loss of Devlin's friendship? *No, you'll miss the shivers of delight that come from his touch.* Shut up. She had been right about him as a child, and she was right about him now. He didn't deserve her friendship, or her body writhing in ecstasy beneath him. And she had stupidly made him her husband. *Well, do what you do best. Charm him into a false sense of security and then attack.* Great advice, she mused. And when I'm through shredding his character, every single member of the commune will know what a despicable bastard he still is after all these years.

CHAPTER TWENTY

A FEW MOMENTS LATER

Devlin pushed his plate back and indulged in an all-out stretch of his arm muscles.

"I have missed good food. I never realized it until just now." His glance swung to Brianna who was staring at the nearby preserve in quiet contemplation. "Okay, spill what you know. I can feel your heightened energy over here. What have you discovered?"

Brianna's gaze swept his face, and he sensed her mind was still elsewhere.

"Not a thing, unfortunately—unless you call the catty bitchiness between Sally and Eileen something."

"Bad blood there?" Devlin asked, tossing a glance over his shoulder.

"Bad vibes. Didn't you feel it between them?"

"No, I was too busy tuning into everyone's auras. They're clean, by the way, no sign of lying."

"You're sure?"

"Positive—which means we've totally wasted today."

"Maybe not. I know I haven't."

Devlin leaned back against the slats of his chair, studying the downward tilt of her lips.

"Okay, but before you spill your news, let me run something by you first. Do you remember earlier when you thought the Guardians were angry at being sent from the circle?" A nod was all the response that Devlin got. "I think now, you were right. After all, why would they be angry at leaving? Their function is to serve and protect, like the perfect soldier. They don't dish out any energy—unless provoked. So, the only reason they'd be angry is if they had been instructed to stay in the circle by your mother."

"Or her attacker."

"No, I've had hours to think back on that moment. The shock waves the Guardians sent your way were meant to warn you they needed to stay, not go. And because you hadn't done a ritual in a while, you didn't get the message."

"Because I'm such an idiot, you mean?"

"No, that's not what I meant, so can the sarcasm."

"Then don't imply that I'm stupid."

Devlin's chair hit the ground with a thud.

"Stop trying to pick a fight with me."

"I'm not. I'm just saying you're not the only one capable of thinking things through."

"Make your point, if you dare."

"The point is, while I've been asking questions of everyone else today, I've not

asked you where you were and what you were doing when Mother collapsed."

"I don't see how that ties into our investigation."

"Don't you?" She began making lazy circles on the tablecloth with her fingernails, and Devlin got the feeling she was purposely trying to sever their aura connection for good. "No, I don't imagine you would," she finally remarked. "By the way, I don't think I've asked you what you do for a living."

Devlin's gaze narrowed. Now what had prompted that question? Had Tommy revealed his identity to Brianna? He studied Brianna's sour expression. No, she had learned who he was some other way. Eileen or Marla. And now she was seething with a quiet rage towards him.

"It's obvious you know the answer already, so why are you asking?"

"I just want to see how many lies you're prepared to tell before I have you banned from the community again."

She rose from her chair, preparing to flee the table, and Devlin caught hold of her wrist.

"I don't give a damn what you say to the Elders about me. After all this time, what they think no longer matters. But I will not let your personal anger at me destroy any chance we have of finding a way to break the spell placed on your mother. Things would be far better if we could find her personal journal … are you sure you don't have it and don't want me to know? I'm having troubling reading your aura."

Brianna unhooked his fingers from her wrist.

"I haven't found the damn journal," she retorted. "But when I do, I won't be sharing it with you."

Devlin's eyes glittered dangerously.

"Don't take that tone with me." His fingers found her wrist again. "I need to see the journal. It's the key to solving this whole mess."

Brianna twisted her wrist from his grasp again.

"Go to hell, Devlin. I have no intention of sharing Mother's journal with you, now or ever. And since I have no intention of ever speaking to you again—well, you get the picture."

She strode from the table without a backward glance. As she hit the incline and disappeared into the darkness, Devlin muttered a curse beneath his breath. He should've come clean with Brianna right from the start. Now, he faced her as an enemy. And worse, without her trust, they stood no chance of finding a cure for her mother.

• • •

Crossing the footbridge, Brianna scrubbed her wet cheeks. It was idiotic to cry over a stupid argument. After all, she and Devlin had never really been friends in the first place. *But you hoped you could be. You hoped to snuggle against him, his hand caressing the curve of your thigh.* She stopped the thought mid-stream. See how empty our life has become? she addressed her ego. We're living on fairy-tale wishes and the lure of "what ifs." No, she was on her own—like always. She brushed away a new set of tears. Devlin was right, though. Her mother's journal was the key to ending this charade, and now that she had both the amulet and Nicodemus, it wouldn't take long to identify the sinner and confront him or her face to face.

"Rrrr-oww."

A flash of black shot by her, and then slowed to a walk as she stepped onto the mulched pathway. Pulling alongside the cat, she voiced her thoughts.

"It won't take Devlin long to start searching for Mother's journal, so how about you show me where the journal is?"

The cat shot off, leaving Brianna standing at the end of the path alone. A minute later, she saw him shoot through the wrought-iron gates on the outskirts of the Main Street Plaza and disappear. Bolting to catch up, she tried to keep his erratic scampering in sight as she jogged. When she reached the Main Street sidewalk, he was missing. And then he dashed out of the bushes in front of her, heading on a straight-line trajectory towards the library. Brianna switched directions, right behind him. Her mother was undeniably smart. What better place to hide a book than amongst hundreds of them?

Reaching the library steps, Brianna glanced over her shoulder. No sign of Devlin tailing her. That was encouraging. *Or pretty shitty,* her inner voice mocked. Annoyed at the thought, Brianna bolted up the steps and through the door. She had to retrieve the journal, and fast.

Rounding the reception desk, she caught the scent of sickly candle-wax, and slid to a halt. What now? She saw a flicker of light casting shadows on the ceiling on the other side of the bookshelf from her. She bit her lip nervously. I see it, she told Nicodemus. A stuttered purr wound around her ankles, urging her to tread cautiously. She followed the advice, reaching the other side of the shelves, and drawing in her breath as she saw the reading tables shoved aside and a chalk circle etched on the floor.

Brianna studied the candles placed at ninety degree angles around the circle. Someone had been extremely busy. Her gaze traveled the chalk markings. What did the circle represent? The candle placement could be a pyramid of folding gateways, but how did they fold in on themselves? She circled the formation, studying the alternating angles and spaces. The circle didn't appear to be finished, and worse, it didn't feel right. Her gaze latched onto the open book lying in the center of the circle. Her mother's journal! A trapdoor out? Or an invitation in? she wondered.

Dropping to her knees, she studied the book placement more closely. Whoever had created this circle was using a disguise. Leaving her mother's journal as bait was sheer genius. Was the bait meant for her? She ran her hand through the air surrounding the circle. The energy field didn't appear to be directed at her.

She craned her head, spotting a scrap of paper peeping from beneath the book. She attempted to read the words. No luck. The only way to read the words was to lift the book and pull the paper out. Straightening, Brianna sat back on her thighs. She'd like nothing better than to cross the barrier and grab the book, but if she did, she might set off whatever had been instigated inside the circle.

Scrambling to her feet, she chewed on her lip thoughtfully. Had Francis built the circle while they had been busy conducting the Weaving ritual? That would explain his conspicuous absence. No, that explanation didn't sit right. In her heart, she knew he would never resort to misusing the Wicca creed. Could she say the same for Rufus? Yes; he was devoted to the congregation one hundred per cent. So who did that leave if not Francis or Rufus? Marla, Eileen, and Sally?

Brianna's gaze lifted to the circle again. Was the circle feminine in nature? It certainly could be. It felt emotional, rather than logical. And God knows, she knew about making emotional decisions instead of rational ones. Her gaze traveled the arc of the chalk again. Had the circle been cast against Devlin? That was certainly likely, given the scrap of paper hidden between the pages of the book. His name could be written on it. But then so could hers. She supposed Sally had the strongest motivation to cast a spell on one of them—as payback for her sister's death. She might deem it justified; taking Devlin out first, and saving her for last. Her pulse skittered suddenly. She didn't relish seeing Devlin on the receiving end of a deadly curse—unless, of course, she placed it on his head herself.

Studying the circle outline again, she decided the circle was meant for Devlin, and the sooner she discerned its final goal, the better. She bent over and scanned the scribbled words again, able to read only the tail end of the last line: "Plus One More."

Her gaze lifted to the book again. The journal could be interpreted as plus one more—a trapdoor built in case things went horribly wrong. But that interpretation felt wrong too. The book had been placed on the floor as bait to come in, not to get out. But who was being invited in, if not Devlin?

A shiver slaked her spine at the question, and Brianna wiped her sweating palms on her skirt. Now that she had read the last words of the mantra, the dynamics of the ritual didn't seem to be aimed at Devlin. If only he was here to … she scratched that thought. It didn't matter what Devlin thought about anything. He was out of her life for good. *Still, two witches against one would be so much more effective,* her inner voice nudged.

"Rrr-ow."

The cat's cry had Brianna rearing back as if stung.

"Good Lord, Nicodemus! Stop sneaking up on people." The cat blinked up at her, seeming not at all repentant as she stared down at him. His gaze never wavered from hers, and because it didn't, she felt a shiver ripple up her spine again. What was he trying to communicate to her? To look beyond her own logic for answers?

Turning her back on his intimidation, she took a step towards the circle. A loud hiss erupted at her movement, and a black paw swiped at her ankle. Falling back, she stamped her foot at the cat.

"Yes, I know, it's dangerous, but I have to determine the circle's intent."

Nicodemus growled at her this time, and giving into his intimidation, she took six steps back, deciding he meant her to view the circle from a greater distance. She let her gaze encompass the total shape. No talisman, no engraved pentacle, no gifts for the Guardians.

Circling left, Brianna began to chew on her lip again. Gateways and guiding words, but no gifts. Why? Only one reason. The circle had been improvised on the spur of the moment and had been interrupted before it could be completed.

"Rrrrrrrr-ooooow."

Brianna looked down at the cat now walking by her ankles. He was studying the circle as intently as she was. Was he suggesting she finally use his magic to get her answer? Nothing ventured, nothing gained, her inner voice taunted. Right. Raising her arms, she reversed directions, walking back along the rim of the markings and offering an impromptu chant.

"I walk this circle thrice about, one for the world within, one for the world without. Here, in this place, beginnings and endings are meeting. What lies ahead, shall be revealed at my greeting."

Giving a half-turn left, Brianna prepared to elevate her chant; however, the cat's mewl had her breaking off. To her surprise, a voice inside her head introduced a new chant.

"Weavers of black fire, heed my call. I bind the man in this circle, and ask that he fall. I bind all gateways in and out, preventing his escape in releasing your wrath. I bind his aura and energies so that my spell will override the one previously cast."

Stunned by the familiar voice, Brianna glanced at the cat at her feet. Was Nicodemus channeling Sally's voice for her benefit? It felt like it. She craned her head and waited for the voice to continue in her head. When it didn't, she leaned over and petted Nicodemus' head.

"You are a true spirit guide, Nicodemus. And you are absolutely right. I have been very stupid. All the signs were clear. The disjointed memories, the subtle grillings, the energy shift during the Weaving ceremony, the smell of sandalwood—clear signs I overlooked."

"Rrr-ow."

"I know I can feel it too. We have no time to lose. Devlin is about to feel the wrath of a conjured demon."

She whirled around, bolting for the front door; however, upon reaching it, she found it locked. She shook the handle and then pounded on the door. A second, louder hammering brought no response, and because it didn't, icy fear snaked around Brianna's heart. She was sealed in, and if she hadn't been so immersed in trying to decipher the circle's intent, she would've heard the rebar being dropped. If only she had listened to her instincts the moment she had spied the circle and retreated back out the front door. Now, she had no choice but to defend herself, rather than going on the offensive.

"Rrr-ooowww."

Brianna whirled at Nicodemus's wail. He darted away—towards the basement door. She moved quickly after him. He had the right idea. Find a way out and take it. In a matter of seconds, she was flicking on the wall light and descending the steps.

Spotting a huge stack of furniture piled against the exit door, her spirits sank. The furniture was much too heavy to move without help. Not to her surprise, Nicodemus took charge, climbing the lower limbs of the furniture and making his way to an open window near the ceiling. Reaching it, he glanced back at her and purred. She grimaced up at him.

"I know I'm too big to fit through. Go get help." He scrambled onto the ledge and out the window before Brianna could finish her instructions. "Wait!" Her yell was two seconds too late and she frowned. He'd seek out Devlin, but he'd be unable to converse with him when they met. Sighing, she turned back to the staircase and re-climbed the steps. How long would it take for Nicodemus to bring help?

Reaching the top step, she found the basement door shut. Odd! Had the door blown shut behind her when she descended? She jiggled the knob. Locked! She would make Sally pay for her treachery.

Giving the door an impatient kick, she whirled around and retraced her steps. Muted light spiraled across the basement floor ahead of her steps, casting misshapen shadows all around her. Brianna shivered, grabbing a discarded chair and righting it. She sank down on the seat cushion, plotting all the ways she would make Sally pay for harming her mother and the community.

CHAPTER TWENTY-ONE

THE HUNT FOR BRIANNA

Devlin slammed the stairwell door. He had been searching for Brianna for over an hour, and at each point of stopping, he had come up empty. How had she managed to slip off the face of the earth in such a short time? And how was she able to hide her energy from him? Since the marriage binding, he felt the pull of her energy no matter how far apart they were. And now, less than a day later, he couldn't read her essence. Had he been wrong in thinking that their merged energies had been a sign from the Sisters of Fate that they had been forgiven for the Dark Time? No, he couldn't feel Brianna because she was pissed at him. And a pissed off Brianna was nothing short of a wild tornado. Why had he been so stupid as to confront her on her mother's journal? It had brought the she-bear out in her again, and now he hadn't the foggiest idea how to catch up with her.

He listened to the echo of his boots tattooing on the pavement and frowned. Sienna's essence could be restored and the energy displacement broken loose of its hold, if he could read her journal. It was foolish to think that Brianna hadn't already worked out some kind of ritual in her head to break the spell. She was that talented. He just hoped she wouldn't try it without his being there to back her up.

He halted his flight, glancing up at the twinkling stars. He had to locate Tommy. He was Brianna's only other ally and it didn't take a dunce-capped wizard to realize that she would seek him out before long. Which direction had she taken after leaving the clearing? He was certain she retrieved the book the moment she left him, but where would she hide it?

A black streak flashed in front of him and into the bushes, and Devlin slowed his steps. Damn pesky cat. Why was he slinking about the sidewalk in the moonlight?

"Rrr-oww."

Devlin jumped as Nicodemus darted from the bushes, and came to a halt in front of him. Now what? The cat sat down, his yellow eyes glued to Devlin's face. If only he could read the damn cat's mind.

"Rrrrr-owww."

A quick sneeze followed the cat-call.

"I don't know what you're saying, you miserable beast," Devlin declared.

The cat meowed in response and then bolted away, through the shrubs again. Watching him go, Devlin gave a wry smile. It was stupid to think the cat knew Brianna's whereabouts, and was attempting to alert him to her location. Women like Brianna weren't devious. They hid in plain sight; he just needed to think like her.

"Meditating? Or contemplating murder?"

Devlin whirled, startled by Tommy's silent arrival.

"Neither. I'm attempting to locate Brianna."

Tommy's smile snaked to a grin.

"Why? Is she lost?"

"Yes."

Tommy's amusement died instantly.

"What's happened? What have you done?"

"I haven't done a thing," Devlin replied. "She's learned my true identity."

"Good God, that's great news."

"She's vowed never to speak to me again. She's turned into a tsunami, and you know what that means."

"Of course. You'll never get her to fall in love with you now."

Devlin's face contorted in anger.

"There was never any hope of that, and we both know it."

Tommy scuffed his toe on a clump of grass.

"I can't believe you were stupid enough to marry her without telling her the truth."

"If you had kept your mouth shut, we wouldn't be having this conversation."

"Hey, don't put this at my door," Tommy fired up. "I had no idea you were a witch in sheep's clothing."

"Can the sarcasm. We need to find Brianna. She's acquired her mother's Book of Shadows, and I need it. It may contain the key to solving this whole idiotic mess."

"Then why are we standing here talking? Let's go find her."

Devlin hissed through his cheeks.

"Have you any idea how large this friggin' compound is?"

"Well then, let's go and demand the Elders start a search for her. The more of us attempting to locate her, the better. We can spread out. She can't be that lost."

Devlin hooted loudly.

"I'm not about to get the Elders involved in this, Tommy. One of them is our sinner. I'm certainly not going to call attention to the fact that Brianna's gone off by herself. I won't put her life in danger just to satisfy my own anger at her. She'd do the same in my place."

"Well then, why don't you do what Brianna would do—if she were in your place?"

"For once, I don't know what she would do."

"Yes, you do. She would be hiding the book in plain sight."

Devlin's head shot up.

"And what better place to hide a book than in a library filled with them," Devlin stated. He bolted off the sidewalk and into the street, gesturing Tommy to follow. A second later, a dark shadow streaked across the road in front of him. Nicodemus. Up to some new mischief, he'd bet. The shadow flashed back across the road a moment later. It would be just like the cat to strike out after them and take up residence beside him as he searched for the journal. What power had Sienna really charged the creature with? Spying the library steps, Devlin gave a shiver. He didn't want to know the cat's power. He didn't like cats, and the thought of them being able to read his thoughts and understand them, well, it was better not to think on it.

Dismissing the feline's erratic scurrying, he crashed through the shrubbery on the left side of the library entrance, skidding to a halt when he spotted the rebar in place. Barreling up the steps, he signaled Tommy for help. Together, the pair shoved the bar up and dove through the door as soon it swung open.

The smell was the first thing he noticed as they crossed the entry-way. Candle-wax—sandalwood, to be exact. His gaze drifted to the ceiling, noticing the alternating prisms of light flickering. What the hell was Brianna doing? Trying to burn the place down? He angled around the reception desk and into the main room, skidding to a halt upon spying the tables shoved aside and a large circle etched on the wood floor of the room. He threw his hand out, preventing Tommy from walking over the sketched lines.

"Stay back." Scanning the circle, he studied the placement of the candles around the borders. Definitely gateways. But for what purpose?

"What the hell is Brianna up to?" Tommy asked. He fanned the air around him. "The air reeks of rotting corpses."

Devlin lifted his hand.

"Give me a minute to think." He dropped to his haunches and inspected the floorboards. "Gateways, no Guardians yet, and no gifts." He felt heat against his shoulder.

"What do you think? Is it one of Brianna's circles?"

"Not likely. It feels wrong."

"Wrong?"

"I can't put my finger on it, but the closest thing I can equate it to is a Venus Fly Trap. There's something I'm missing here, though."

Devlin felt the heat on his shoulder vanish.

"I can't imagine what. Even with my limited knowledge, I can see candles representing doorways," Tommy bent down and inspected the center of the circle. "What do you suppose this book represents?"

"Book?" Devlin's heart leapt at the word and he bolted to his feet, knocking Tommy out of the way. "It's not just a book, Tommy. It's Sienna's personal journal. No, don't touch it. It's the trigger."

"Trigger?"

Devlin shot to his feet, ignoring Tommy's question. The ritual was underway, though not yet in full motion; however, when the designated trigger set off, the true intent of the circle would kick in. And it wasn't hard to imagine who the target would be when it did set off. Like mother, like daughter. He felt his arm snatched roughly, followed by a husky growl.

"Talk to me, Devlin. Tell me what the circle means."

Devlin brushed the fingers from his sleeve.

"We're out of choices."

"I'll go with you."

"You have to stay here."

"The hell I will!"

Devlin's gaze softened.

"Look, I'm thinking of Brianna. If the book is meant to lure her, as I believe it is, she needs to be warned. One of us has to stay here in case she attempts to touch the circle."

A cranky sigh emanated.

"Well, in that case, take your ass out of here."

Nodding, Devlin pulled out a chair.

"Sit here and wait for Brianna. And whatever you do, don't let your curiosity get the better of you. If you interfere with the circle, you'll be lying alongside Sienna Sage."

Tommy dropped into the chair, pulling out a handkerchief and wiping his beaded brow. Devlin spun about, angling back around the reception desk, sliding to a halt when he spied Nicodemus barring his way.

"Rrr-oow!"

Ignoring the cat's cry, Devlin sidestepped him. He didn't have time to cater to a crazed cat. A second later, a heavy pressure hit the back of his calf. What now? He looked down at the black bundle righting itself on the floor and taking a surly stance in front of him again.

"Get away, Nicodemus."

"Rrrrrr-ow, rrrrr-ow."

"It's no use talking to me. I have no cat skills."

As if understanding his words, the cat spun about and scampered to the basement door. He paused in front of it, looking back at Devlin, and then at the door again. Devlin studied the glow of the overhead light, assessing the cat's posture. Was the obnoxious pest trying to converse with him?

"What the hell's going on? Why haven't you gone?" Tommy asked, coming around the reception desk.

"The damn cat's keeping me here," Devlin replied.

The eerie sheen of Nicodemus's fur underwent a drastic change as the cat raised its hackles and hissed at the pair. All at once, Brianna's aura floated through Devlin's senses. She was below. He could feel her essence once again. Had the damn cat relayed it to him? He stepped forward, trying the door handle, not at all surprised to find it locked. He jiggled the doorknob, looking for a key. Suddenly, a large pounding erupted from the other side of the door.

"Devlin!"

Hearing Brianna's muffled voice, incredible relief washed over him. The she-bear was still alive. Scanning the area around the door, Devlin hunted for something to break the handle with. He spotted a fire extinguisher on the wall next to the reception desk, and headed towards it.

"Devlin!" The door handle rattled.

"Hold your horses," Tommy called through the door. "We're working on it."

Devlin returned with the extinguisher, and with one fell swoop, smashed it down hard on the knob. The metal tore from its hinges, and hit the floor with a loud clank. The door flew open, bringing a stumbling Brianna with it. Devlin tossed the extinguisher to the floor.

"Thank God! I thought you were dead." He swept her into his arms, and in a split second, his lips were devouring hers in a punishing kiss. And then he was lifting his head. "If you ever scare the hell out of me again like that, I'll chain you to a damn chair." He saw the dangerous glint in her eye as she wriggled out of his arms, and whirled around the front desk and into the main part of the library. Following, Devlin watched her stop before the painted circle and study it intently. "I haven't touched it, if that's what you're thinking."

Her answer was breathless.

"I wasn't."

Devlin settled beside her.

"Has it been cast against me—as payback for Brenda's death?" He saw her mouth turn down, followed by a fast shake of her head.

"That may be the end result, but it is not the reason it was cast." She stepped across the chalk markings, and scooped up the book inside. "Mother's journal was left as bait, an invitation of sorts."

Devlin hauled her out of the circle, snatching the book from her fingers.

"You idiot! The book isn't bait, it's a trigger. And now, you've set it off."

Her scoff echoed as the book was snatched back.

"Don't you dare tell me how to read circles, or what flux they're in. I've been reading circles since I was nine."

"And I've been reading them since I was six. So what's your point?"

"You didn't learn to read them from my mother. And since you didn't, you have missed the fact that Mother gave her journal to someone for safekeeping."

"Someone she obviously never suspected was the sinner," Devlin stated.

"Someone she suspected *was* the sinner," Brianna corrected. "She chose to bait that someone with a false journal."

". . . which is why the circle feels unfinished," Devlin remarked suddenly. He gave Brianna a curious stare. "You've figured out the name of the sinner. Who is it? Francis?"

"Right house, wrong person," Brianna replied. "The book was a ruse to confuse Sally, but it backfired." She broke off as Nicodemus sat down beside her ankles. "Yes, I know," she told the cat. "I can feel it. She's half-way into the spell."

Catching the exchange, Devlin's puzzled gaze came up to study Brianna's face, and then dropped to the cat. A disquieting thought raced through his mind and he stepped forward, grabbing Brianna and spinning her around. He saw the amulet around her neck immediately, even though she attempted to shield it from him with her fingers. In seconds, he was jerking the chain from her neck. He dangled the amulet in front of Tommy.

"You gave her the amulet?"

"She said she needed it."

Devlin's mind veered sharply to anger, and rearing back, he rammed his fist into Tommy's jaw, sending the man stumbling backwards. Appalled by the attack, Brianna rushed to Tommy's side. Shielding him, she glared at Devlin.

"Are you insane? How could you hit Tommy?"

"I couldn't very well hit you, now could I?" Devlin answered. He took a step forward. "Did you even bother to tell him the truth before taking the amulet?"

"What truth?" Tommy asked, wiping his bloodied lip, and staring at Brianna.

Devlin's retort hardened his features.

"She's merged her essence with the damn cat, and in doing so, she has become the leader of this Coven. She has thrown her life in Washington away, and worse, she has thrown mine away too."

"I didn't do it on purpose," Brianna said, "Sally conjured a spell on Nicodemus and the only way to save him was to merge our essences."

"Unfortunately, that reckless act has made it impossible for me to trust you anymore. And since I don't trust you, I don't intend to stay married to you." His gaze scorched Brianna, and rancor sharpened his tone. "You've gotten your wish, Cinderella. When this madness is all through, I'm through with you."

"What's going on here?"

The voice, though quiet, had an ominous quality to it, and the trio turned, startled to find Francis and Rufus staring at them with baffled glances. Rufus was the first to take stock of the situation, his gaze landing on Tommy's bleeding lip. His expression shriveled as Eileen, Marla, and the doctor joined them.

"You've resorted to violence—a thing that can't be allowed. You will leave the property at once—all of you." His voice held a hint of steel, but then so did Devlin's as he snarled.

"We're not going anywhere!" His glance bounced from face to face, and Devlin sensed that for the first time since their arrival, the group was intimidated by him. Realizing it was best to soften his approach, Devlin took a step towards the front door, signaling Francis.

"Come with me. We've not much time."

"I can't come with you," Francis responded.

Annoyed, Devlin rounded on him.

"Can't or won't?"

"I can't come with you."

"Look here," Devlin stated. "There's no time for your bullshit. We've got to find Sally. You're coming with me." He took a step towards Francis and so did Brianna. She laid a hand on Devlin's arm and her voice held a depth of authority.

"It's not that he won't. It's that he can't." She studied his face intently. "What type of spell has Sally bound you with? Air magic? Earth magic? What? I need to know and I need to know now."

Baffled by the question, Rufus glanced from Devlin to Brianna, and then, catching on, he stepped between Brianna and Francis, laying a hand on Francis' sleeve.

"Has Sally placed a binding spell on you? You must answer; the Ancients decree it."

Francis's mulish expression collapsed under the gentle probing of his father's words.

"It's not her fault. She didn't ask for such pain."

"I'm not accusing you," Rufus replied. "If I was in your place, I might do the same. But if she has misused magic for her own personal gain, we are all in grave danger."

Francis's gaze shot to Devlin.

"Her rage is spotty, but when it comes, it's directed towards Devlin for Brenda's death, and for taking Brianna away from her."

Devlin took a step back. He had never expected to hear himself condemned so openly. Yet, for all his surprise, he knew he deserved Francis's derisive scorn. His banishment had allowed a hidden evil to fester in Sally's essence and take root. Not against Brianna, but against himself. They had to disrupt the ritual drawn on the floor without delay. Whirling, he moved to the circle, finding his elbow snatched back roughly.

"What are you going to do?" Francis asked. "Sally has no memory of these psychotic breaks. Any confrontation may cause irreparable damage to her soul."

Devlin didn't bother to respond. Francis's face said it all. He felt compelled to save Sally from her dark psychosis, but in trying he had managed to become part of her spell-making.

"We've got to short-circuit this circle immediately—throw her off her game," Devlin stated. "If she is as unstable as you imply, she will target whomever she can, whenever she can. It's clear her psychosis is accelerating. When it finally splits off, her ritual will come full circle."

Spinning back, Devlin studied the circle, discarding option after option in his head. A loud purr soon echoed from beside his ankles. Damn cat. He oughta be shot. And so should his mistress. But he had the right idea. They had to disconnect the circle by any means necessary.

"Any suggestions on how we disconnect it?" Eileen asked, settling beside him and studying the markings.

"I'm fresh out of ideas," Devlin remarked. "What do you think, Brianna?" He turned, expecting to find Brianna studying the circle as well. When he didn't see her, he scanned the room. A door slammed, followed by the sound of a rebar dropping. He flew around the reception desk, emitting a vindictive curse on all stubborn she-bears. Reaching the front door, he tried the handle, knowing full well he'd find it sealed shut. Exasperated, he whirled on his heels and dove back around the desk, dragging Francis forward.

"Have you any idea where Sally might erect a circle to match this one?" he asked.

"It isn't possible for Sally to deceive us, Devlin," Eileen stated. "There is too much foot traffic in the gardens for her to do so.

Members are always cutting through, meditating on benches, or greeting guests strolling the footpaths."

"And there's always nighttime vigils," Brad added. "No one can be everywhere twenty-four seven, no matter how many of us there are."

Devlin's gaze shot to Francis again.

"You know Sally the best, Francis. How much time occurs between these fugues?"

"Sometimes years, but each episode is more severe than the last—and lasts longer."

"There's always Green Glen," Eileen stated, suddenly.

"Don't be ridiculous," Francis stated. "No one uses the original gardens anymore. It's off-limits."

"Is that the old Sacred Circle site?" Devlin asked, a frown emerging on his lips. Eileen answered for Francis.

"Unfortunately, yes. But you can cross it off your list. The ground is contaminated. Not even Sally in her madness would dare to initiate a ceremony there."

"But how did the ground get contaminated?" Devlin asked. Looks of horror marred each face, as they supplied their own answer. Their expressions were enough for Devlin. They had to find a way out of the library and fast. A pull on his sleeve had Devlin turning to Tommy.

"The cat's on to something," he stated. He signaled the floor behind them. "Something in the circle."

Devlin twisted around, spotting Nicodemus sitting in the center of the circle. His mind clicked into focus.

"Not in the circle, Tommy, but beneath it," he muttered. His gaze collided with Francis's and held.

"The emergency tunnel," they said, simultaneously.

Devlin dove forward, shoving Nicodemus aside. The cat hissed its displeasure; however, in seconds, the floorboard was raised, and the cat was diving down the steps into the hole. Peering into the darkened space, Devlin called after him.

"You better wait for us, you miserable beast!"

Devlin heard a chuckle from beside him.

"Are we relying on that creature to show us the way again?"

Devlin's lips twitched, but he sobered instantly.

"If you say one word of this to Brianna, I'll do more than bust your jaw. Now, hang back and stay with the others."

"The hell I will. I'm going with you."

Devlin frowned, but made no other demand as he dropped down on the first step, and began his descent. Time was once again his enemy, rushing forward like a raging river gone wild. He listened as his boots stomped on the wood, wondering why he hadn't kept his attention on Brianna. The circle was meant for her and she had sensed it from the get-go—which meant he would've sensed it too, if Nicodemus hadn't blocked her essence from him. What would she find when she arrived in Green Glen?

He didn't want to think that far ahead. He had to cut her off and prevent the confrontation Sally was obviously intending. He heard a light wheeze from above him and knew Francis was dogging his footsteps.

"Hang back, Francis. I can handle this one without you."

An out-of-breath stutter floated in his right ear.

"Yeah, just like you did fifteen years ago."

His meaning was clear, and it stung Devlin to the core; however, he didn't lessen his pace. Instead, he reached the exit door, jerked it open, and headed for the wooded pathway off the Crystal Gardens. If he cut through to the Sage cottage onto the old path outside the back door acreage, he could shave off at least four minutes of their running time. Brianna was no more than five minutes ahead.

Increasing his stride, he barreled down the garden path, and into the old orchard bordering the Green Glen cove.

CHAPTER TWENTY-TWO

GREEN GLEN CLEARING

Brianna crashed through the underbrush and into the hatchery clearing, skidding to a halt when she spied the figure draped in glittering black, kneeling over her father's prone body inside a painted circle. Tuning into the buzz of energy alive in the air, she realized she was a total idiot. Sally had been waiting for her arrival. And thanks to the dark entity who had latched itself to her essence, she was bent on making the entire Sage family pay for the death of her sister.

Feeling a tremor beneath her shoes, Brianna glanced down at her feet. She was standing inside an outer circle similar to the inner one, and Sally had already called the Quarters. By stepping into the clearing she had triggered the second circle outside the inner one. Taken back by the tremendous flow of energy bouncing around her, she glanced at the woman straightening in the circle. Her change in posture and Gothic looks were staggering as she took a defensive stance and threw her tattooed arms out towards Brianna.

"If you want your father, cross over and get him," she taunted.

Brianna realized that initiating any counter-attack while inside a double circle would backfire on the person inside the outer circle, not the one in the inner circle. And that was just what this new Sally was hoping for. She glanced at her father's prone figure and took a step forward.

"Papa?"

His head rolled towards the sound of her voice; however, before he could reply, Sally stepped over his torso, and blocked his face with her cape. She waved her hands toward Brianna again.

"I bind thee from doing magic to aid this spell; I bind thee from entering all gateways as well. You cannot stop the motion I have set into place. From sister to sister, you will suffer his fate."

Ignoring the chant, Brianna stepped to her left, catching sight of her father attempting to lift his hand. That he had been condemned to some awful mental fugue by Sally's psychosis was clear. A band of black auras surrounded his prostrate frame. It didn't take any magical skill to see that his earlier illness was preventing him from throwing off the stupor he had been paralyzed with.

"You can't save him," Sally mocked. "I have seen to that."

A surge of anger welled in Brianna's chest. She wasn't about to give any credence to this Sally's threats. This Sally was simply too unfocused and in-experienced to maintain two magic spells at once. Besides, she didn't have the power of six generations of High Priestesses as her back-up.

Realizing she had to do a quick assessment of the circle she was in, Brianna made a hurried walk right, then left, studying the markings on the ground as she went. She had to give the appearance of being in control—even if she wasn't. And she had to trust she'd be shown any error this Sally might've made in the construction of the spells.

"You'll never figure it out," Sally jeered, mirroring Brianna's walk along the markings. "I have seen to that as well."

"The day I can't beat you at casting spells hasn't arrived yet, Sally," Brianna retorted. "You've never done anything on your own that I didn't do first, and better. Once a copycat; always a copycat."

A maddening shriek echoed in the clearing, proving Brianna's taunt had found its mark. The hair around Brianna's ears crackled under an influx of static electricity, and she felt the tendrils lift from her face.

"I forbid you to say such things to me. I hold the power of the Queen of the Witches!" She raised her hand, and Brianna felt a spray of pain along her right arm. She clutched her wrist, rubbing the sore spot. She had to think of a way to throw Sally off her game. If she didn't, her time in the clearing would be filled with non-stop pain. But what to try?

The sound of crashing shrubs erupted behind Brianna, and she spun about, horrified when Devlin dove into the clearing and skidded to a halt beside her. A moment later, his legs buckled, and his knees hit the ground. The aura around his frame went from white to grey to black, and she knew his entry into the clearing had been anticipated as well. Hearing a second series of crashing twigs, Brianna flew to the edge of the circle and flung out her hands to the arriving group.

"Stay back," she warned. "The clearing's in flux."

The group's faces registered alarm; however, Brianna had no time to worry about their fears. She had to think and think fast. Devlin was already thirty seconds into his binding. Whirling about, she dropped to her haunches beside him. How far gone was he really?

"Can you hear me, Devlin?"

He didn't answer, and the fact that he didn't made Brianna's pulse shift into overdrive. What horror had Sally concocted for him?

"Rrr-owww."

Brianna jumped at the sound of Nicodemus's wail. She looked down at the sleek black fur brushing against her thigh. Nicodemus, ever vigilant. Thank the Goddesses, Sally's spell couldn't keep him out. Cats had an affinity for skirting the fabric of spells.

She heard a light chuff, followed by a sneeze, and watched as the cat sat down abruptly by her right side. His gaze centered on Sally, and Brianna had the feeling his presence was one of intimidation. When he gave a low growl in his throat, Sally moved away.

"Not even a spirited cat can halt what's been set in motion. The Weavers of Death have been called, and their vengeance cannot be undone."

"She's bluffing," Eileen called from behind Brianna. "Rituals can always be undone. All you need is a trigger."

Brianna hopped to her feet quickly. Should she attempt a counter ritual without knowing what the original curse started off as? She glanced at the area around the circle. This Sally had been clever in building the circles, she'd give her that. Devlin's head suddenly knocked against her thigh.

"The ritual's … too far … gone … " he muttered. "Let me … go down."

"I'm not letting you go down," Brianna stated, tartly. "Not you or Papa."

"It's … too … late."

"It can't be. Otherwise, Nicodemus wouldn't be … " Brianna's gaze shot to the cat. Of course, that was it. Nicodemus had the power to cripple the original curse. A busted sneeze echoed, sending her gaze skimming along the angles of the quadrants. There was no sign of a trapdoor anywhere between the first and second circle. Sally must've been truly riding the edge of insanity when she created her spells. She had left the book as bait in the library, forgetting the most important quality it held—the wrong essentials for a ritual.

"Rrr-owww."

"Yes, I'm wearing it," she said, aloud. Reaching into her dress, she withdrew her necklace. Why hadn't she thought of it before? Crystal energy had restored Nicodemus's essence before; her necklace had the power to poke holes in the fabric of time. She glanced at the markings in front of her again. Eileen was right. No circle was absolute. They could always be re-programmed, especially by a High Priestess with the right tools.

The first gateway was built with two boundaries, and Devlin had triggered the first with his sudden entrance into the clearing. Now, it was time for her to take a leap of faith and trigger the second gateway. To do that, she had to act without thinking of the consequences. Dropping her left hand to Devlin's shoulder, Brianna placed her Pentagram against her forehead with her right. If she merged her energy with Devlin's, and used it to tap Nicodemus's power, she should be able to harness enough power to rework Sally's ritual.

"Heed me, Saviors of doubt. Shower me with light, within and without. No other use may be made of this channel, except for the energies your goodness does handle. I ask that my aura be protected from ill. So mote it be, this is my will." She opened her eyes, bent, and placed the Amulet in front of Nicodemus, and then straightened. "From witch to witch, and mortal to immortal, I invoke the Guardian to open a portal. Switch without to within, and awaken the Towers, as above, so below, transfer their power."

"Stop! You will not call the Towers to arms," Sally shrieked. She moved to a spot in front of Brianna. "If you dare to coax them any further, I shall end your father's life."

Brianna ignored her shrill tones and continued chanting.

"Mind the threefold law you should. Three times bad, and three times good."

Sally's counter-attack came on top of hers.

"Heed the shadows' mighty gale, lock the door, and drop the sail."

Brianna immediately countered her chant.

"Recast the circle thrice about, all evil spirits ferreted out. I beseech the Guardian to un-barricade this gate and reverse the curse ... "

". . . Weavers of Death, initiate her fall. From sister to sister, ignore her call."

Brianna felt a sudden tingle in her fingers, and realized the Weavers were having difficulty deciphering her life force from Devlin's. Buoyed by the knowledge, Brianna bent down and patted Nicodemus's head.

"Without to within, awaken the Towers."

She felt the rush of energy as soon as her fingers left his fur. Don't panic, her inner voice warned. *Nicodemus needs time to clear the blockages in and around the gate so the switch can take place.*

Feeling a soft ripple of air fan her hair, Brianna knew her leap of faith was paying off. The gateway could be switched without it caving in on itself—if she didn't let up on her chanting. It was time to raise the stakes—with Devlin's help. Brianna squeezed the fabric beneath her fingers.

"Listen to my voice, Devlin. Focus." His head rose at her words, but slumped down again immediately. Her heart skittered, seeing the motion. *Don't let him die, she prayed to the Goddesses. I need him to make mad, passionate love to me for the rest of his life.* "Stay with me," she urged, panic-stricken. "Focus on my voice. If you don't, we'll die." His head lifted again and she heard a stuttered whisper.

". . . still ... here." His head dropped, and Brianna knew he was drifting off again. "Stay with me, I said! Focus on my voice."

His head sprang up, and his hand lifted and settled on her fingers. A hefty jolt of electricity suddenly passed between them.

"I bind you, Devlin. I bind you."

Sally's call seemed confident; however, Brianna heard a small quiver in the pitch as she focused her gaze on Devlin's hunched form. Was Sally beginning to doubt her powers? She hoped so. A witch who had sudden doubts would be hard-pressed to keep the negative energy from a total backlash.

A surge of energy rippled through her fingers, and encouraged by the sign, Brianna shifted her body closer to Nicodemus. Nicodemus and Devlin were doing their part. Now it was her turn.

"From witch to witch, I invoke this vow. One shall win, and one shall lose ... "

Sally's voice over-pitched hers.

"Weavers of Darkness, vanquish her plea. Show her no mercy, until I grant a reprieve."

". . . one shall sleep, and one shall choose … "

"Stop! I forbid you … "

A huge blast of wind careened from the north quadrant of her circle, and spiraled upward. A second blast followed the first, this time from the south quadrant. Two more blasts followed the pair, and Brianna knew the cones of power were switching places. Sally's knees buckled at the switch, and she hit the ground, totally surprised by the sudden attack.

"No, I won't be denied." Her cry was tortured as she clutched her head and then doubled over. Brianna felt a sudden surge of pity well up; however, she quickly dispelled it. No matter how sorry she felt for Sally, she couldn't show any feeling or remorse until the curse had been severed. Raising her voice, Brianna addressed the Guardians.

"Standing between the worlds of the known and unknown, I call to the Ancients to rise from the river. Come from your resting place, your light to deliver. I am your daughter, a sister of light. Respond to my call and show yourselves bright."

She paused, waiting for a response. None came; however, she felt a change in energy levels as Nicodemus stood and approached the inner circle. He sat in front of Sally's hunched and sobbing form, and Brianna heard a loud purr begin to bounce off the cone of power.

A jarring bolt of electricity suddenly erupted in the middle of Brianna's palms, and she marveled at the awesome rush of adrenalin that suddenly shook her body. She had never expected to experience a healing wash in her life, and here she was being totally cleansed and purified by the arriving Masters. Was Devlin being cleansed by the same waves of light?

She closed her eyes, and felt an immediate connection to his life-force. A second later, an unexpected transfer occurred from his body to hers, and back again. The exchange was so powerful that it was all she could do to remain on her feet.

For a moment, she saw two sparkling lights slamming into each other and then, by magic, both merged into one bright, white light. Immediately on the heels of the first vision, the Masters sent a second one, filtering the image through a scrim of blue light. This time, the vision that swept over her didn't stay hers alone. Instead, bits and pieces of it washed over Devlin, who clutched his head in self-defense. Ten seconds later, he blacked out under the powerful assault. He hit the ground with a thud, severing his connection with Brianna, who ended up taking a full hit of energy as it looped back around to find an alternate source.

It took all her self-control not to wither under the onslaught that began jamming her thoughts. And then, out of nowhere, a peaceful euphoria saturated her entire being, and she knew the Ancient Ones were powering down the wash and preparing to respond to her request.

Ahead of her, in the circle, Sally's tortured sobs turned to full-scale weeping. Hearing the sobs, Brianna knew Sally's spell was imploding, and so was her psychosis. It was impossible to maintain a spell against the Ancients, and she was learning that lesson the hard way.

Nicodemus stood then and entered the circle, brushing past Sally and jumping over Brianna's father's motionless form. Swinging about, he raised his paw and laid it on her father's chest.

"Rr-roow."

His cry was directed at Brianna, who immediately responded. Snatching up the Amulet, she placed it in the middle of her forehead.

"Givers of light, let me share in your glory. I seek your light for one who comes from a long line of stories. Send your daughter, Sienna, back to the light of the earth. Restore her to all who know her true worth. Remove all discord, trauma, and strife. Make these distresses unable to pierce her new life."

A spiral of wind buffeted Brianna's body, and she knew the ascended Masters were assessing her second request. She braced for the administration of their powers, aware that the Ancients waited on no one, not even High Priestesses. Her hair rose from her shoulders and billowed around her face, and Brianna marveled at the pure joy of being at one with the River of Souls. Directing the stone towards the inner circle, she addressed the Masters.

"Live and let live, fairly take, and fairly give. Bide the Wicca laws you must, in perfect love and perfect trust. I ask that all be released from their river of dark. Their spiritual essence once more energized by your powerful mark. I ask that you dispatch my sister Sally's pain to the earth. And align her once again with the renewal of birth. Thank you all for this healing. Your work now is through. Return to your resting place, to refresh and renew."

The wind rushed up at the dismissal, swirling into a cyclone above Brianna's head, and then splitting off into the separate quadrants and dissipating. The sudden loss of power in the clearing brought Brianna to her knees, and she hit the ground alongside Devlin. Her vision clouded at once, and a huge buzzing erupted behind her temples. She clutched her head in self-defense. She had temporarily forgotten about the after-effects of releasing powerful entities from a circle.

"Brianna?" The voice sounded far away, but she recognized it.

"Brad." She turned her head in the general direction of the voice. "I'm b-b-lind as a bat."

"What do you need me to do?" The voice came closer, and Brianna felt a presence settle beside her.

"Check Devlin. I tried to protect him, but he got hammered by the Masters." Brianna heard movement and queried anxiously. "Is he alive?"

"Alive and breathing; although, he's going to have a whale of a headache when he wakes."

Brianna suppressed a grin. A gigantic headache was just what he deserved for following her to the Glen and triggering the ritual. *He was attempting to keep you from getting yourself killed,* her ego chided. *He loves you.* She did grin then. Well, he's going to get a sizeable shock when he wakes and remembers the healing wash vision.

"Is it safe to check Sally's vital signs?" the doctor queried. "She seems to have passed out."

"Yes, but be careful. I can't be sure how much payback the Masters administered to her. And don't forget about Papa. He will need medical help as soon as possible."

Brianna heard movement, followed by Francis's voice.

"Let me take her, Brad. She's my responsibility."

Brianna heard boots scrape on the ground, and knew that Sally was being carried from the clearing by the one person who loved her more than life itself. Francis may have been at fault in keeping silent on her increasing paranoia, but she'd not judge him harshly for that. After all, Sally's madness had resorted to a binding of the worst kind.

A hand landed on Brianna's shoulder, and she jumped.

"Sorry," Tommy stated. "I forgot about the left-over energy thingy. Is the circle safe for you to leave?"

"Yes, but give me a minute anyway."

A companionable silence descended, and Brianna was grateful not to be rushed into leaving the circle. She felt as if the Pentagram had dissolved inside of her, and reset the relays of her mind. The buzzing in her head was finally lowering its volume, allowing her to hear the sound of bubbling water and swaying branches in the distance.

A loud groan shattered the silence and she felt a bump against her knees.

"I hope you got the license plate of the truck that hit me," Devlin muttered. "I've got a headache the size of Texas." His fingers fumbled for her legs. "You?"

"Grateful to be alive."

"Amen," Brianna heard another groan and assumed that Devlin was rolling onto his back and studying the stars. "How do you go back to the real world after experiencing that?" he asked.

Brianna didn't need to ask what he was referring to.

"You take all the love and light with you, and you do your best to make this world a better place to live in." A thoughtful silence descended, and Brianna sensed Devlin was digesting her words.

"Help me up, Tommy," he finally mumbled. "I need an aspirin as soon as possible. By the time Brianna reaches the clinic, her vision should have cleared."

"Righto."

A flash of white moved in front of Brianna, and the blurred image sprang from the ground. In a matter of seconds, she felt strong hands yanking her to her feet. The touch sent an intense physical awareness of who was lifting her. Not Tommy, but Devlin. Fleeting thoughts of his naked body claiming hers pranced through her head, and she shut the image out. Backing out of his arms, she patted his chest.

"On the mend." A new pair of hands whirled her around and nudged her forward. Tommy's voice assailed the top of her head.

"Can I make a suggestion now that I'm temporarily in charge?"

"I'm listening."

"Don't you ever scare the hell out of me like that again, do you hear?" His fingers squeezed her collarbone. "My heart can't take it."

"Trust me, next time I'll let someone else rush in where angels fear to tread."

His fingers left her shoulders, and she heard a light growl.

"There won't be a next time. I'm taking you back to Washington where they've never heard of Sacred Circles—or demons who want to rip your heart out and eat it." His mention of Washington had Brianna's pulse skittering. "Sorry," Tommy said, a moment later. "I forgot you can't go back to Washington."

To her surprise, Brianna laughed at his sarcasm, and then spying Devlin's blurred form striking off through the trees, she sobered. Where was he going in such a hurry? *Leaving you behind,* her inner voice nudged. *He's through with you.* The observation was a stab in her heart and she felt as if her breath was caught in a whirlpool. He wouldn't leave her, not after all they had been through together. *He would and he is,* her voice pressured again.

"Rrr-owww."

The wail was at her feet and she looked down at the black blob keeping stride with her steps. Nicodemus—ever faithful. The blob streaked away from her ankles; however, Brianna was sure she would soon find him tailing her again. So mote it be, she thought, as her vision suddenly cleared. She searched the tree line for Devlin's retreating figure, only to see him falling into step with Eileen. He flung his arm around the woman's shoulders and bent and whispered in her ear. *Your pulse is racing like a mad man,* her inner voice chided. *You're jealous of the attention he's showing Eileen. Do something. Make a move on him. Prove to him he's not the only one who can deliver a killer kiss.*

A flicker of a smile rose on her lips and with it, a new determination. She would kiss Devlin very soon. And when she did, the pleasure would be pure and explosive—for both of them. Glancing back, she saw her father struggling to sit up and gave a sigh of relief. Her father was moving like a slug, but at least he was moving.

Entering the tree line, she lost sight of the clearing, and by the time, she arrived in the Main Street Plaza, Devlin was nowhere in sight. Her mind floundered, once again—as dark as the night sky around her. She felt a warm touch on her arm and, seeing Tommy's keenly, observant stare, she burst into tears.

CHAPTER TWENTY-THREE

THE CROWNING

Brianna sat in the dimly lit room, deep sobs rocking her insides. For twenty-four hours, it had been touch and go; her mother on the verge of slipping away permanently. And then she had stunned them all by regaining consciousness—moving out of the dark, and into the light again. So why then, was she sitting in the dark crying? *You know why. He's leaving—without acknowledging the vision.* Brianna gave a choked sob. Perhaps he doesn't remember the vision. *It happens sometimes,* her cynical voice added. *Besides, why should he stay? You've never shown him a lick of kindness ever.*

Brianna swallowed hard and her clamped lips imprisoned a wail. She was facing a desolate future without Devlin, and it was just what she deserved for not discussing the binding with him. *Beg him to stay,* her inner voice urged. She snatched up another tissue and wept into it. Beg him to stay? No, he wouldn't like it if she begged him. She had to sheath her inner feelings and shore up the old Brianna—the one who was in perfect control. The bedside lamp snapped on, startling Brianna. She scrambled forward in her chair, capturing her Mother's trembling hand. She stuffed it back under the covers, scolding her lightly.

"You must rest, Mother. Doctor Ellis's orders."

Her mother's whisper was raspy.

"What's wrong? You're crying. Are you ill?" Hearing the concern laced in her Mother's voice, Brianna emitted a convulsive sob.

"He's leaving, Mother, without remembering the healing wa ... " She broke off, covering her face with her hands. Her Mother couldn't know about the healing wash. No one could. Her

Mother's fingers exited the covers and found her manicured ones. She squeezed the digits.

"Is he going without acknowledging the healing wash?"

Dropping her hands, Brianna drew in her breath.

"How did you know?"

"I'm ill, dear, not blind," Her voice faltered. "And of course, your father has told me some of what's occurred while I was comatose."

"Devlin won't talk to me; he won't let me beg his forgiveness for consenting to the binding with Nicodemus. He refuses to believe I had no choice."

Her mother jiggled her fingers.

"Correct me if I'm wrong, but did you or did you not vow to love, honor, and obey Devlin when you married him."

"Yes, of course, but that was days ago, when I still had his respect."

Her mother's voice turned irritable.

"Oh, for heaven's sake, Brianna, the boy has been your constant shadow since you were three. Surely that should tell you something about his character." She paused to catch her breath, and Brianna saw a stab of pain cross her features.

"Rest, Mother, you need rest."

Her eyes closed and Brianna sensed she was drifting off to sleep.

"Tell Devlin you love him, dear," her mother said, sleepily. A second later, she wafted into sleep.

"It's too late," Brianna whispered, watching her features relax.

"RRR-owww."

Brianna turned at the meow, studying the cat sitting outside the hospital room. She swiped at her wet cheeks.

"It's alright to come in. She's asleep."

"Rrr-oww."

Brianna sighed.

"Alright, have it you way. Sit out in the cold corridor all night. I'm sure I don't care."

The cat yawned rudely at her, and then standing, he meowed at her again. He moved then, out of her sight, and Brianna stood and crossed to the door. Peeking around the doorframe, she saw him slip into a second room. She followed his path, surprised to find the room occupied. She glanced at the two men shaking hands, and drew back.

"Come in, Brianna," Tommy's voice hailed her. She peered around the doorframe again to find Tommy's hand beckoning. She entered the room, hearing his added mutter. "Help me convince this stubborn fellow that he should stay a few more days."

Brianna blushed at Tommy's words.

"We have no hold on him, Tommy. He's free to stay or go."

"Rubbish! You two need to talk to each other. You belong together, and it's time you both admitted it—to each other!"

"Tommy!" Brianna's cheeks turned scarlet and she began twisting her hands nervously.

"Leave it alone, Cloisters. You're making matters worse."

Brianna's heart sank at Devlin's rebuke. He hadn't lied in the library; he was through with her, and worse, he'd never know the Ancients had given their approval to the marriage. *Tell him then,* her inner voice pressed.

Brianna tore her mind from the thought. She couldn't tell him. In her bid to protect him from Sally's curse, she had inadvertently diverted the vision. And since there was no way to shore it back up, it was useless to go on fighting anymore.

"It's best this way, Tommy," she finally said. "The Coven can't have a leadership that is divided. The community is built on harmony. It cannot have a High Priestess who wishes harm on another." She took a step forward. "The annulment papers are ready for your witness signature. As a witness to the marriage, you must witness the divorce."

"I won't do it. I may not have been for this marriage at the start, but after seeing the two of your together over the last couple of days, I know this marriage is right for both of you."

Brianna gave a huge sigh, stepping forward, and laying her hand on Tommy's sleeve.

"If you love me, Tommy, you'll do this for me."

His scowl was fierce.

"It's not fair to play the 'L' card against me."

"I know it isn't, but it's the only card I have to play." He nodded this time and Brianna knew there'd be no further argument. A second later, he was exiting the room, and she was alone with Devlin. She craned her head, studying his back as he finished zipping his suitcase.

"Have you said goodbye to my parents at least?" she finally quizzed. He turned then, giving her a nod.

"I talked to them a little while ago—told them my intentions."

"You could stay a few days longer, you know—for Mother's sake. I can make myself scarce to give you time with her."

"Let's not push our luck, shall we?" he replied. "I'm pretty sure the Sisters of Fate have washed their hands of us once and for all." A black streak flashed by Devlin's ankles and he sprang back. "Damn cat!" He eyed Nicodemus as he vaulted to the windowsill and began washing his paws. Devlin's gaze returned to Brianna. "I promise to take care of Sage Industries for at least a year. After that, I make no promises." Briana frowned at his words, but didn't offer a retort. "You aren't regretting how this all played out, are you?" he asked, suddenly.

Surprised that he had asked her that, Brianna gave a choking laugh.

"Good heaven's no, I've been tired of my life for a long time, and spirit has now given me an opportunity to mend some overdue bridges—especially with Francis and Sally."

"They have a long road ahead of them," Devlin murmured.

A huge lump formed in her throat at his words. Their road was nothing compared to the road she would be facing now that Devlin was abandoning his responsibility as a High Priest. His annulment would force her to choose another husband in the upcoming months, and the prospect was as depressing as a monsoon rain.

"Earth to Brianna … "

Brianna shook off her reverie.

"Sorry. I was just thinking of the long road ahead."

He felt silent, and Brianna wondered if she should tell him that before he had dammed their union, the Council had reversed their opinion of the marriage. Would he even care that the Elders were willing to accept him as their High Priest now? No, that piece of news would stay buried—like her love for him.

A moment later, he dropped his suitcase to the floor and lifted the handle. Turning, he stepped to Brianna and lifted his hand to her cheek.

"I wish it could've worked out for us, Brianna."

She plastered a smile on her face, giving a shrug.

"Wrong fairy tale, I guess."

"It would seem so," he replied.

His hand left her cheek then, and he skirted her shoulders, heading towards the doorway. As if crushed beneath a heavy boot, Brianna felt her heart shatter in two. It was over without even starting, and the knowledge would fester and gnaw at her for the rest of her life—just like the evil that had corrupted Sally's soul. She spun suddenly, shoring up a last bit of courage.

"You do understand that if you don't mend your ways, a powerful High Priestess will be forced to place a curse on your head that can never be removed."

He glanced over his shoulder, and then held up his fingers in a Boy Scout salute.

"I promise to mend my ways, Cinderella. After all, I've seen firsthand what a High Priestess can do with just a sweep of her hand."

He didn't give her a chance to reply. Instead, he executed a mock bow and strode from the room. Watching him go, Brianna's vision clouded with tears. That was that. *Swallow your pride and go after him. Beg him to stay,* her inner voice nudged. Not that. She'd not ask him to sacrifice all he had worked for in Texas for her.

Whirling on her toes, Brianna hurried across the room to the bay window. She swatted her eyelashes, waiting for Devlin's tall frame to emerge on the steps below. When he didn't appear, she brushed Nicodemus's fur.

"I can't ask him to give up his old life to stay with me, can I? It's too big of a sacrifice. Isn't it?"

"Rrr-oww."

"Well, what do you suggest I do to make him come back?" She glanced out the window, still not seeing Devlin's tall frame on the steps. Where was he? Why was he dawdling? She craned her head, studying the area around the Jeep. When she still didn't see him, that same, crushing pressure exerted itself in her chest. Another set of tears sparkled on her eyelashes. She drew back from the window, with a sob.

"Rrr-owww."

"Don't be absurd," she murmured. "You cannot make him remember the healing wash. He's got to remember on his own. The Ancients decree it that way." A chuff and a sneeze emanated, followed by a series of stuttered throat vibrations. Brianna glanced down at the ring on her finger, and twirled it absently. "Well, at least I won't need this anymore. I'll use another one when I remarry."

"If you do, your new husband won't live long enough to kiss you," a deep voice said, from behind her.

Brianna whirled, startled to find Devlin lounging in the doorway, a lop-sided grin on his face. Her pulse skittered at once. *Thank you, Nicodemus. I owe you one.* The cat mewed its disgust at her, but she didn't have time to react, as Devlin hoisted himself from the doorframe and came her way.

"Do you actually think I would divorce you—now that I've finally got the only thing I've ever wanted?" he asked. Brianna's mind whirled at his question. His hands snaked up her arms, and hauled her close to his body. "Good God, woman. We shared a healing wash."

A sob tore from Brianna's throat.

"I thought you didn't remember. I thought I diverted it."

"Divert a healing wash by the Ancients? You're not *that* good." He wrapped his arms around her midriff and held her snugly. "I have loved you since I was ten, you moron. And I have wanted to marry you since I was sixteen."

"What?! Then why the divorce?"

"To bring you to your senses—so you'd admit that we belong together. Even that obnoxious pet of yours knows it." Bending, he planted a wet kiss on her lips, and then, lifting his head, he met her gaze. "Do we belong together, Mrs. Janus?"

She thought of saying no just to tease him, but her heart was hammering so wildly that all she managed to get out was a simple, breathy "yes."

Hearing the word, he released her waist, stepped around her, and scooped Nicodemus from the windowsill. Crossing the room, he tossed the growling cat into the hallway, shut the door, and locked it.

"What are you doing?" Brianna queried, choking up.

He headed back her way.

"I'm going to have hot, steamy sex with my wife."

"Don't be absurd."

He stopped in front of her.

"What? You don't think I can arouse you to a fever pitch a second time?"

"Don't be an ass. We're not having mind-blowing sex in a hospital bed."

He gathered her into his arms and his grin was devilish.

"So you admit the sex was mind-blowing?"

Brianna tossed her head at him.

"Change the subject, or there won't be any sex between us ever—hot or cold."

His voice softened as he lifted her chin and gazed deep into her eyes.

"If you think that, Snow White, you're not the smart High Priestess I know you to be." The last of his words were smothered on her lips and, to her delight, this time the kiss was slow and erotic. She savored every moment of the burning fire on her lips, and then his mouth left hers to nibble on her earlobe. Brianna's trembling limbs quickly clung to him, and then, scarcely aware of her own voice, she whispered in his ear.

"We have to let the Council know we're not divorcing."

He ignored her words, his mouth wandering down the tingling cord of her neck.

"They already know. They got the message when I tore up the papers," he finally murmured.

His mouth wandered back up along her jawbone, and then, with a soft sigh, he settled his mouth on hers again. Caught up in the pleasure pulsing through her, Briana nestled against his supple strength and parted her lips in mute invitation. His tongue swept inside immediately, and overwhelmed by the spreading heat, she broke the kiss and buried her face against Devlin's throat.

"If the stars are in a favorable conjunction tonight, I might let your naked body claim mine."

"Even if the stars aren't in a favorable conjunction tonight, my naked body is going to claim yours," he responded. "That's a promise, and as a High Priestess, you have to do what your High Priest thinks is best."

"I'm more interested in knowing what Mr. Janus thinks is best," she murmured.

His fingers fumbled with the buttons of her blouse.

"He thinks Cinderella should keep Prince Charming satisfied, day and night."

His lips recaptured her mouth, his fingers skirting inside her bra, to magically stroke the smooth flesh. The caress was so male and so bracing this time, that for a long moment, she lay drowned in a melting sweetness. This was what it was to be blissfully happy, and fully alive. Her arms slipped around his neck and she caressed the tendons she found there. He broke the kiss, his breathing labored.

"You're killing me here, Rapunzel."

"I certainly hope so." she murmured.

Her lips met his half-way this time. Soon, nothing else mattered, except the strong and vivid desires that shook both their bodies and claimed their hearts.

EPILOGUE

High on the rise, overlooking a painted circle, Nicodemus stood guard, ears twitching, waiting to be summoned. Alongside, Devlin watched the scene below, listening to the raucous giggles reverberating in the night air. Brianna's laughter soon joined in, and Devlin saw her lift her hands toward the full white moon hanging low in the sky.

"Begone!" she ordered.

The moon slipped behind a cloud, and the five young girls in the circle clapped and spun, not the least bit frightened by the orb's sudden disappearance. Instead, they began a silly chant for the moon to return and chase away the darkness. When it re-emerged from its hiding place a moment later, showering them and the clearing with a neon brightness, they giggled and twirled. Oohing and aahing, they attempted to catch hold of the prisms of light bathing their raised arms.

Seeing the bright rainbow, Devlin grinned. The girls were about to experience a last, shocking surprise. Brianna's hand waved towards the moon again, catching the girls' attention and directing it upward.

"Abra … ca … dabra … " she began. The girls giggled in delight at her silly reference.

"No, it's hocus pocus, Mrs. Janus … hocus pocus, stinky, okus … " The youngest of the girls twirled on her toes, and her cohorts joined in. "Hocus pocus, stinky, okus … "

The girls squealed at their own silliness and then fell silent, eager for the surprise Brianna would shower on them. Devlin knew Brianna wouldn't disappoint. She pointed her finger skyward.

"Oh, magic genie, I order you to open sesame … " The girls held their breaths, their glances shooting back and forth along the skyline in anticipation. And then a loud "rrr-oww" split the air, and the group looked down, startled to find Nicodemus lying peacefully in the center of the circle, staring up at them with his bright yellow eyes. The girls clapped in unison.

"It's Nicodemus," Miranda O'Connor cried first. "What a clever, clever cat."

Joining hands, the girls began to dance and twirl around Nicodemus' outstretched form, chanting his name over and over. Lifting his gaze, Devlin spotted Brianna striding the rise. Reaching the crest, she slipped into his arms.

"There'll be no living with Nicodemus now," she scoffed. "Their flattery will go to his already over-stuffed ego."

"Rotten cat for a rotten brat," Devlin muttered. Turning her face up, he deposited a wet kiss on her lips, and then spun her around. Slipping his arms around her waist, he dropped his head on her right shoulder, and studied the giggling figures below. The shrill chants revved up, allowing the pair a moment to savor the energy surrounding the clearing, and bask in the power of spirit. Finally, he heard a contented sigh.

"The joy in magic still lives, Devlin. Can you feel it?"

"I can feel it." He molded her curves closer into the contours of his body, and his mouth grazed her earlobe. "It's right here in my arms." His lips seared a path down her neck to her shoulder, and then with a quick spin, he swept her, weightless, into his arms. He immediately devoured her lips, reveling in the shared intimacy of the kiss—until, to his annoyance, a strong pressure knocked against his legs.

"Rrr-ooww."

The kiss ended abruptly, the pair springing apart.

"Damn cat," Devlin drawled.

Brianna's laugh echoed as she backed out of his arms.

"He means well. He's reminding me, I must close the circle." She spun around and headed back down the incline. Reaching the circle, she gathered the girls together and began powering down the energy cone.

Watching the group from the ridge, a grin overtook Devlin's features.

"Rrr-owww."

"Yes, I know. It's not at all proper to envision my hands roaming intimately over a High Priestess's naked breasts."

Nicodemus sneezed his dislike immediately, and Devlin's grin turned up a notch. No one was going to keep him from rousing his wife to a frenzied state of love-making in the next hour. Not even a damn, magical cat.

More from This Author
(from *The Kindred* by Rachel James)

THURSDAY—10 A.M.—ASPEN, COLORADO

A shadow of alarm touched Janice Kelly's face, and she stepped back from the three-legged easel, tossing her paintbrush into a jar of cloudy water. The painting before her had changed background colors again. On its own. No, she brought herself up sharply. Paintings did not change colors by themselves. She had done it. She had changed the colors. She let her gaze travel across the now bright yellow background, struggling with the uncertainty it aroused. Had her divorce from Jimmy finally sent her mind over the edge? If so, this mind-fugue was dangerous. She might hurt someone. She might hurt Sarah. Horrified, she raised a hand to her temple. Damn! If she weren't careful, she'd work herself into a full-blown migraine.

Unaware of the streaks of brightly colored paint she was dabbing into her flaming red hair, she rubbed the sore spot vigorously. This was no regular headache she was battling. That's why the pills she'd taken this morning had done nothing to quiet it. No, she'd experienced this kind of pain before, and she knew what it meant. Now, more than ever, she could not put off her trip to Maine tomorrow. She had to go and not just for the debt she owed to her mentor.

Fingers trailing down her temples, she strode back to the easel and began to pack up her paints. She needed sleep desperately— the dead-to-the-world kind. She had been on a five-state gallery tour for months, skipping meals, signing autographs and hopping trains. And now, just when she got home, she was leaving again. No wonder her face had looked pale and pinched when she woke this morning. She was so tired her nerves throbbed. "Mama, what's a Si-Pip?"

Janice jumped at the sound of the high-pitched voice and quickly brought her gaze from the paints to the open doorway. Her eyes lit with pleasure as she spied her daughter, Sarah, bouncing from foot to foot in the middle of the alcove.

"Sarah, sweetie, I don't think I know that word. Where did you hear it?"

"From Aunt Bibi." She bounded through the doorway and sailed onto a cushioned workbench beside Janice. Once there, she eyed the huge canvas. "Is that my Daddy, Mama?"

Janice grinned, amused.

"No, sweetie, I don't know who the man is."

"Aunt Bibi told Uncle Roddy he's your dream lover."

Janice's grin vanished, replaced by a quick frown.

"I've asked you not to spy on your aunt and uncle, Sarah, remember?"

"Uh-huh." She tucked her feet beneath her rump and tipped her face to Janice. "Who is he, Mama?"

Her persistence brought Janice's focus back to the painting, and she let her gaze sweep the dove gray breeches and matching topcoat. An absolutely gorgeous rake. And her sister was right. She was becoming enamored with the handsome figure she had painted, seemed inexplicably drawn to him.

"Mama?"

"He's just a man I've been seeing in a dream, sweetie."

"He's handsome."

"Yes, he is. Devilishly handsome."

"Is he as devilish as me?"

The question was cheeky, and Janice chuckled, tweaking one of Sarah's bright red curls. Sarah was an adorable poppet, no doubt about it. She took a moment to study the snow-blasted cheeks as Sarah began to riffle through her paints.

"Aunt Bibi says you're a Si-Pip, Mama."

Janice lightly smacked the prying fingers and gave a sarcastic laugh.

"Little pitchers have big ears."

"What's that mean, Mama?"

"Nothing, sweetie. C'mere."

Dropping to the workbench, Janice opened her arms and wiggled her fingers. She must divert Sarah's attention from the tubes of paint. Sarah toppled forward and sprawled across her legs eagerly. One hand flew beneath her cheek to wait patiently for an answer to her earlier question. But which question? Janice wondered. A contented sigh singed her ears, and Janice gave another bright laugh, tickling the round belly peeping between the folds of the yellow flannel jogging suit. Sarah squirmed and giggled, their hands entwining.

"Stop, Mama ... you know that tickles."

"But you have such a yummy laugh, I can't help myself." Janice cooed. She slid her fingers along Sarah's tummy again, eliciting more spontaneous giggles.

"Stop ... Mama ... please!"

Hearing a serious hiccup, Janice stilled her fingers and, with a swift tug, righted Sarah to a sitting position in her lap. She dropped a quick kiss on her warm cheek and gave her a light bear-hug. Sarah's face sobered, and Janice knew her attention was back again on getting answers to her questions.

"What *is* a Si-Pip?"

"Psychic. The word is psychic. I'm a psychic."

She saw the flash of alertness in the eyes studying her face.

"What's a Si-Kick?"

"It's a person who can see things before they happen, see things that are way off in the future."

"Like the gip ... gip-sies who look into the ball?"

Janice craned her head thoughtfully.

"Umm … more like a television set. I see pictures in my head, sweetie, kinda like our television set downstairs. The pictures can be funny, sad, scary … "

"Mon-sters?"

Janice smiled, once again brushing back a stray curl along Sarah's temple.

"No, no monsters. At least not the kind you mean."

"Does the television set hurt your head?"

"Why no, sweetie, what makes you think it does?"

"Aunt Bibi's gettin' you some ass … ass-prin from the drawer. She says your head aches."

Janice rolled her eyes.

"Bless your Aunt Bibi."

She gave Sarah's cheek another brief kiss then slid her back onto the padded bench. Rising, Janice returned to the portrait and picked up her paintbrush. Why did she feel compelled to embellish on the yellow hue when the painting was already quite perfect? She didn't know, but found herself less than a minute later ignoring the mocking voice inside and dressing up the background with a few flourishes of her brush. Beside her, she heard a light humming and joined in. It was marvelous the way she could tune into Sarah's boundless energy. Recharge from it. Without warning, the sound of spit bubbles began to mingle with their humming.

"Pa-tew … pa-tew."

Janice looked over in amusement.

"Whatever are you doing, you silly bear?"

"I'm spittin'."

"I can see that. But why?"

"Aunt Bibi says I'm the spittin' image of you, Mama."

A choking laugh bubbled out before Janice could stop it. What a delightful ragamuffin she and Jimmy had produced. And so infinitely precious. Yet her sister's comment was true. She and

Sarah were unmistakably related. She swished her paintbrush into the water jar, stealing a peek at the appealing face now displaying Janice's own familiar signs of thoughtfulness. Their faces were identical delicately carved facial bones, both blessed with the Mignon family trait of a full-bodied lower lip.

Scanning the young features, Janice sensed the face so pink with eagerness at the moment would eventually showcase high, exotic cheekbones like her own. As for their hair, Sarah's was bright red, too, but not quite so crackling red as her own. She decided they were as alike as two peas in a pod—except for the eyes. Sarah had extraordinary blue eyes, as blue as the Aspen summer sky, while her own eyes gleamed emerald, like deep green ice.

There was another difference between them. But as of yet Janice couldn't bring herself to discuss it with anyone, not even her sister. She knew without question Sarah did not possess second sight. She would hold no psychic tremors in the coming years. And that relieved Janice immensely. Not that she would have changed things for herself. But she was glad Sarah's carefree nature would not be hindered, her eyes lose their sparkle when carrying the weight of the gift.

She looked at those eyes now, twinkling with untold mischief, and she heard the giggle, unmistakably Sarah's own. Responding, Janice made a sudden dive for the workbench. Sarah screeched in delight and vaulted from the bench. She hit the floor running, and Janice marveled at her fleet-footedness. Was she raising a future track and field star? Perhaps not, since in the next instant Sarah collided with a pair of long, tanned legs. Janice's sister, Bibi, glass in hand, reared back to absorb the unexpected impact, and Janice heard her call out sharply.

"Hey, slow down! I'm carrying a full glass."

Sarah's giggles echoed louder as she grabbed Bibi's knees, using the tall, sturdy body as a shield.

"Mama's gonna tickle me, Aunt Bibi. Don't let her."

"Have you been teasing her while she's painting, you naughty munchkin?" She attempted to shake Sarah loose of her leg, but the motion only managed to slosh water over the rim of the glass. Seeing the juggling act, Janice sank onto the workbench in convulsive laughter. Across the space, Bibi prodded Sarah more sternly.

"Sarah Anne Kelly, you let go of my leg this instant! Your mother and I need to talk. Go help Peter out of his snowsuit this minute." She gave a last shake of her leg, and Janice heard her say even more sharply, "Go!"

Janice caught a brief flash of yellow as Sarah bounded out on the landing and tripped down the hallway. Her sing-song call to Peter echoed back gaily.

"Come out, come out, wherever you are."

Bibi entered the loft, her face finally turning up in the smile she'd fought from showing.

"She's a sunny little thing, Jan. She reminds me a lot of Anna sometimes."

Janice propped herself on the bench, swiping at her eyes.

"Anna?"

Her sister came forward, offering Janice the glass of water plus two aspirin tablets in her palm.

"Oh, she's you through and through, but she has a tiny little imp inside her that jumps out every now and again. Like Anna."

Janice took the tablets and glass with a nod and tossing the tablets to the back of her tongue, she swallowed them down quickly. Wiping her mouth, she handed the glass back with a sigh.

"Her temperament resembles Anna's, too. She accepts things so easily. She pouts but never frets."

"Or throws a nasty temper tantrum like you know who."

A bemused smile trembled on Janice's lips.

"Peter has his good qualities, Bibi."

"Yes, he does." Her voice became tender, almost a murmur. "I'm lucky to have him, aren't I? Dr. Walsh said I wouldn't carry to term, being the old broad I am. But I proved him wrong."

"Dr. Walsh meant well, Bibi. Truly. Having your first baby in your forties is risky. Of course, he didn't know you as well as I do. There was never any doubt of miscarriage."

At her words, Bibi spun around and plunked the half-empty glass onto the worktable behind her.

"I hate it when you go all psychic on me, Jan. You know I have no defense against your damn second sight."

"Does my being a psychic bother you after all these years?"

"Hell, no. I'd love you if you had two heads and fourteen arms. And as for your psychic powers, they awe me." She broke off abruptly, and Janice saw her lift a photo frame from the worktable. "Lord, Jan, I didn't know you still had this photo."

Janice dipped her head.

"Ummm, next to Sarah, it's my most treasured possession."

Bibi caressed the glass, and Janice heard a wistful sigh.

"God, we were a trio back then, weren't we? How old was Anna?"

"Thirteen."

"That's right. I remember now." She raised her chin, and Janice saw a faraway glaze cloud her eyes. "You were a funny little twit then, Jan. You'd stand in the corner of your crib and stare and stare at Anna, who couldn't help crying out in pain while Mama forced her lifeless legs to exercise. You'd stare as if sending her some kind of healing thought. And she'd be better. No one could see it outwardly, but I could. I knew you were gifted and special even back then."

Janice crinkled up her face, determined not to cry. She hated that she always got teary-eyed when reminiscing about Anna.

"I don't seem to remember that time clearly, Bibi." she remarked. "Sometimes it seems so important that I do."

Bibi replaced the photo quickly and moved away from the table.

"Hell, you were only Sarah's age at the time—three or four—how could you? But you'd stand by her bed. And she'd be better … no, I swear it! Mama didn't believe it, of course. She never believed anything she couldn't taste, touch, or see."

"Now, that I DO remember. " Janice replied, sliding to the edge of the bench and hoisting herself up. Moving back to the easel, she ran a finger across the canvas. Was there now a hint of red streaks clogging the pores? She felt a warm presence beside her.

"You've changed the painting again, Jan. I like what you've done."

"Do you?"

"Yes, don't you?"

"I don't know. I don't remember repainting it."

Distressed, Janice turned from the canvas. She wasn't going to breakdown and blubber. Not over a stupid painting.

"You're scaring me, Jan."

She whirled back at the sound of her sister's stricken tones.

"I'm being stupid. I'm sure I made the changes to the painting. I just don't remember doing it."

"That's exactly why you should cancel this trip to Maine tomorrow. You're burned out, and this memory lapse proves it. Why don't you let me call Lloyd and tell him you're too exhausted to attend this seminar?"

"Because I gave Lloyd my word I'd be there. I can't renege now. I'll be back in four days and rest then. Besides, Sarah and I have plans."

"That's why she's a giggling idiot."

"She's the dearest, most precious thing in the world and don't you dare criticize her!" Bibi grinned broadly at her, causing Janice to let out a long, audible breath. "When I come back, I'm going to stay put for a very long time. Enjoy Sarah's company." She reached out her hand to Bibi, who took it readily. "I don't know what I would have done if you hadn't been there after Jimmy walked out on us."

Bibi flushed, and for once Janice realized she had caught her sister completely off-guard.

"Hell, Jan, I'd walk through fire for you and Sarah."

She would too, Janice knew, through hell and back again. They exchanged warm smiles.

"Hearing her constant giggles thrills me, Bibi. She's such a silly little bear, happy and alive."

"And she teases you on purpose. She certainly knows which buttons to push on you." Bibi's face sobered again. "Anyone interesting going to be at this big seminar in Maine?"

Janice crinkled her nose.

"Well, let's see … there's Lloyd."

"I said interesting. Not stuffy."

"Lloyd's not stuffy … he's … " She gave a smart ass little grin. " … intellectually stimulating."

"Forget the intellectual stimulation." Bibi responded. "You need a red-blooded male with active sperm to stimulate you physically."

"Bibi!"

"Don't sound so shocked! I know you didn't find Sarah in a cabbage patch. You've had your share of blissful nights beneath a man."

Janice felt a warm rush steal across her cheeks and knew she was blushing.

"What's got into you today, Bibi? Have you been reading those naughty romantic novels again for pointers?"

"Nope. I got Roddy. He's all the outside stimulation I need. You want to get rid of your headache, Jan? Make love. Does the trick every time."

Janice gave a hearty laugh, amused by her sister's foolish banter.

"Sex with a stranger is dangerous these days."

"Damn! You're right. Guess your only hope *is* aspirin." They broke into shared laughter again until Bibi prodded. "Go on. Who else will be at the seminar?"

"Jasper and Muriel Grisomb. She did the television series *Dream Robbers* a few seasons back. Her husband is a Lutheran minister."

"Ummm … go on."

"Adrian Magus … "

"Aaahhh!" Bibi's squeal was ear-splitting as she bolted upright on the bench. "You can't mean that gorgeous hunk Roddy and I saw perform in Las Vegas last year?"

"Yep." Janice dropped alongside her, gesturing for her to scoot over. "Was he as good as you said he was … as the papers say he is?"

Bibi shifted on the bench, and Janice saw her expression grow wistful.

"Are you kidding? He was incredible. And lord, what a bod!"

Janice took a swipe at Bibi who ducked.

"Will you stop already! If anyone's hormones need adjusting, it's yours!"

Laughing, Bibi hoisted herself up from the bench and struck a dramatic pose. Grinding her hips, she ran her fingers suggestively over her body.

"Well, if you don't *ska-rew* that gorgeous hunk, danger or no danger … " Janice snickered loudly. Bibi would never change. She would always be outrageously outrageous. At her snicker, Bibi dropped her pose. "Don't think he won't ask. That red hair of yours is like a magnetic flame. One look and they burn!"

"Burn out, you mean."

Disgusted, Bibi took a swat at her arm.

"Don't joke. I mean it. You need a man, Jan. Sarah needs a father."

"She has a father."

"Balderdash! I mean a father, not an asshole."

"Bibi!" Janice's voice turned brittle.

"All right, alright! I won't harp on Jimmy."

"Thank you."

"Peter's ready, Aunt Bibi."

The shrill voice held a rasp of excitement, and both women turned simultaneously. An astonished shriek rent the air as Bibi bolted to her feet. Janice's hand flew to her mouth, attempting to stem a ripple of laughter as she spotted her near-naked nephew poised in the doorway, clinging to Sarah's hand.

"Sarah Anne Kelly!" Her sister flew across the space, and with a swift tug, scooped Peter up from the carpet and rubbed his goose-caked arms. "Stop laughing, Jan. It's not funny. You know how delicate Peter is."

Janice made an effort to contain her laughter by sitting upright. She knew Bibi was right. Peter's health was fragile. However, one look at Sarah's impish face, and she found herself dissolving into laughter again. Sarah joined in, all girlish giggle. Swiftly, she sailed in through the doorway and pounced onto the bench into Janice's arms. Together, they studied Bibi, who Janice saw was alternating between keeping a straight face and trying to look outraged. Finally, she tore into the dimpling pair.

"You are naughty, Sarah Anne Kelly. Just like your mother." She caught Janice's eye. "And I hope you get snowed in at Carrington House with no one to make love to!" Janice's laughter pealed again, and she began tickling the flesh wrapped in her arms. "Jan?" She looked up quickly. "Seriously, Jan, have you remembered to pack everything? Anna's compass?"

Janice tilted Sarah and reached into her slack pocket. Withdrawing the small object, she held it up for Bibi's inspection.

"Never leave home without it."

Bibi nodded, clucked to the bundle in her arms once, and disappeared into the hall landing. Watching her go, Janice felt a tremendous surge of pride well within her. Bibi was right. She had been blessed. Only Bibi didn't realize that she, Roddy, and Peter were the blessing. Feeling grasping fingers on hers, Janice released the compass into Sarah's tiny palm.

"What's this for, Mama?"

She peered down at the small face intently studying the arrow wheel pointing to a big red "N."

"It helps people who go away to come back safe and sound."

Sarah mulled that thought over for a few seconds, and then to Janice's surprise, she bent her tousled head and kissed the plastic face. Janice reached out and brushed through a stray curl, touched by the gesture. Sarah had such an innocent abandon about her. She envied her that innocence. Cradling her closer, she placed her cheek atop Sarah's head.

"I'll be back in four days, sweetie. And then we'll go to Hollow Lake."

"And you'll teach me to skate, Mama, right?"

"That's right."

"When I grow up I'm gonna be the bestest skater in the ekopades."

"Escapades."

"Ess-ca-pades," Sarah mimicked, snuggling closer. A moment later, Janice heard a warm sigh and craned her head to view Sarah's face. She was dozing already, eyes closed, her lips tilted at the corners. Janice began to rock her gently. Four days and she'd be back. Four days and she'd teach Sarah to skate. She gave a long, exhausted sigh and began to hum one of Sarah's favorite ditties lightly. Four days. Not so long.

She felt a ripple along her left temple and lifted her gaze to the painting. Was there another change of colors? No, not this time. The breeches and topcoat were still surrounded by a yellow flecked background. She looked away hastily. She was tired and distracted and had repainted the background without thinking. That was all there was to it. Nothing mysterious, nothing abnormal. Still … her gaze swept back to the easel and she chewed on her lower lip thoughtfully. If there was nothing mysterious going on, why hadn't her gift of premonition set off in its usual way? Why all of a sudden had her gift chosen to be secretive, leaving her to feel as if she were the proverbial Alice about to tumble headfirst into the looking glass? She didn't know, and not knowing could mean only one thing. She wasn't going to like what was coming one little bit.

In the mood for more Crimson Romance?
Check out *Touchdown* by Yael Levy at *CrimsonRomance.com*.